ABOUT THE AUTHOR

David Chadwick is an acclaimed author, historian and award-winning journalist whose work includes *Tin Soldiers*, the first of his Nixon's America trilogy, *Liberty Bazaar*, his debut novel, and *High Seas to Home*, an historical account of the Battle of the Atlantic. David uses his experiences reporting politics, crime and business to inform his fiction. He divides his time between homes in Greater Manchester and southern Spain.

ALSO BY DAVID CHADWICK

Fiction
Tin Soldiers
Liberty Bazaar

Non-fiction
High Seas to Home – Daily Despatches from a Frigate at War
(with Shirley Morgan and Allan Seabridge)

Short stories
Panopticon (edited with Nicky Harlow)
Weird Love (edited with Nicky Harlow)

HEADLOAD OF NAPALM

DAVID CHADWICK

Copyright © 2024 David Chadwick

The moral right of the author has been asserted.

Apart from any fair dealing for the purposes of research or private study, or criticism or review, as permitted under the Copyright, Designs and Patents Act 1988, this publication may only be reproduced, stored or transmitted, in any form or by any means, with the prior permission in writing of the publishers, or in the case of reprographic reproduction in accordance with the terms of licences issued by the Copyright Licensing Agency. Enquiries concerning reproduction outside those terms should be sent to the publishers.

This is a work of fiction. Names, characters, businesses, places, events and incidents are either the products of the author's imagination or used in a fictitious manner. Any resemblance to actual persons, living or dead, or actual events is purely coincidental.

Matador
Unit E2 Airfield Business Park,
Harrison Road, Market Harborough,
Leicestershire. LE16 7UL
Tel: 0116 2792299
Email: books@troubador.co.uk
Web: www.troubador.co.uk/matador
Twitter: @matadorbooks

ISBN 978 1805143 765

British Library Cataloguing in Publication Data.
A catalogue record for this book is available from the British Library.

PPrinted and bound in Great Britain by 4edge Limited
Typeset in 11pt Minion Pro by Troubador Publishing Ltd, Leicester, UK

Matador is an imprint of Troubador Publishing Ltd

*For my fabulous friend Shirley Morgan
whose advice and support have enriched
my work from the beginning*

PRAISE FOR DAVID CHADWICK

'A political mystery thriller with great pace and intelligent analysis of Nixon's America'
— *The Bookbag, Top Ten Self-Published Books of 2023*

'A terrific crime genre debut … I am looking forward to seeing what next David Chadwick has up his sleeve'
— NetGalley 5 star review

'Powerful, twisty and smart'
— Nick Jackson, *Manchester Evening News*

'Offbeat, refreshingly absorbing … twisty and well-realized … Features impeccable research'
— *Kirkus Reviews* (starred review)

'A compelling story with a profound moral dimension – and a political page-turner that transcends the genre of historical fiction'
— Faber Prize winner Livi Michael

'First class storytelling. An addictive novel with a tremendous feel for its time and settings – lived out by characters with real passion and true human complexity'
— Paul Du Noyer, founding editor of *MOJO*

'Chadwick shares that light touch intensity of the king of this genre, John le Carré … the claustrophobia … the intrigue, the rules of engagement and the double dealing'

— Michael Taylor, *The Marple Leaf*

'Much to please both thinker and those demanding entertainment.'
— *The Book Bag*, five star review

'Chadwick pens a story with precision and poise'
— *Readers' Favorite*, five star review

ONE

Thursday September 13, 1973

The two men lay in the parking lot between the Desert Diner and New Life Episcopal Church. The first had fielded a big one through the chest, two more in his belly. The second man's head was hamburger, hit flush by two rounds. Positions of the bodies suggested they'd approached from different directions: one from the diner, the other the church. It looked like a professional hit with bad collateral. But who was the mark?

The woman was even more of a puzzle. She was sprawled on rough ground outside the Million Dollar Nugget Bar, a beat-up dive seventy or eighty yards away. One side of her head was missing and a second bullet had gone into her chest.

Mid-afternoon. Naked sun beat hard. It stung exposed skin like nettle-rash and melted tar-seams on the street. Cover of an easy listening standard drifted from the diner: *A World Without Love*.

I hadn't seen so many dead people since I rode the liftbird out of Saigon and came home to the Land of the Cheeseburger. Sure, a body count of three was chump change in the Nasty. But this wasn't Viet Cong country. This was Hicks, California – a little town somewhere between no place much and no place at all. Pitched in the western Mojave desert, Hicks had a population of fifteen thousand and two main career opportunities: Los Angeles 120 miles west, and Las Vegas a similar distance east.

Yet this remoteness was why I took my job here.

Shane Phillips, the first cop to arrive, had rounded up half a dozen of people I assumed were witnesses. They stood in a patch of shade near the church while Shane fished some yellow and black tape from the trunk of his cruiser. The kid's face was lard-white. His fingers fumbled with the plastic tape. Almost certainly his first homicide.

Lyrics from another easy listening cover floated from the diner: *What the world needs now is love, sweet love...*

'You okay, Shane?'

He gave me a startled glance. 'You got here pretty fast, Mr Tyler. How'd you find out?'

'City desk got a tip off,' I said.

Of course this was from one of my sources at the cop shop, but Shane was too preoccupied to push it.

I nodded toward the nearest body. The guy was lying on one side in a reservoir of blood, chest and gut opened up. And yet the back of his navy-blue suit coat was undamaged. Large calibre rounds had gone in and stayed in.

I looked more closely at his face: flat features and deep-tanned complexion, framed by dense black hair, long over his collar, with pork-chop sideburns. 'That's Ray Carmody, isn't it?'

Shane made a helpless shrug. 'Sorry, Mr Tyler. You know I ain't authorized to give out information to the press.'

He didn't need to. All that surprised me was that I hadn't identified Carmody earlier. As the entrepreneur behind the country's newest silver mining corporation, I should have recognized him instantly. But it was all about context: I never expected to see Ray Carmody in the context of having gotten shot to death. The story I'd already written in my head suddenly acquired a new, much stronger angle. And urgency. The big hitters from LA would be rolling into town all too soon.

I still needed more names.

Shane started sealing off the crime scene with his barricade tape.

Now the soundtrack was *I'd Like to Teach the World to Sing*. Seemed the compilation record was trying for a feel-good deal with 'world' in the song titles. But the hippie harmony sounded flat-out sinister in the vicinity of three homicide victims.

I glanced back at the second guy. Poor bastard no longer had a face.

Distant howlers silenced the diner music. More black-and-whites on their way.

I focused instead on the rest of victim number two. He was a heavy-built man, dark blue suit pants and a white shirt. Nothing there to help me recognize him.

Something familiar, though, about the plaid necktie.

I tried to remember.

The sirens grew louder in the blowtorch air.

What little time I had was running out.

I looked at the body again, up and down. My eyes locked on the crocodile-skin shoes with brass-coloured toe tips.

The realization slammed into the front of my mind so

hard I quit thinking, let my brain finish playing catch-up. When a deal like this goes down, you need to be sure you got your facts straight.

But there could be no doubt. This was the guy I interviewed four hours earlier. This was Congressman Frank Hazeldene – pegged by many of my colleagues as the most anti-business politician in the United States.

In that instant I pictured his animated features as he'd given out on workers' rights between bites of beefsteak in Fred's Fast Feeder. I'd sat opposite, making notes. Smells of deep-fry fat and stewed coffee. Grand Funk Railroad laying down *American Band*; other diners' chatter; the clatter and clink of tableware.

'There's a lot of scared people up here in Hicks.' He'd paused to pick up a paper napkin and wipe a fleck of ketchup from his cheek. 'They figure forming a union will put their jobs on the line – because that's what the bosses keep telling them.'

'Think they'll listen to you?'

'I'll make them listen.'

'You'll make enemies.'

'Already have.'

I recalled him reaching into his pocket…

…And right there, standing over what was left of Congressman Frank Hazeldene, I saw my story go from big to colossal.

TWO

The irony of me being the hack who'd get to break it was something else.

I had to move fast, though. Those cop cars would roll up any moment and put the whole scene off limits. So I walked toward the woman in hopes of getting my final name. As I crossed the lot, I noticed a sprinkle of shell casings at the side of the kerb – almost certainly from the shooter's weapon. I stooped and counted eight of them gleaming on the cracked concrete. Inserting the tip of my ballpoint into the open end of one, I tilted it so I could read the head stamp: *Federal .45 Auto*. The killer had apparently emptied an eight-round pistol clip. Judging by the absence of exit wounds on Carmody and the extreme trauma to all three victims I guessed they were hit by hollow point rounds – the kind designed to shred and tear and stay inside the target. You want handgun ammunition that really makes a mess, the .45 jacketed hollow point is your baby. I guessed the shooter was making a statement. And having made it, he split real fast – on a motorbike headed toward Interstate 15, according to my source.

Glancing at the bodies from the shooter's perspective, it was obvious that Hazeldene and Carmody were easy targets. The congressman got hit from five or six yards, the businessman from seven or eight. The woman, though, was seventy or eighty yards from the casings. That sort of distance, a pistol loses a lot of accuracy. Looked as if she walked out of the bar at precisely the wrong moment. Maybe the shooter fired his last couple of rounds in her general direction to scare her off. If that was so, it was the worst kind of bad luck.

As I got closer, I took in a half-way attractive woman, nearer forty than thirty, with tawny hair, dark at the roots, and a face bearing the tread-marks of hard living. A frayed cotton tank top and cheap nylon skirt with big platform shoes added to the impression of someone who didn't care too much about her appearance. Her injuries were grievous. One shot had taken away the right side of her head, just above the hairline; the other hit below the sternum. I guessed she might have survived that one, but not the head wound.

Failing to identify her came almost as a relief. After seven years in Vietnam I'd seen every type of violent death I could imagine and some I couldn't. Yet the murder of two people I'd interviewed here in Hicks – one of them that lunchtime – was somehow more shocking. Gazing at the bodies, I got an adrenaline hit I hadn't known since my first firefight. That was in the fall of '65 when I was a grunt in the 101st Airborne. Old stinks returned to the back of my nostrils. Blood and napalm and phosphorous. I closed my eyes and I was back there with the dead Viet Cong fighter, his face pulverized just like the congressman's.

Except this was downtown Hicks, not some shell-cratered hill with a three-digit name. And Charlie was the whole Pacific away. So I had to wonder who could have done this. I had to wonder why.

Black and white howlers reached a crescendo. Three Dodge Coronets came bouncing along the uneven surface of First Avenue and swung onto Main Street. They pulled over outside the diner, red lights flashing, cops baling out both sides.

At the same time a stumpy Plymouth Cricket approached, in no big hurry, from the opposite direction and backed into a parking space on Second and Main.

The woman who got out was tall and slender, righteous enough to grab my gaze and hold it. She wore a light blue cheesecloth shirt and bellbottom suit pants that covered her shoes. Fawn hair fell straight to her shoulders and her features were keen, maybe a little bookish.

I stood up, realizing she was walking toward me – and the butcher block of a parking lot.

'Hey, baby, you don't wanna come any nearer.' I held up my arm to ward her off. 'There's stuff here you won't wanna see.'

She ignored my warning and came up close. 'You from the coroner's office?'

'*High Desert Herald*,' I said. 'You?'

Pushing back her sunglasses, she looked at me through smoky brown eyes. On a different day they might have been mellow. Right now, they were straight from the freezer. I guessed she'd be early-thirties – same as me. 'I'm Detective Sergeant Caraway,' she said. 'You got ID?'

I showed her my press card and she glanced at the details with a sullen expression.

She handed it back. 'You still shouldn't be here.'

I'd never seen her before, which meant she'd arrived in town very recently. And the rank of sergeant would make her head of Hicks Police Department's small detective division. A woman taking up a high-profile position at the cop shop would have made a page lead, maybe a front-page lead. Conservative place like Hicks, there'd be an outcry about a woman taking the sort of job normally reserved for men. Odd, then, that none of my police sources mentioned her appointment.

She stooped to examine the woman's body and her expression stayed businesslike. Gotta say this surprised me. Sure, women cops had been riding patrol cars since the mid-sixties, but despatchers generally routed homicides to male officers. And I'd never come across a female detective. She stayed totally focused, though, no argument there.

I put my pen to my notebook. 'You got a name for this lady?'

Her voice was icy. 'You got no shame? She's been brutally murdered and you're hovering around like a goddamn buzzard.'

'Just doing my job.'

'That what you call it?'

I said nothing – what was the point?

Caraway looked at me hard. 'You see any of this go down?'

'No, sergeant, I did not.'

She turned her back on me and summoned two of the cops helping Shane string out the crime scene tape.

'There'll be a press statement in due course.' She spoke to me over her shoulder, her tone dismissive. 'In the meantime, I'd be grateful if you'd remove yourself from my crime scene.'

'Just one thing, Sergeant – '

'You still here?' Still kneeling by the body, Caraway squinted up at me against the harsh sunlight.

I was about to tell her what the congressman produced from his pocket when I interviewed him. Its implications had been way too paranoid to use in my story – until he got his head blown open.

She hollered to Shane. 'Hey, Officer! Escort this guy to the other side of that police line – pronto!'

Well screw you, I thought. *You can read it in my paper just like everybody else.*

THREE

I figured the murdered woman just left the Million Dollar Nugget Bar when she got hit. So I started toward the place in hopes of finding out her name.

Up close, the joint looked even more beat-up than from across the parking lot: a rusty tin roof and crumbling clapboard façade, patched up with offcuts of corrugated metal. Faded ads touted *Regal Whiskey 'The Liquor of Kings'*, and *Billy's Beers – Hicks' Best*.

The scene indoors was no surprise. Cluster of barflies on tall stools down the far end. Two guys shooting pool on a red baize table, ripped in so many places the balls couldn't move without jumping. A crackly juke box sound – Townes Van Zandt's *Pancho and Lefty* – laid its melancholy vibe on the fug of sour booze and dried-in sweat.

The moment I crossed the threshold I got good news and bad. Good news was the owner was a fan of mine. Bad news was he the last sort of fan I needed.

He set down a half-poured glass of beer and hurried around the bar, greeting me like the brother-in-arms he considered me to be.

Norm Dibbitts was junkie-thin with rodenty features

and unstill eyes. He was wearing a burnt orange polyester shirt and reeked of Hai Karate aftershave. The high and tight buzz-cut seemed a little weird for somebody who'd not seen the inside of a uniform for a lot of years. When I left the army, first thing I did was grow my hair.

'Lemme get you a drink, Wat. On the house, goes without.' Norm shepherded me to a table. 'I guess you know about the shooting out there?'

'Sure do, Norm. I was hoping you might help me out with some information.'

'Anything, buddy. Anything at all – but let me get you that drink.'

I asked for a cold ACME and he scurried back around the bar to fix it.

I first met Norm in February when he called at the *Herald* office the day I arrived and introduced himself as a fellow veteran – though I later discovered he'd been a rear echelon clerk who never saw combat. He'd brought a clipping from a previous edition announcing my appointment as interim editor while my buddy Dave Tomaszewski took a sabbatical. (Dave was in an Arizona detox clinic, though this had not been mentioned in the paper.) His article mentioned that I was an ex-*New York Examiner* police reporter, which was fair enough. But he'd also revealed I was a former Green Beret captain and Medal of Honor recipient, which was not fair at all. See, the thing with Uncle Sam's top medal during the Vietnam War was that it made folks want one of two things: They wanted to buy you a drink because you were a hero; or they wanted you to get lost because they thought you'd gotten the medal to make a bad war look good. For a reporter it wasn't helpful either way because *you* became the focus of attention instead of your work. So it had proved with Norm.

When he brought my beer, I said, 'That poor lady who just got shot, Norm, do you know her?'

My buddy nodded. 'You betcha. One of my barmaids.'

'Sorry to hear that, Norm.' I began scribbling shorthand in my notebook. 'What's her name?'

'Marsha. Marsha Houtrelle.'

I asked him to spell the first name and the last. 'Age?'

'Said she was thirty-seven when I give her the job. That would've been six months back.'

'Can you tell me what happened?'

He made a little shrug. Despite the tough-guy stuff I could tell Norm was badly shaken. For the first time I saw him as something other than an irritant. 'She just walked outside to take a break and – *bang-bang-bang*. Six, seven, eight shots, I dunno. Looked out the window and there she was on the ground with the other two. Didn't know what to do. I figured the shooter might still be out there and I don't have no gun in here. So I stayed indoors and waited for the cops.'

Norm glanced at me as if seeking approval.

'You did the right thing, Norm.' I gave him a reassuring look. 'You couldn't have helped any of them.'

He seemed happy with that.

I asked, 'Was Marsha a local girl?'

He shook his head no. 'She was from outta town.'

I smiled. From a Hicks perspective, outta town meant the Rest of the Universe. LA, New York, London, Mars, it didn't matter. They were all equally outta town.

'Where'd she live?'

''Cross the street. Had an apartment in a block I own. Paid me rent from her wages.'

I took a swig of beer. 'Can you give me a quote, Norm? What sort of person was she?'

Norm lit a Chesterfield cigarette. The smoke lingered around his stubbly face as he appeared to consider a proper response. 'Marsha was a great gal. Always happy to help. Nothing too much trouble.'

'So the folks here liked her?'

'Sure did.' He leaned toward me and lowered his voice. 'Off the record, they kinda liked her a little too much, and she *liked* 'em liking her, if you know what I mean.'

I knew what he meant. I didn't judge folks, but this was useful background.

'You got a picture of her? Maybe behind the bar?'

Norm shrugged. 'Sorry, Wat. Can't help you there.'

'And there's no family here in Hicks?'

'Bit of a drifter, I guess.'

I chewed on that. 'Could I take a look around her apartment? Maybe she has a picture of herself there. Or some indication of where her family's at. You have a key don't you?'

'Sure.' He looked doubtful. 'But what about the cops?'

I took another mouthful of beer before making my Vietnam play. 'One old soldier doing another a favour? Nothing wrong in that. Cops won't ever know. You got my word.'

'Well, I guess...'

A comradely slap on his shoulder sealed it.

FOUR

From what Norm told me, Marsha Houtrelle got short-changed on forty years of life expectancy because she picked the wrong time to take a ten-minute break. The thrust of my piece had to be about the controversial politician Frank Hazeldene, with got-rich-quick entrepreneur Ray Carmody close behind. All the same, Marsha deserved some recognition. The tragedies of ordinary folks oftentimes grabbed my attention more than the misfortunes of high-ups. Not a good trait for a newshound, yet it was weirdly comforting. It showed that a small part of me could get a jolt of real emotion.

On my way to Marsha's apartment, I passed the eight-year-old VW Beetle that I'd parked on Main Street.

I made a lopsided grin when I saw the busted tail-light and bumper. That may sound like a strange reaction, but there was a good reason. See, this electric blue Cadillac rear-ended me at the Fifth and Jepson lights, just after my interview with Frank Hazeldene. The Caddy driver was a pasty-faced fellow, maybe mid-forties, John Lennon glasses, with a receded hairline and frizzy ginger rug grown long over his collar. No doubt the idea was to compensate for the baldness up front with extra hair out back, but it just looked as if he was wearing a wig that had slipped. He was clearly in a hurry to be someplace else. Didn't even look at the dinted fender of his Coupe de Ville. Instead, he riffled through his wallet and thrust a bunch of dollar bills into my hands. The guy vamoosed before I had time to count the compensation, but I wasn't about to chase after him. He gave me $150 – a lot more than my rusty old Bug was worth.

'Hey, Mr Tyler, wait up!'

Looking over my shoulder I saw the wiry figure of the *Herald's* trainee photographer, Suze Carter, hustling down the sidewalk. Must have been mighty hot under that big Afro hairdo: sweat was streaming down her broad brown face.

She made an apologetic smile. 'Sorry I took so long. Got stuck on a job at city hall. Came over the moment I heard.'

I told her to forget it. Even if she'd arrived when I did, the photos would have been way too graphic to publish.

'Just get some shots of the cops working the crime scene,' I said. 'Then come with me.'

The apartment block Norm rented out was as run-down as his bar, though its origins had been grander. It was a two-storey place with stucco walls and a terracotta tiled roof, built in the 1920s when this end of town had been relatively prosperous. Brickwork was crumbling, much of the mortar flaked away and missing roof tiles were covered by tar paper and plastic sheets.

Marsha's apartment was on the ground floor. It wasn't much: small, cheerless and revealed little about the woman who had lived there. A black and white TV set stood in one corner of the living room, a portable mono record player in another. A half dozen empty beer bottles had been left on a coffee table and an unemptied ashtray on the couch.

'Hey, Mr Tyler, I think I found what we need.'

Suze was in the bedroom hunched by bottle of Charlie perfume and a framed colour photo on the nightstand.

The picture showed a young woman and a middle aged one standing next to each other on the lawn of a suburban duplex. I pegged the younger woman as Marsha. Judging by the resemblance I figured the other woman was her mom. Anyways, we could crop the image to give us a headshot of Marsha. First, though, I needed to get the picture out of the glass-fronted frame so Suze could get a clean shot. As I removed the cardboard backing I realized there was another, smaller picture concealed behind the mom-and-daughter snap. Flipping it over, I saw a monochrome image of a woman on a street corner leaning into the driver's window of a light-coloured Ford Pinto with a peace symbol bumper sticker. The woman was facing away from the camera and the only clue to her identity was a floral pattern dress. There also appeared to be someone at the wheel, though the face was just a shady smudge.

The picture was useless for my story, though I did wonder why Marsha had gone to such lengths to hide it. Maybe she'd taken it as evidence that the guy – if it *was* a guy – in the driver's seat had been cheating on her. Maybe *she* was the woman leaning into the car window. Maybe he was a married guy and the photo was part of some shakedown routine. Maybe I was overthinking this.

All the same, it would be worth taking a copy. I laid both pictures on the chest of drawers by the window for Suze to get a shot of each.

The *Herald's* final edition deadline was coming at me fast and I needed to file my copy. I left Suze at the apartment and headed back to my car.

Across Main Street, Detective Sergeant Caraway and the uniformed cops were still at work. Very soon I'd have competition from the nationals as well as the TV people, and she'd have the FBI to deal with. Political assassination goes down, it's bound to draw the Feds.

I went to the phone booth on Second and Main. Lifting the receiver, I saw that I had a clear view of the front entrances to the diner, the church and the bar. Even if some dramatic development went down at this late stage, I could still fit it in my report.

But the cops continued their crime scene routine and I called in my copy off the top of my head. This literature-in-a-hurry deal still gave me a hit, even as a seasoned hack. By the time folks clocked off that afternoon my exclusive would be on the streets. The military coup in Chile, Skylab 3, even the latest on Watergate would take a vacation from the lead slot of every paper in America.

Even so, I wondered how pissed off Caraway was going to be as I dictated the lead paragraph:

Local congressman Frank Hazeldene was slain today in a triple homicide – two hours after revealing exclusively to this newspaper that he had received a death threat.

FIVE

With the final edition on the newsstands, I lit a Camel cigarette and looked out the front window of my office at the *Herald*. First time I saw this view I was impressed. Then I realized almost everybody in town had a very similar one.

See, Hicks was surrounded by mountains. Everyplace you went, splintered peaks stalked the horizon. From their summits you looked down on a land at war with itself. You saw ochre valleys scored by washes of arid mud – all that remained of floods that raged and died like reckless adventurers. And you saw dry lakebeds shimmering white as if their alkaline sinks still held water. On top of this, whiplash winds stacked sand into dunes so high they drowned rusting car wrecks and filled up ravines. Even the desolation was deceptive. Look a little closer, you'd see blooms of rabbitbrush and flax, desert willow and cattle spinach scribbled in purple and gold and pink on the late summer landscape. Then there were cottonwood and juniper and Joshua trees. I'd seen some far-out plants in the jungles of the Nasty but I never saw anything as ugly and messed-up as Joshuas. They reared from the earth, twisty boughs with fists of bayonet-shaped leaves stabbing the sky. Like the desert, they looked mean and crazy. They'd gotten named by Mormon settlers after the Hebrew prophet Joshua who waved his arms as he led the Israelites into Canaan. Silhouetted by sunset or moonshine, they had an otherworldly appearance – like something out of a sci-fi movie.

This was a land of chaos, a mind-fuck of a place, and that suited me fine.

The newsroom was deserted except for Tom Ferris, the copy chief. With three years to retirement, he had no regrets about a career spent exclusively on the *Herald*. Squat, potbellied, with a head of thick grey bristles, Tom could edit and lay out pages as fast and accurate as anyone I'd worked with in New York City. He rarely had anything good to say about the young reporters whose stories he corrected, and any piece of writing he considered substandard would be screwed into a ball and hurled at the hapless writer.

I returned to my desk and picked up the news budget for the next day's paper. There was a half-decent court story about a botched robbery downtown and a bunch of local government pieces that read like they dribbled all the way down the city hall steps.

A strong AP piece had also come down the wire. Richard Nixon was flipping the bird at the Appeal Court over the release of the Watergate tapes. According to the latest article, Tricky Dick was continuing to deny prior knowledge of the burglary at the Democratic National Committee headquarters in the Watergate complex in DC last June – even though a string of Whitehouse officials clearly knew a lot.

Then, of course, there was my follow-up on the triple

homicide – which was something of a problem in that my original page-one splash had undoubtedly ticked off the city's chief of detectives.

With this in mind, I felt a little concerned when I saw Caraway's Plymouth Cricket swing off Coldstock Lane and head for the *Herald's* parking lot.

Expecting trouble, I straightened my tie then buzzed Sheila on reception and had her send Caraway through to my office.

I watched the gentle sway of her hips as she picked a path through the newsroom – every bit as chaotic as the Mojave landscape.

The woman was a conundrum. When I first saw her outside the Million Dollar Nugget I figured she had to be new in town but hadn't found time to find out why no one at the cop shop mentioned her arrival. New head of the detective division rolls in, you'd think Bull Turner, the police chief, would want the publicity. Maybe there was some reason why Bull wasn't on board with her appointment.

Although I got that she'd be unhappy with me, I totally underestimated the extent. Stepping into my office she slapped a copy of the final edition on the desk. 'Think that's smart, do you?'

I made my best disarming smile. 'Well, it's the biggest national exclusive out of Hicks in living memory.'

Her eyes narrowed. 'I found you poking around at the scene of a triple homicide. Then you walked away with material information concerning one of the victims.'

'I did try to tell you.' I stubbed out my cigarette and returned to my desk chair. 'But you had an officer escort me from the area.'

'You could have tried harder. You people have no problem cranking up the goddamn volume when it suits.'

I tilted my head to one side. 'What are you accusing me of, Sergeant?'

'Obstructing justice has a ring to it.' She placed her palms on my desk and leaned toward me. 'Just who are you, Mr Tyler?'

Man, was she angry. I held up my hands in a gesture of appeasement. 'I'm the acting editor of the *High Desert Herald*. Everybody in the police department knows that.'

'Everybody in the police department isn't asking. *I* am. You sure don't speak like any newspaper editor I ever came across. So what's your story?'

'*My* story?' I was someplace between baffled and rattled. 'Am I a suspect?'

'Let's say I want to know who I'm dealing with.'

This was tedious, but I could see there'd be less grief all around if I just gave her what she wanted. 'Okay, Sergeant, since you're so interested, I grew up in Fayette County, West Virginia. My dad was a coal miner. He lost his job and started beating my mom, so she took me to New York City. I'd have been fourteen. Pretty soon she was on Skid Row and I was off the rails. That lasted a couple of years before I caught a lucky break.'

'You telling me you're back *on* the rails?'

She was riding me hard, but I let it pass.

Her gaze didn't leave mine. 'So, what was this lucky break?'

I made a longsuffering shrug. 'A journalist, name of Maggie Call, took me in and trained me up. I worked hard and became a news reporter on the *New York Examiner*.

Then I got drafted. No rich family; no formal education; no surprise.'

'You must've felt bitter.'

Was that sarcasm or sympathy?

'Didn't much matter what I felt. Went to Vietnam with the 101st Airborne in August '65 and made buck sergeant mid-tour. After that I moved up through the ranks in short order – nothing gets you promoted faster than catastrophic attrition. Transferred to the 5th Special Forces Group – that's the Green Berets – in '67 and got a direct commission during the Mini-Tet offensive.'

'You must have done something real special to swing that.' She just couldn't keep that hint of mockery from her voice.

'Chopper carrying a rising star of the US Army named Laurence Westerby went down in enemy territory and my A-team pulled him out. Our captain got killed and I ended up in charge. We spent two weeks cheek by jowl with Charlie and the general liked the way I worked. We bonded too, I guess. Anyways, he wanted me in command of my own team. And what Westerby wanted, Westerby got.'

I didn't expect the idea of an Appalachian country boy becoming an army officer as well as a newspaper editor would sit so well with her.

But she didn't react, so I finished my piece, 'Mustered out at Fort Bragg last year, rejoined the *New York Examiner* as a crime reporter and left for personal reasons back in February. That was when I got to sit in this editor chair.' I made a sarcastic smile. 'Hillbilly accent and all.'

'I'm not a snob.' Her tone softened some. 'But I'm not a fool either. So why did you make me look like one? Thanks to your *national exclusive* my boss knew about Hazeldene's death threat before I did – not to mention the FBI.'

I nodded slowly. With Bull Turner *and* the Federals breathing down her neck, I got why she was so pissed. And with the nationals about to arrive on my beat, it was in our mutual interest to patch things up. We were working in the same small town. We needed to cooperate.

'I didn't mean for that to happen,' I said. 'I'm sorry it did.'

'Apology noted.'

'But not accepted?'

She took a seat opposite me and gave me a curious look. 'That depends on what you can give me on this death threat.'

SIX

I sat back. 'What do you know about Amalgamated Metals?'

'Assume nothing.'

'Well, it's a big defence company that makes tank suspension components for the Man and doesn't welcome organized labour. Hazeldene was in town supporting a meeting of Amalgamated workers who wanted to form a union.'

She nodded. 'What sort of audience did he get?'

'The gig bombed. Fewer than two dozen showed up from a workforce of more than twelve hundred. Hazeldene claimed folks were bullied into staying away.'

'You think that's true?'

'Possibly. But the fact is I got no evidence and Hazeldene is dead. So it's an allegation I can't print without copping a libel writ.'

'Any sign of trouble at this meeting?'

'Negative. It was held on public land outside the factory gates and passed off real quiet, so not much of a news angle for the *Herald*. But I interviewed Hazeldene forty-five minutes before he gave his speech. He said he was on his way to meet me when a piece of paper was stuffed in his coat pocket by someone he didn't see. He showed it to me and I made a note.'

I riffled through my spiral notebook and read from the shorthand. 'It said, 'This union shit gonna put us outta work – so we gonna put your commie ass in the ground.' It was signed "'True Worker Brotherhood"'.

She studied me across the desk. 'Did it strike you as genuine?'

I shrugged. 'What does a genuine death threat look like? The handwriting was poor and the grammar bad, but that's easy enough to fake. Hazeldene put the paper in an ashtray and set fire to it. Guess he was making a point.'

'How about Hazeldene? Did *he* strike you as genuine?'

'I don't think he manufactured the note if that's what you mean.'

'Did he seem scared, anxious?'

'No he didn't. But he was a politician – putting on a face is what they do.'

'How would you assess him as a politician?'

Again, I flipped through my notebook and found some background material. 'Pulled off an impressive coup last year when he got elected on the Democratic ticket in a traditionally Republican district. Didn't get too many votes here in Hicks, but the folks down in San Bernardino and Victorville – his home town – backed him big time. In Congress he strengthened his reputation as a champion of unionisation and workplace reform. None of this played well with corporate America and he got tagged as the country's most anti-business politician. He was also a member of the House armed services committee. Called for cuts in defence spending, but nothing you'd call outrageous.'

She gave me a hard stare. 'Apart from these anti-union people, would you say he was a threat to anyone? Business interests, for example?'

This was the crossroads. The moment I had to decide.

Question was, did I keep Hazeldene's other disclosure to myself, or trust a cop who minutes ago walked into my office threatening to arrest me? One part of me said to keep what I had to myself. Problem was I didn't have very much, and Caraway could help me find what was missing. Besides, her owing me a favour would be no bad thing. So I went ahead and laid down what I knew.

'I think he enjoyed being seen as a threat,' I said. 'Until today. Today he *became* a threat.'

She pinned me with those smoky eyes. 'To whom?'

'I don't know.' I went back to my notes. 'But he told me he was mighty close to getting hold of highly confidential information that could – and this is a direct quote, "Change the balance of the Cold War".'

Caraway gave me a puzzled look. 'Why didn't you put that in your story?'

I closed my notebook. 'Without context it's just a wild claim. I need substance. Also, if I *had* used it, Hazeldene's source would likely have gotten spooked and vanished – if they haven't already.'

A small smile nudged her expression from flat out starchy to vaguely amused. 'Restraint from a reporter. Whatever next?'

I went to the percolator and poured myself a cup of stewed coffee. She shook her head no when I offered her the jug.

'There's another reason,' I said. 'If this information is as serious as Hazeldene claimed, my printing it would alert the people it threatened – who may well be the folks behind the hit.'

She tilted her head to one side, as if still weighing me up.

I took gulp of coffee. It was lukewarm, with the consistency of tar, but I'd had a long day and needed the fix. 'So it *was* a hit?'

She gave me a what-do-you-think? look. 'Someone empties a .45 automatic into three people and doesn't take anything, it sure isn't a wallet snatch gone bad.'

'Those wounds looked big and mean – what sort of ammo are we looking at?'

'Jacketed hollow point.'

This was what I'd suspected. 'You figure the shooter was saying something? Leaving a message?'

She made a sour expression. 'Could be. But I'd say his top priority was making sure nobody was left alive. All those hollow points caused massive internal trauma. The coroner had a tough time finding them.'

'You attended the autopsy?' I spoke with a little too much surprise.

'I am the chief of detectives.'

'Yeah, but...' Words fizzled out as I realized I was deepening the hole I just created.

'I'm a woman, that it?'

'I'm not a sexist.' Now *I* was on the back foot.

She gave me a dubious look. 'You sound like one.'

How to sound reasonable? 'Look, you're the first female detective I met. That was this afternoon. Now you're the first female cop I met who observed an autopsy. Sure I'm surprised, but that's not the same as being sexist.'

It was a decent recovery, and she made a tolerant expression.

I made the most of the respite. 'You got anything more on the shooter?'

She shook her head no. 'None of the witnesses saw anything until the shooting stopped. Guy seen fleeing the scene was a biker-type, maybe from a motorcycle gang. Long brown hair, beard, shades. Wearing a beat-up leather jacket with the sleeves cut off. Took off toward the interstate.'

'Anything on the bike?'

'Only that it was a regular road bike. No ape-hanger handlebars or other customized features.'

The tone of her voice told me she wasn't optimistic and I understood why. This was a planned hit and catching the killer was going to be a tall order.

'Any developments on the other victims?'

'On the record, no. Off the record, maybe.'

'Off the record, then.'

'How do I know I can trust you?'

Seemed she wasn't used to working with reporters. 'Setting aside my ethical commitment to protect my sources, the way it works is real simple: I betray your trust just once, you don't ever tell me anything again.'

'Okay.' She seemed to get the practical deal if not the moral one. 'We're working on the assumption that Hazeldene was the mark and Ray Carmody the collateral. But we're also looking into whether it could have been the other way around. Did you know Carmody?'

I drank more coffee and felt the sour brew lock onto my taste buds. 'I did a couple of interviews, but I wouldn't say I knew him.'

'Any information you can give me would be appreciated.'

'Help yourself.' I lifted the *Herald's* clippings file on Ray Carmody from a stack of paperwork on my desk and pushed it toward her.

She started going through the deep pile of clips – every type of story from page leads on big capital investments to stories with pictures of Carmody opening fund raiser events.

'He came over as friendly and businesslike. Charismatic too, in a showy sort of way. Very much the local hero. Create all that wealth, you're gonna be the Man in a place like this.'

'Is it right he had no previous experience of silver mining?'

I nodded yes. 'Until three years ago Carmody was a small-time entrepreneur with the gift of the gab. Raised finance from a venture capital investor in LA to buy the old High Rock Mine and turn it into a Silver Rush visitor attraction. Development was under way when a contractor who *did* know something about mining found a vein of high-grade silver. Carmody called in mineral exploration specialists and they soon established that he was sitting on a substantial lode – my more enthusiastic colleagues called it the New Comstock. Value of the business went from chump change to more than $20 million in two years.'

'Did Carmody own all of it?'

'Not all, but most. He made sure he kept a majority shareholding. That way he got the investment he needed to develop the mine without giving up control.' Coffee grounds stuck to the back of my throat as I drained the cup. 'Corporate financier I spoke to reckoned Carmody got real lucky in the first place, but then had the business savvy to play a shrewd hand. Luck ran out today, though.'

She looked up from the pile of clips. 'You make that much money that fast, you'll likely make enemies, right?'

'I guess. But the suits in downtown LA don't normally call a hitman if somebody puts their nose out.'

It was time I got some information in return so I asked what Carmody had been doing in the diner before the shooting.

'Eating lunch,' she said. 'He was alone, but I'm told that wasn't unusual. A manager up at the mine called the diner with a message. Seems Carmody had to get back there fast. On his way to his car when he was shot.'

She went back to sifting through the clips.

'Could Carmody have been lured out by the shooter?'

'The call was genuine. The manager confirmed making it.'

'And the third victim – Marsha Houtrelle?'

'At the range she was hit, she must have broken a boxful of mirrors and kicked a dozen black cats before stepping out that door. Marsha as the mark doesn't make any sense from any point of view, especially the shooter's.'

She paused, as if figuring out whether to share her thoughts, then added, 'Besides, the FBI has ruled her out.'

I lifted an eyebrow. 'Feds here already?'

'Soon enough. But in Marsha's case they don't think they need to be.'

'What do you think?'

She glanced up from the clips. 'I don't always agree with the Bureau, but this time I do. Marsha was a dive bar girl who liked the sauce and was popular with men. But not in the sort of way that makes enemies. Just the opposite. Everybody I spoke to said the same. She'd break up a fight before it got serious, and listen to the barfly blues all night long.'

What she said made sense and chimed with my own information from Norm Dibbitts.

'So we're back to Hazeldene.'

She nodded yes. 'His itinerary was public knowledge – your paper printed it. The shooter knew exactly where he was going to be, and exactly when.'

She was right. By using the press release I'd effectively pinned a target on the congressman's back.

'So is Wat Tyler your real name?' She was poring over the clips again. 'As in Wat Tyler's Rebellion?'

'Yes it is.' Her knowledge surprised me. 'I used to be Walt but one day a sloppy copy editor missed out the 'l' in my byline. Some history professor at Columbia wrote to congratulate the *New York Examiner* on hiring the leader of the Peasants' Revolt, all the way from England and all the way back to 1381. I thought it was a righteous tag so I kept it.'

'See yourself as a rebel?' She made a teasing smile.

Just for a second, I glimpsed a sexy woman behind the cold cop.

I mustered a grin. 'Don't know about that, but I guess I am the modern day version of a peasant. And my mom was from England – she met my dad when he was a Merchant Marine sailor in World War II.'

I paused, studying her with fresh interest. 'Anyways, how come you know about the Peasants' Revolt?'

She closed the clips folder and I noticed there were no rings on her fingers. 'I minored in popular insurrection from the Middle Ages to the 20th Century.'

'Wow – that's not something you hear every day from a cop.' She'd blown my mind, no doubt about it. 'What was it you majored in?'

'Police administration.' She pushed the clips file back across the desk. 'Although I'd have been better off sticking with medieval upstarts.'

I was about to ask her why, but she pushed the chair back and came to her feet.

Chief Turner wanted a full report before the Feds arrived and that meant her working through the night. She thanked me for my help and saw herself out.

SEVEN

I finished up and left the office an hour later.

The four guys were waiting in the sodium-lit parking lot. All over forty, all over-weight. Tangs of booze and armpit stink. They stood in a rough horseshoe between me and my car.

One of them stepped forward. He was a heavy unit, six-four and 300 pounds to my six feet one and 180 pounds. Bowling ball deltoids and Popeye forearms. Impressive – until you realized the Los Angeles Dodger jersey was stretched more by his belly than anything else. More ab work and fewer pies was what he needed.

'You're the bastard who wrote that piece, ain't you?' he said. 'About Hazeldene getting some death threat before he got shot.'

'Well the story had my name on it.' I kept my smile in place. 'Fair assumption I wrote it.'

'You shouldn't print shit like that.' The short guy behind Dodger Jersey piped up. 'It don't make us look so good.'

'And who might you be?'

The short fellow shuffled forward. 'We're workers who don't want no union folks getting us laid off.'

He sounded genuinely worried so I spoke in a tone I hoped might reassure him. 'Organized labour tends to improve workplace conditions and that has the effect of boosting productivity. That means job creation, not job losses.'

Dodger Jersey stepped sideways, cutting out the short guy.

My smile stayed. 'You gonna give me a death threat too?'

'Not a threat. A fucking lesson.'

Now I could smell ketchup and fried onions on his breath.

'And if you print any more of that garbage in your asswipe newspaper, there'll be another fucking lesson, and another after that.'

'You should go home.' I stood my ground. 'I don't need lessons.'

'Special Forces crap don't scare us none.' Dodger Jersey was jacked on booze and brimming with bile. 'And that Medal of Honor guff don't mean shit neither. All you done was stiff a few gooks on your pansy-ass way to losing the war.'

My expression switched from amiable to rueful. 'You sure you wanna jive with me?'

'I wanna.' Dodger Jersey's nostrils flared, neck muscles tightened. 'Real bad.'

This was hardly an engagement with the Viet Cong but I treated it the same: recon; plan; execute.

Recon told me these guys had been drinking, and this – along with their four-on-one advantage – made them figure me for easy meat. That in turn told me they were dumb. Fact that they knew something of my service record and still pegged me as a push-over told me they were dumber yet.

My plan was straightforward enough: take out Dodger Jersey fast and watch the others sky out.

Now came the execution.

Dodger Jersey pumped out his chest and drew back his head, giving himself a little extra height. He thought that was what counted – size.

His punch was hard and straight.

But way too predictable.

Slipping inside the swing, I endured a blast of ketchup and onion fumes, then jabbed his throat with a finger knuckle, just above the sternal notch.

His gag reflex went spang and he folded, clutching his throat.

His buddies didn't move. Hadn't reckoned on this and didn't know what to do.

I helped them reach the correct decision. 'You boys better take your pal home. He'll have a sore throat for a while, but he'll be fine.'

Short fellow seemed glad of the route out. Urging his two compadres to help, he grabbed Dodger Jersey by the arm and hauled him to his feet.

They loaded him into a pickup parked on Coldstock Lane and started the engine.

They were about to light a rag for home when one of the two guys who hadn't spoken yet called out the window. 'This ain't over, newspaperman.'

*

I headed back to my place on the edge of town. It was a ten-minute drive and I switched on the radio in hopes of catching a news bulletin.

The DJ was playing golden oldies and the one he picked was the oldest and goldenest I ever heard: Burl Ives' *Big Rock Candy Mountain.* It threw me right back in a way only music can. It was my seventh birthday. I was lying in bed in our house in Fayette County, West Virginia, and that old bluegrass song was playing on the radio downstairs.

My mom loved it. She turned it up loud. Louder still when my old man came home drunk and she knew he was gonna lay into her. I heard Burl's satiny voice above the thuds and screams the neighbours heard but never heard. The song never upset me though. Just the opposite. Whenever it came on the radio I focused on the lyrics. I sang along. It was my hymn. And that wasn't really surprising. Years later, after my mom took me to New York City, she told me it was the lullaby she sang when she put me in my crib.

When the song ended I left the Bug on my driveway and walked two blocks to a little bar called the *Say When*.

It was almost empty, although the guy I hoped to see was exactly where I expected him to be.

'Been wondering when you'd show.' Grover Burdick didn't look around as I took a seat on a bar stool next to his. In the gold-tinted mirror behind the liquor bottles, I watched the fleshy canyons on his lugubrious face settle into an amused grin.

I ordered a refill for the glass of bourbon he'd been cradling, and one for myself.

'I got nothing for you, Wat.' He accepted a Camel as well as the whiskey.

'What made you imagine I was here for anything other than the pleasure of your company?'

Burdick answered with an exhalation of cigarette smoke.

He was the senior sergeant at Hicks PD, a by-the-book copper who'd sooner break his own arm than the rules. If he liked you, though, he would sometimes bend them. And for all his gruffness, he had a soft spot for me. Why? Because we came from the same dead-on-its feet coal mining town in West Virginia. Not literally, but in the sense that every dead-on-its feet coal mining town in West Virginia was the same.

Like my dad, Burdick had been a coal miner who lost his job in the early fifties. Unlike my dad, though, Burdick had the savvy to quit the Mountain State and come to California.

Burdick took a long drag on his cigarette. 'So what's new on Nixon and Agnew?'

'Depends whose brand of news you wanna hear. Crookedest president and VP in American history; or victims of the most injustice.'

'Which one plays right to you?'

'Doesn't really matter. They're both dead meat. After Watergate nobody will ever trust Nixon; and the more Agnew denies tax fraud, the more credible it gets.'

Burdick ran his fingers through his wiry rug and gave me an amused look. 'Power of the press, huh?'

Shook my head. 'Listen, man, I just write stories as strong as I can based on the best information I can get. But when the President of the USA goes on TV in Disneyland and tells the nation 'I'm not a crook', folks wonder why he needs to say so.'

Burdick was clearly enjoying this. 'I got you pegged as a Democrat. Am I wrong?'

'Yes you are. I'm not a Republican either. They both shafted me like they did you. But I gotta credit Nixon for replacing draft deferments for rich kids with the lottery system. It's still a bum deal, but at least it's a democratic bum deal. And he is trying to scrap conscription altogether. Way too late for me, but he's done stuff that Lyndon Johnson never did.'

'Another bourbon?' He waved the bartender over.

'On me,' I said.

Burdick nabbed another of my Camels. 'So you *do* want something.'

I waited until the refills arrived. 'This new chief of detectives,' I said at last. 'What's the skinny?'

My source winked. 'Lee Caraway? Pretty, ain't she?'

'I guess. But how come there was no press release?' I read his dubious expression. 'Anything you tell me is strictly not attributable.'

He examined the long stack of ash that had built up on his cigarette, tilting it this way and that to see if it would fall off. 'Bull Turner didn't want her. Scuttlebutt is he was forced to give her the job because Stokes Honeysett had a word with the mayor, and the mayor had a word with the chief.'

This left me flat-out perplexed. Stokes Honeysett was the founder and president of Amalgamated Metals. Same firm Hazeldene wanted to unionize; same firm whose workers just tried to beat the shit out of me. 'What's Honeysett got to do with anything?'

Burdick loved it when he had one over on me. Made me wait while he drank some whiskey and, ever so slowly, laid his glass on the bar. 'Lee Caraway is his daughter.'

Not for the first time that day my mind got blown.

'Changed her name some time gone. Old Man Honeysett was none too enjoyed, but what could he do?'

'Why didn't Chief Turner want her here?'

'She's one of them feminizers. Bull don't like women cops, period. Never mind feminizers.'

'You mean feminists?'

Burdick chose not to hear me. 'Went to a fancy college – Princeton or some such like. Then seven years in LAPD including three in the detective division. Top marks in her sergeant exam, but no promotion. I heard was she was gonna take LAPD to court. Then her daddy got to hear about this head of detectives job in Hicks. Story I heard is that he persuaded her to drop the lawsuit and apply here.'

'Apply? So she doesn't know her old man pulled the strings?'

'Not as far as I know.' Burdick finished his bourbon. 'Ask me, she's better off out of LAPD. Full of biggoty bastards.'

I made a small grin. 'Never had Grover Burdick down as a feminizer.'

'I ain't. But I *do* know what it's like when you're a better cop than the next guy but still get passed over. I got a hillbilly accent; Caraway burned her bra. But it stacks up to the same pile of shit.'

He banged his glass down with unusual force. 'Wanna know what's worse? This is Caraway's first week on the job and already she got the first triple homicide in the history of Hicks. Hell, we never even had a double homicide before this. So on top of Chief Turner, she has the Federals on her back.'

I finished my whiskey. No wonder Caraway was curt with me at the crime scene and mighty pissed when I didn't tell her about Hazeldene's death threat. It put a lot of things in very different perspectives.

'Thanks, Grover. That's real useful to know.'

I got up to leave but he called me back. 'Did you know you got a busted taillight?'

'Yes, I did. Crazy thing happened.' Told him how I got rear-ended by the Cadillac at First and Jepson.

Burdick made a wry grin and I suspected this wasn't just on account of my $150 worth of good fortune. 'That Caddy, was it a '71 Coupe de Ville, electric blue?'

I nodded yes and gave him a puzzled look. 'Who are you, Uri Geller?'

'Fellow who went into the back of you picked up a speeding ticket a few minutes later. Yardstick Road, headed toward the interstate. Like you say, in a big hurry.'

I thought again about that panicky-looking dude with John Lennon glasses and ginger hair like a pulled-back wig. 'What's his name?'

'Gary Gerwitz.' My source's grin went wider. 'Stokes Honeysett's right-hand man over at Amalgamated – and dollars to donuts known to Lee Caraway. Small world, ain't it?'

'Microscopic more like.'

This latest revelation pulled me dead to the kerb. Gerwitz was apparently headed for Vegas at warp factor six when he got stopped by a speed cop two and a half hours before the Desert Diner shooting. If Caraway thought he was involved in any way, she'd have hauled him in for questioning whether he was a family friend or not. And Burdick would certainly have been wise to that.

Yet my curiosity had gotten stoked. If Gerwitz was a big cheese at Amalgamated Metals, he'd have known all about Hazeldene's union meeting. Had Gerwitz put those boys up to making the death threat?

So instead of going home for some overdue sleep I drove back to the *Herald* office and searched the clips library for the file on Gary Gerwitz.

Not much to go on: a handful of picture stories of him presenting cheques to local charity and community groups. All good PR for a firm in the armaments industry.

Then my eyes settled on a single column story at the back of the file. The small point-size of the print and tight packed decks of the headline told me this wasn't a recent piece. A closer look told me it had been clipped from the *Herald* on December 18, 1964.

The lead paragraph was dull, bordering on soporific. Amalgamated Metals had hired Gerwitz, a former applied metallurgy professor at the University of California, Berkeley, as its head of research and development. My news-antennae started twitching, though, when the second paragraph told me Gerwitz, aged thirty-five in '64, quit to protest the university's treatment of students involved in the Free Speech Movement. The story went on to explain that five years earlier, Honeysett provided cash backing for Gerwitz's research project to develop a steel alloy for use in tank suspension systems.

Didn't take a superbrain to figure out that Honeysett helped out his old pal Gerwitz by giving him a job just two weeks after he made himself unemployed. Seemed this act of loyalty paid off, though, because Gerwitz soon became Amalgamated's senior vice president.

It was late when I finally got back to my place. It was a modest wood-frame bungalow with a shady porch and front yard where I'd planted all sorts of local flora. Right now was a good time for tamarisk and scale-broom, princes plume and golden bush. All those still and silent hours on recon patrol deep in Charlie country gave me an appreciation of botanical species that followed me back home.

I stopped halfway down the pathway and was enjoying a modest hit from those nocturnal aromas when I became aware of the figure standing very still on the porch steps.

Even in the dark, even eight thousand miles from where I last saw him, I recognized my visitor immediately. Nothing changed, from the potato-sack belly and cascading chins to the crazy-cut buffalo hair and 300-pound frame.

Last time I saw Finn Sheldon he was walking into enemy territory after my team delivered him to a rendezvous with a double agent he was running.

That was four years ago.

So what was the CIA's most overweight field officer doing at my house in Hicks?

EIGHT

'I'm not getting short-changed on surprises today,' I said.

He pivoted toward me, the movement of his gut calling to mind a tin globe revolving on its stand.

'I hope this is a pleasant one.' Sheldon voice was low-pitched, his accent well-to-do New England.

'Always a pleasure, Finn.' I stepped up onto my porch and took the clammy hand he extended. 'But this can't be a coincidence.'

'It's exactly that.'

I knew this was bullshit. A congressman and two other folks get murdered and a senior spook shows up the same day, that's not happenstance. But I let it pass for now.

'So what *are* you doing here?'

'Debriefing the commander of an armoured division up at Fort Irwin. He got held up in West Berlin, though, so I'm kicking my heels. Saw your byline on the front page of the local rag and thought, heck, I'm gonna look up my old compadre Wat Tyler.'

'At this time of night?'

He gave me the look I remembered from Vietnam, the

look that said, '*I* know that *you* know I'm bullshitting, but this is the way it's gotta be.'

I showed him into my living room and watched his familiar gait: upper body so spherical it made his arms seem too short to reach his waist; and a walk that came mostly from the knees down – thighs functioning mainly as support columns for the heavy torso. Despite his weight he was light on his feet and a better shot with a handgun than me. My A-team had gotten him into Laos and Cambodia as well as areas of Charlie-controlled Vietnam. Each time we saw him fade into the tree line we thought he'd never get out. Yet he always did. Mission accomplished. Whatever that was.

'Can I get you anything?'

He took a seat on my couch and placed his tatty leather brief case on the glass-topped coffee table.

'Cold beer and a sandwich would be good. Pastrami and cheese if you got it.'

Ask that question of Ordinary Joe, he might ask for the beer but never the sandwich. This was Finn Sheldon, though – he consumed food in agricultural quantities.

'All I got is salami.'

'Then that's what I'll have.' My guest squinted, as if assessing my appearance. 'You look in good shape, Wat. Seems you slotted right back into the groove.'

'Up to a point.'

'I read about you leaving the *New York Examiner*. What's the story?'

I made a resigned sigh. Main reason I came to Hicks was to get away from questions like this. But Sheldon had a right to ask. 'You recall Maggie Call, the reporter who took me off the street and under her wing?'

He nodded his wide buffalo head. 'You called her your surrogate mom. Member of the sisterhood if memory serves.'

'Maggie never made a big secret of it, but she was always discreet. Then she crossed some bigoty shirtbird on the city desk and he decided he was gonna use it against her. Tipped off a rival paper that had already criticized her reports on gay liberation. The opposition did a hatchet job. Accusations of bias, deviancy, corrupt practices, you name it. Folks who never had anything good to say about the permissive society just loved it. Damn near wrecked her career.'

'And you put this city editor straight?'

I made a what-do-you-think expression.

'And got fired?'

'The executive editor said I could stay on if I apologized.'

'Which, of course, you didn't.'

'I'll get you that sandwich.'

He made a wan smile. His face hadn't got any prettier since the Vietnam days. Sandy hair looked like Art Garfunkel's if he cut it himself using sheep shears. Eyes and mouth seemed small in a tumble of fleshy mounds. No chin, just a U-shaped outline in the pink flab spilling over his collar. Last time I saw him he was wearing olive drabs. Now he was decked out in a lightweight cotton suit, concertinaed at the knees and elbows, and a tie that dug so deep into his neck that the knot was half-buried.

When I returned with the beer and sandwich he took a swig and a bite.

'Where you been, Finn, since you left the Nam?'

'Mainly desk-work in Europe.' He gathered some crumbs that had fallen on his chest and placed them, one by one, in his mouth. 'Fat, fucked and forty. What else can they do with a guy like me?'

'Come on, man. You flipped more enemy agents than hamburgers. You must've been running a dozen assets on Charlie's beat.'

He pushed a wedge of food into one of his cheeks so it looked as if he had a big tooth abscess. 'I'm still the fat man. That's all they see. That's how I get defined.'

'That's the most shit I ever heard. You deserve better.'

I meant it. First time we crossed the Ho Chi Minh Trail together he dropped a Viet Cong who would probably have killed me. I was the last man out and making for the whirlybird when the VC came out of nowhere. Sheldon took him out with one shot at thirty yards with a .45 Browning. That was how I knew he was better with a handgun than me.

He seemed to pick up on my thoughts. 'You miss Vietnam?'

'I'd be lying if I said not. But I miss the time I used to get for reading more than anything.'

He laughed. 'Hart Crane, John Crowe Ransom, Wallace Stevens. Never went into your hooch without seeing their stuff spilling out your duffel.'

I recalled those stretched-out days between missions when I soaked up anything I could lay my hands on – poetry most of all, but also fiction and biographies.

I mirrored his smile. 'You pulled my coat to Ted Hughes and Elizabeth Bishop. They were good company too. Damn site better than the officers' club.'

'Even those weird plants you brought back from the jungle were better company than the O club.' He hesitated, then gave me a slightly worried look. 'How about the post-combat shit? You okay with that? No flashbacks, bad dreams?'

'I'm cool.'

'You sure?'

'One hundred per cent.'

This was true, though I appreciated his concern. People who served in the Nasty, they often got broken in places that wouldn't go back together. Me, I was broken before I got there so it made no difference. Like pre-shrunk jeans. See, I learned before I could talk that scared never stopped my dad hitting my mom. When my mom took me to New York, scared never stopped her ditching me to go suck canned heat on the Bowery. Scared never saved me from the street gangs in New Lots who had a special kind of hatred for a hillbilly kid. Scared only ever made things worse. Of course I had a price to pay. Take away fear, you take away other stuff too. You leave a big empty space where there shouldn't be one. Poetry was one way of filling it, rock music another. And if the lyrics had a poetic dimension, like Bob Dylan's or Paul Simon's or Leonard Cohen's, that gave me a double hit.

'You still in touch with Leaping Larry?'

Shook my head no.

'He's a three-star general at the Pentagon now. Word is they're grooming him for chief of staff.'

'News to me, but I'm not surprised.' Laurence Westerby was the general who got me my field commission after his chopper went down deep inside Charlie Country and my unit got him out – along with some vital intel. He got called Leaping Larry because he was a capable and aggressive commander. A third star was nothing less than he deserved.

'I thought he might have offered you a job Stateside.'

Gave him a puzzled look. 'Why would he do that?'

'He owed you his ass – and more. I know about those black ops you carried out on his say-so; the work in other theatres – including the stuff back home; and of course the face to face debriefs in Saigon.'

'He swung me my captain bars. That made us even.'

'From what I heard the intel you got for him was worth major, maybe even light colonel.'

That made me chuckle. 'Yours truly on the staff of a three-star general? You gotta be putting me on.' We both knew the type of job Sheldon was hinting at wasn't behind a Pentagon desk, but I could toss the jive too. I knew Sheldon was fishing and I sure wasn't going to give him anything on the ops I carried out for Laurence Westerby.

He seemed to lose interest. 'You got mustard?'

I jabbed a thumb over my shoulder in the direction of the kitchen. 'Help yourself – on the shelf by the stove.'

As he went to pep up his sandwich my eyes were drawn to the briefcase on the coffee table. Whatever was in there might tell me what he was really doing in Hicks.

The case was a regular design, fastened by two slide-and-spring clasps.

His voice carried through from the kitchen. 'On the shelf you say?'

The reporter in me locked horns with the wartime comrade but the struggle was brief and only ever going one way. Sheldon had his agenda. I had mine.

I called back to him. 'Left hand side of the stove as you stand facing it.'

Moving quietly to the case, I slid the spring mechanisms that released the clasps. It should have been locked. But it wasn't.

'Can't see any mustard here.' I heard him rummaging around the stuff on the shelf.

'Might be behind the ketchup. Can see you the ketchup?'

I opened the case and peered inside. Just one manila file. Quick glance over my shoulder confirmed he was still poking around in the kitchen.

'Still can't see it.'

'Definitely there.'

I took out the file, flipped it open and found myself looking at a slim document with *Top Secret* stamped in faded red ink on the facing page. Under the CIA crest, the title of the document was typed in bold:

Organized Crime Money Laundering:
Offshore Investment into Los Angeles Venture Capital Funds

Not exactly snappy, but it sure said a lot.

'Oh yeah, I got it.'

I closed the wallet and put it back in the case. But I could hear Sheldon moving back toward the living room. No time to shut the case before he was onto me.

'Do me a favour, Finn,' I called. 'Fetch me another beer.'

I counted one beat, two...

The sound of approaching footsteps stopped. I heard him moving back into the kitchen, then the fridge door opening and the clink of beer bottles.

'I'll have another beer too if that's okay?'

'Sure.'

I closed the case.

Seconds later he appeared in the kitchen doorframe with two beer bottles and his mustard-laden sandwich.

We continued the small talk, but my mind was someplace else. It was working overtime on the implications of that document in Sheldon's case. Ray Carmody raised the cash to buy High Rock Mine from a private equity investor in LA. The acquisition cost twenty thousand bucks and the mine wouldn't have been worth much more if Carmody's plan to turn it into a silver rush tourist attraction had been where the story ended. But the discovery of high-grade silver three years ago changed all that. Now, it was valued at $20 million. Now, Carmody was dead. And now, the CIA was investigating a mob caper involving LA venture capital firms.

NINE

My phone rang. It was Sheila on the front desk, 'Gentleman here wants to see the editor.'

I made a silent sigh. Somebody rolling up at the front desk was rarely good news. Journalists were often the last resort of the desperate, the deluded and the demented: Folks who'd gotten nowhere with their lawyer, shrink, local council member or congressional representative. Just occasionally, someone swung by with a good story. But you had to get real lucky for that to happen and today I wasn't feeling so lucky.

I said, 'Does this gentleman have a name?'

I heard Sheila relaying my question, then she was back, 'Mr Schwenk. Says he's from the FBI.'

I asked Sheila to send him through and sat back in my chair to wait.

Through the glass wall of my office I watched Schwenk move through desks and trash cans and stacks of newsroom junk. Unlike Lee Caraway, this guy was every inch plainclothes law enforcement: dark brown gabardine suit, slightly out of shape, with a white shirt and sober tie. Everything was ten years out of fashion, but in a way that suggested he wasn't so much behind the times as resentful of them. The bulge on the left side of his coat meant he was packing heat and was happy for people to know it. Big-framed fellow, maybe five ten and two hundred pounds. A few reporters and copy editors gave him curious looks as he moved among them. They didn't know where he was from, but they knew it wasn't the Rotary Club.

As he came closer I made out a cuboid head with blunt features and dark eyes set in razor-cut apertures. His complexion was pale, his hair short and slick. I guessed he was mid-fifties, which meant he probably served in World War II. Wanna know what the far side of the generation gap looked like? This guy was the complete picture.

He came into my office. 'You Tyler?'

'Who's asking?'

'Supervisory Special Agent Schwenk, FBI.' He flipped his shield.

'I'm Tyler,' I said. 'Take a seat. Not often I get a personal visit from the Bureau. What can I do for you?'

He took a seat in the chair opposite my desk and stretched his legs in a lazy A. 'You can stay away from my investigation.'

'*Your* investigation?' I put on a quizzical smile. 'What does Sergeant Caraway say about that?'

'Doesn't matter.'

'Does to me.'

He lit a cigarette. 'This is now a federal matter. Possible assassination of a US congressman means we got a national security issue. All press information has to come through the Bureau.'

When the Feds come to town a lot of people think they take over from local law enforcement. In reality, though, the FBI is supposed to work alongside police officers, not instead of them. Of course a lot depends on how much control the locals are willing to hand over. Sometimes there are sound operational reasons for letting the Feds take the lead. With Caraway, my guess was she'd sooner die.

I maintained a friendly tone. 'I take my information any way I can get it.'

'Well you won't get anything unless I say so.'

'We'll see. But so far I've given more than I've gotten.'

The G-man blew smoke out his nostrils. 'Listen, Tyler, I know you were a big shot crime reporter in New York. I know you like to chase down your own angles and I know you think you're smarter than guys like me. But if I catch you interfering in this case I'll hit you with an obstruction of justice rap that'll make your eyes water.'

'I'm real flattered you did your homework.' I leaned forward in my chair. 'But I bet you don't run background checks on all the reporters you come across, still less drop by their offices. Think of all that taxpayer money going to waste.'

I waited a few seconds. 'So why are you here, Agent Schwenk? What makes this case so different?'

He stabbed out his barely smoked cigarette. 'As I said, there are questions of national security.'

'Care to elaborate? There's some crazy shit going down, I can tell that much.'

He stood up, clearly rattled. 'You need to watch yourself, Tyler. You don't want to piss me off.'

'Nor you me. This little paper might not be the *New York Examiner* or the *LA Times*, but we reach into every home, every organisation, every business in a thirty-mile radius. You wanna talk to the local community, you gotta talk to us. Happy to work together, but it has to be mutual.'

He made a snort someplace between contempt and frustration and left.

*

I got off the phone with Stokes Honeysett's personal assistant and drove out of town toward Interstate 15. Hicks' great patriarch had agreed to a face-to-face interview after I told his PA about my encounter with his anti-union employees.

Hard to tell what I was in for. On the one hand it could be soft soap about his inability to control individuals outside his factory gates; on the other, he could threaten me with a libel writ if I published anything suggesting he sanctioned intimidation.

How I was going to approach him was another matter. Like me, Honeysett had been awarded the Medal of Honor and perhaps this would give us some common ground.

Leastways I had some time to think. The Bug's ageing 1100cc motor could just about muster 50 mph. Any faster and I risked overheating. And with the air temperature north of one hundred degrees, the idea of waiting on the shoulder for a tow-truck was not appealing. So I rolled down the windows, sat back in the slow lane and watched the Mohave unspool. Flats of khaki dirt, mottled by mesquite and sagebrush, gave an impression of bobcat pelt. The dusty expanse was corralled by the Cronese Mountains in the north and the Cady range to the south. At this distance the peaks laid low, serrating the horizon like the jaws of a bear-trap. Someplace over to my right the Mojave River took cover beneath its alluvium bed, flowing in an upside-down sort of a way towards the dry playa of Soda Lake. There, any moisture that made the ninety-mile journey from the San Bernardino Mountains evaporated in seconds.

My soundtrack was David Bowie's *Aladdin Sane* on an eight-track stereo system that was worth significantly more than the car. I'd never heard an album more hip to the LA scene of those years, though the title track might have been written for the Mohave. Like the desert, the song was jagged and sometimes jarring and just about hung together, but in a way that was perversely righteous.

I took the Field Road off-ramp and drove south and east. Bowie sang *Cracked Actor*, then *Time*.

Which was something I didn't have to spare.

Making sense of the CIA and FBI arriving on my remote desert beat was going to be tough, though I was certain it was no coincidence.

The two organisations had a history of enmity. The Bureau's long-time boss, J Edgar Hoover, had died last year. But there was too much bad blood to make collaboration likely or even possible. I had to assume they weren't working together. In theory, the CIA's job was spying on other countries, while the FBI was responsible for stopping other countries spying on the USA. But on the ground, it wasn't so simple. The CIA routinely spied on American citizens and the Feds posted agents abroad. You want to muddy the water, bring in the Agency *and* the Bureau. That's what Nixon did with the Watergate investigation and, man, that had gotten to be one complicated crock of shit.

Of course this rivalry wasn't necessarily a bad thing. Maybe I could make it work in my interest – when I figured out what my interest was.

As far as information sources went, I was ahead of the

field: I had Caraway in the local police department; Sheldon in the CIA; and Schwenk in the FBI. The spook and the G-man were what you might call passive sources in that I'd seen Sheldon's file without him knowing, and Schwenk's unsubtle attempt to make me toe the line told me there was much more at stake than he was ready to admit. This was the thing with sources: what they didn't say was sometimes more revealing than what they did.

Sheldon's appearance was the most baffling because it went against Caraway's entirely logical assumption that Hazeldene, not Carmody, had been the mark.

No great surprise that the CIA was investigating the mob's use of offshore bank accounts to scrub up dirty cash before bringing it back into the USA. Even the news that LA venture capital had gotten implicated was hardly shocking. Folks who invested big in high-return crapshoots didn't ask too many questions. But what did make my radar ping was that Ray Carmody's silver mine enterprise was financed almost entirely by private equity cash from LA. If a deal involving mob money turns sour, you better make your peace or bug out fast. Maybe Carmody's deal *was* funded by the mob; maybe something *had* gone wrong; maybe he *had* been hit and Hazeldene got in the way.

Of course this was just speculation based on a ten-second glance at Sheldon's file. I hadn't seen anything of the documents it contained.

Mick Ronson was cranking up the guitar riff on *The Jean Genie* when I realized I was outside the home of Stokes Honeysett and still had no plan.

TEN

Sometimes, no plan is the best plan.

Anyways that's what I told myself as I pulled up at the tall wrought iron gates and announced my arrival through an intercom speaker.

A few seconds later the gates swung open and the voice of a woman with a Mexican accent told me to park near the house at the end of the drive.

Honeysett's place was a churrigueresque mansion fronted by arched colonnades and flanked by landscaped gardens. There were regimented lines of royal palm, eucalyptus and bougainvillea – and certainly none of the tough Mohave weeds I grew in my yard.

The old boy was watching me from the shade of a carved stone portico.

He cut a lean, unstooping figure as he started toward me with the distinctive gait I'd read about in the library clips. See, Honeysett had lost both legs in World War I and wore prosthetics that required a swinging motion from the hip to carry him forward. A lot of old timers would have taken to a wheelchair long ago and I was impressed by this guy's sheer cussedness.

As he came closer I made out a suntanned complexion and thick white hair that seemed to accentuate one another. Hazel eyes nestled in shawls of loose flesh either side of a slender nose. Despite the oppressive heat, he was decked out in a worsted navy-blue business suit, starched white shirt and perfectly knotted necktie. For a guy of 77, he looked in real good shape.

I took the hand he extended and examined his features for similarities with his daughter. She certainly had his eyes and fine-boned face, but not the thin lips or fleshy ears. Difficult to imagine her at home in this lavish setting and I wondered what sort of relationship she had with the old man. Why had he gone behind her back to pull those strings at city hall and get her the chief of Ds job? Did he fear for her safety on the streets of LA? Was this a control thing? Was it any of my damn business? If it wasn't, it would be very soon.

He invited me into the house and made a gracious smile that reminded me of Cary Grant's. 'I must apologize for the unacceptable behaviour of my people, Mr Tyler.' His voice was resonant, the accent suggested a long pedigree and old money. 'And I can assure you there will be no repetition. I won't tolerate intimidation.'

I returned his smile. If this was bullshit, it was the most convincing I ever heard. Maybe it was his patrician manner; maybe he was telling the truth; maybe both. 'That's good to hear, Mr Honeysett. But given that those men acted independently, how can you be so sure there won't be more trouble?'

I followed him into a lobby with a vaulted timber roof and marble floor. It was furnished in the Spanish colonial style and spoke of affluence, but not in a loud or flamboyant way. If anything, the atmosphere was ascetic. 'I know my people, Mr Tyler. Amalgamated Metals is a family. I have personally made clear to each member of my workforce that further incidents will result in immediate dismissal.'

As we moved into his office suite I switched to the tack I wanted to steer him on. 'Fear of losing your job can rouse powerful emotions, Mr Honeysett. And Congressman Hazeldene's speech outside your factory gates did just that.'

He went to a big mahogany desk with an inlaid leather surface and picked up the phone.

'Refreshment, Mr Tyler? Coffee? Something cool, perhaps?'

'Water would be good, thanks.' Behind the desk were framed photographs of Honeysett with every US president from Harry Truman to Richard Nixon. Wanna make a statement about your business credentials? Getting yourself snapped with half a dozen US presidents is a hell of a way to do it.

He spoke into the receiver and asked for two glasses of iced water.

Then he turned to me with a concerned expression. 'Surely you don't think one of my people carried out those appalling murders?'

'The police believe Congressman Hazeldene was the primary target. And you have made it very clear to your workers that unionisation would threaten jobs.'

Honeysett frowned. 'That's hardly the same thing as saying, "go shoot a congressman and anybody else who happens to get in your way".'

'I'm not suggesting it is, sir. My point is that Hazeldene scared a lot of people at your company when he came to town. And scared people are capable of crazy things.'

'Even so, I hope you're not going to print any intimations of that nature?' Now there was a hint of threat in his tone.

'If I did, Mr Honeysett, I'd choose my words carefully and you'd be wasting your money on a libel writ.'

I hung back as a Mexican woman came into the office with two glasses of iced water on a tray.

I took one and gulped a few mouthfuls. The sensation of the cold liquid sliding down my throat after the hot drive was real welcome.

'My attorney might advise differently,' he said. 'And I have deep pockets.'

The old boy had salt, I had to admit it. But there were better options than riling him. 'That would be your call, Mr Honeysett. But your stance on unions is a matter of public record, and in any case I'm more interested in *why* you're so dead set again them.'

'I'm not against unions, Mr Tyler. In appropriate circumstances I'm in favour. There's simply no call for unions at Amalgamated Metals.'

I took out my spiral notebook. 'Can I quote you on that?'

'I see no reason why not.' A conciliatory smile. 'Should we take a seat?'

He led me to a leather couch and armchair by some french windows. Outside, a stone birdbath stood at the centre of the smoothest lawn I ever saw and an Hispanic gardener stooped over a bed of purple fuchsias.

'You recall what caused last year's strikes at General Motors' Ohio plants?'

I nodded yes. 'From memory, United Auto Workers walked out for better conditions, as opposed to better pay.'

'They wanted dignity, Mr Tyler. They wanted to be respected.'

My host gestured for me to take a seat on the couch, then eased himself into the armchair. Feeling through the cloth of his pants, he located the mechanisms in his prosthetic legs that enabled them to bend at the knee.

When he was sitting comfortably, he looked up with a friendly expression. 'You must understand that Amalgamated is a business like few others. Of course my people are well paid, but just as importantly, they are valued. They work in excellent conditions; they enjoy generous benefits; and they are represented on a shop floor committee that includes workers and managers.'

He took out a pipe and started filling the bowl with tobacco from a tin. 'I'm sure you did your research before driving out here and are aware that I served in the Great War before steering my company through the Great Depression. Those experiences were not ones I'd care to repeat. But they did teach me the importance of comradeship; of looking after your own. As I said, we're a family. If people have problems, they come to me.'

Striking a match, he held the flame over the bowl of his pipe and briefly vanished in a fug of smoke.

'I get the wartime leadership stuff. I can even understand how it might have worked in the Depression era. But a paternal approach to industrial relations at a time of big workforces and collective bargaining is, well...'

'Old fashioned?'

'I was going to say idealistic.'

'Let me tell you something about my company, Mr Tyler. That way you'll better understand – what is it you young people say? – *where I'm coming from*. You see, I didn't simply start my firm *after* my experience in the Great War, I started my firm *because* of that experience.'

I scribbled more shorthand notes. Wasn't sure where this was leading but it would be useful for background.

'I commanded a company of tanks when Uncle Sam first sent them into action against the Hindenburg Line in the fall of 1918. We'd barely engaged the Germans when five of my tanks got bogged down in muddy shell craters. They were sitting ducks. I had to run from tank to tank to make sure each one could get going again.' He tapped his pipe on one of his prosthetics. 'But all that running around in the open exposed me to enemy fire. That was how I lost my legs – and how I came to get my Medal of Honor.'

My host took a moment to gaze at a disappearing scrawl of tobacco smoke. I suspected he was back there in the bloody, muddy killing grounds. 'After the war I faced an unpromising future. Employment opportunities were limited for a double amputee. So I studied the thing that had gotten me into that fix – tank design – and figured out how I could use it as a business proposition.'

I made a note of this comment and underlined it. Here was the nub of a feature story. Anybody who could use the loss of both legs as the inspiration for a multi-million dollar business was worth fifteen hundred words in anybody's newspaper.

He continued in a more reflective tone. 'In the inter-war years everyone agreed that tanks were the future of land warfare, but contemporary models had major problems: they were too unstable to fire accurately while moving; they were prone to losing mobility in rough terrain; and they were vulnerable to anti-tank mines.'

He gave me a quick look, like a teacher making sure a kid was paying attention. I was listening carefully enough, though I had no idea where his story was headed. All the same, I was well versed in the art of faking it. 'So what was the answer?'

He took a suck on his pipe. 'Developing better suspension systems. Effective suspension produces a smoother ride, so firing accuracy improves; road-wheels are independently sprung so they can handle challenging terrain; and you increase the ride height – every fraction of an inch higher, the greater the chances of the crew surviving a mine blast.'

I finished my shorthand note and waited for him to continue.

'The firm I founded in 1926 focused on vertical springs but we moved over to torsion bars during World War II. We were small in those early years, but a real team. Mainly ex-tank fellows from the Great War. But even as the business got bigger, that team ethic remained. It still does. It's what defines and drives us. We're in it as one; we all get a fair share of the rewards; no one gets left behind; and we make a real contribution to keeping our country's tank crews as safe as possible.'

He turned to me, this time with a penetrating stare. 'Now do you see why I don't want union zealots poking around, upsetting what I've spent a lifetime building?'

'I don't necessarily agree about organized labour being a problem, but I can see where you're coming from.' I made a one-sided smile. 'As we young folks say.'

He nodded approvingly and struggled to his prosthetic feet.

'Let me show you something, Mr Tyler.'

I followed him across the room to a glass display case by the window. It contained a polished steel rod, maybe ten feet long and three inches in diameter, with grooved sections parallel to the bar at each end.

'Can you guess what it is?'

'Got to be a torsion bar.'

'Doesn't look like much.' His voice was soft, almost reverential. 'But it's been the main weight-bearing spring in every American tank since World War II.'

'Sure doesn't seem very spring-like,' I said. 'How does it work?'

He glanced at me as if I should have known this, but his explanation was patient rather than patronising. 'One end is anchored to the hull of the tank and the other is connected to a road wheel on the opposite side of the vehicle. When the wheel moves up and down over rough ground the bar twists around its axis and springs back due its resistance to the rotation. The M60 main battle tank is driven by six road wheels on each track, so that's a total of twelve torsion bars configured laterally.'

I made more notes. This was the opposite of sexy but if I went ahead with the feature that was taking shape in my head I'd need to explain to my readers how Honeysett's company made its money.

'The bar you're looking at is a high-hardness steel alloy that we developed in record time for the M18 Hellcat tank destroyer in Normandy. Our product was so successful that we received a presidential citation.' He pointed to a framed letter on the wall above the glass case. Under the tight-packed typewriting was the seal of the president of the United States.

His voice quavered slightly and I got a sense of why this guy was so turned on by metal science. 'I tell you straight, Mr

Tyler: this product, this citation, means as much to me as my Medal of Honor.'

He seemed to compose himself, as if embarrassed that he'd revealed too much. Regardless, I was impressed. Gottasay. And perhaps a little jealous that he'd gotten something solid, something true, that justified his life's work.

His tone became more laid back as we returned to the seats.

'Of course you were awarded the medal much more recently, and in a very different war.' He gave me a skewering stare and I realized the tables were about to be turned.

ELEVEN

'Sounds like you did a little homework too, Mr Honeysett.'

'I thought it would be a sensible precaution if I was going to invite a reporter into my home. What, if I may ask, was your experience?'

I gave him a sidelong look as we sat back down. 'Of winning the Medal of Honor?'

'Not winning it, *possessing* it.'

'Much the same as everyone else's, I guess.'

I recalled Lyndon Johnson placing the sky blue ribbon around my neck, standing in front of me and adjusting the small gold star. I recalled him saying he'd rather have that medal than the presidency and me thinking *Sure you would*. I recalled the camera flashbulbs popping in a rippling silver dazzle, my picture and story appearing in *Stars and Stripes* and almost every news outlet across the country.

Honeysett chuckled. 'You couldn't wait for some other joe to get one so you'd be out of the spotlight, could you?'

'Off the hook, more like.' We exchanged a knowing look, and I laughed too. 'And I was used to media hype – I'd been a newspaperman in New York before the war. I guess I was used to dishing it out but I wasn't so good at taking it.'

Leaning back in his seat, he looked at me as if in a fresh light. 'Why *did* they give it to you?'

Shook my head. 'I honestly don't know. To this day I can't remember any part of the action. Just the before and after.'

In a crazy kind of way, the memory gap was reassuring. It meant some of my emotional circuitry was still connected: that I wasn't completely unshockable. I'd read the citation, sure I had. It told me I'd 'displayed extraordinary heroism in the face of extreme personal danger'. But that was just a bunch of lofty words that didn't mean very much to my reporter's brain.

Even so, I felt obligated to tell the old man something.

'An infantry company had gotten surrounded in the Đăk Tô area, where the borders of Vietnam, Laos, and Cambodia come together. My unit was sent in to get them out. I remember debarking the chopper, but then it all went blank. I was told I charged an enemy formation and smoked a significant number of NVA regulars. I was never told how many and I was never interested to find out. They also told me I brought back a lot of casualties.'

I took out a Camel but didn't light it. 'My memory started working again after the firefight. I was in the whirlybird with a bunch of medics and wounded guys. They were giving me strange looks, but I couldn't figure out why. Then I realized I'd gotten this pink goo plastered all over my arms and chest. At first I thought I was covered in bits of some poor bastard I'd cut up in close quarter combat. Later I learned it was skin and soft tissue from wounded grunts I carried from the foxholes.'

Honeysett leaned forward, resting an elbow on one prosthetic leg. 'Saving your own is always better than killing the enemy. Leastways, that's what I've always told myself. Perhaps it makes the actuality of taking human life easier to accept.'

'Perhaps.' Truth was that killing people never troubled me. It was my job. I took out Charlie like I took out the trash. But I didn't get any sort of high from it either. If anything, danger made me feel normal in the way I thought ordinary folks felt normal. My mom once told me she didn't drink to get drunk; she drank to feel normal. Maybe I got addicted to Special Forces ops in the same way. Maybe that was why I stayed so long. But there was nothing normal about the Nasty.

'Want a light for your cigarette?'

I remembered the unlit Camel between my lips and accepted his offer.

'You might be interested in attending a demonstration up at Fort Irwin next Saturday. A company of M60s fitted with our torsion bars are going to show what they can do. We've already supplied the Chrysler Tank Plant in Detroit with a major consignment and will close another substantial deal next month.'

I glanced up from my notebook. 'Would that mean more jobs for Hicks?'

'Two hundred to start with, rising to five hundred within a year. We'd start hiring before Christmas. Just as importantly it would safeguard the jobs of the twelve hundred employees we already have.'

'Could I bring a photographer?' Job creation stories always sold papers, but I was also thinking about potential page one artwork. Tanks could be photogenic and Suze Carter could work on a dramatic shot, perhaps of an M60 ploughing up a plume of Mohave dust.

'I'm sure that can be arranged. I'll have my office send you a couple of press passes.'

The interview done, he walked me back to my car.

I'd deliberately left the subject of Gary Gerwitz until the end so I could drop it into the conversation like an afterthought.

'I ran into your senior vice president yesterday,' I said. 'Or, more accurately, he ran into me.'

I explained how Gerwitz rear-ended me.

'That's too bad,' he said. 'But I'm glad no one was hurt, and that Mr Gerwitz compensated you for the damage to your car.'

'He gave me way too much – more than my old rust bucket is actually worth. Is he at work today? Thought I might call around and offer to repay some of it.'

'I'm afraid won't be possible. Mr Gerwitz is on vacation.'

'Oh, I see. When is he back?'

'I don't know. Couple of weeks maybe. He cleared his diary.'

Gerwitz sure hadn't looked as if he was setting off on vacation, but I let it pass.

I parted company with Honeysett at the front door and headed toward my car.

TWELVE

A woman was standing by the Beetle with one hand on her hip, apparently waiting for me. She looked early thirties with blonde feather-cut hair and a deep suntan. She smiled as I came closer: vivid lipstick and shiny white teeth. Blue eyes pinned me with sharp curiosity. A floral pattern dress showcased figure-eight curves and head-turning legs. She had a luminous quality that stopped me looking in any direction but hers. She wouldn't get called beautiful; hot, you'd hear that plenty.

'Dad never told me he was entertaining.'

I hadn't realized Honeysett had *two* daughters. But then the library clips were all about the old guy's business activities. There was next to nothing about his personal or family life.

She extended a hand. 'I'm Stacey Honeysett.'

Her grip was firm. 'Wat Tyler, editor of the *Herald*.'

Her high-wattage eyes locked on mine. 'Of course you are. Formerly a police reporter on the *New York Examiner*. Prior to that, a decorated hero in the war of imperialist oppression in Vietnam.'

I let the Vietnam jibe slide and smiled back. 'For someone

who didn't know anyone was calling, you sure know a lot about me.'

'If you recall, I said my dad didn't *tell* me you were calling. He rarely tells me much. So I have to find these things out for myself.'

'What did you discover?'

One of her precisely shaped eyebrows tilted a fraction. 'Some factory boys didn't like your newspaper story because it suggested pro-union politicians like Frank Hazeldene aren't welcome in Hicks. So they attacked you and came off the worse. You naturally wondered if my dad put them up to it; and he naturally wanted to assure you otherwise.'

'You're remarkably well informed.'

'I make it my business to be.' She turned to my Bug. 'Love your car. It's so I-don't-give-a-fuck cool. So blue collar. That's what you are, isn't it, a blue collar guy? Not really a military guy.'

Her blend of rich girl and anti-war protestor carried a whiff of Jane Fonda – Hanoi Jane as she'd been tagged after visiting North Vietnam. But Stacey Honeysett seemed forthright enough, so I played along. 'Only work I ever did was white collar – excepting Vietnam, of course. And even there – as you probably know already – I ended up an officer. So I don't really slot into any conventional stereotypes. What about you, Stacey? You a Hanoi Jane?'

She made a gurgling laugh. 'Ooh! Touché, Wat. Tou*ché*.'

Slinging open the driver's door, she peered inside and pegged the eight-track.

'That's a cool sound system. Bet it cost more than this old Bug.'

I smiled. 'You gotta get your priorities right.'

In truth, music wasn't so much a priority as an obsession. It grew out of the fucked up world I lived in when I was a kid and my dad beat the shit out of my mom because, well, that was what he did. The country tunes I heard on the radio didn't make any of that easier to cope with, but they did help me to dig that the world had some good stuff in it if you looked hard enough. Later I discovered the sweet alchemy of words in poems, novels, even news stories. They all became obsessions, but music was the deepest, perhaps because it was the oldest.

'I couldn't agree more.' Stacey touched my arm. 'Music is right in the groove. Materialistic shit like dick-surrogate cars, they're for jerkoffs and losers.'

She picked up the *Aladdin Sane* tape. 'Bowie's right on the beam, isn't he? I dig that androgynous thing, that blurring of sexual identity. What do you make of Lou Reed and Iggy and the Stooges and the New York Dolls? They your scene too?'

I told her sure, I liked Lou and Iggy and the Dolls.

'I'm into soul music. Right now I'm listening to a lot of James Brown and Marvin Gaye. They're the most, aren't they? Did you interview James or Marvin?'

'I was a crime reporter. But I did interview Johnny Thunders from the Dolls one time after his place had gotten burglarized.'

Her mind was someplace else before I finished speaking. 'Marvin's so right about Vietnam, isn't he? On *What's Going On?* I mean.'

'He makes some valid points.'

'My dad doesn't approve of anything left-leaning. He claims to be tolerant but he hates my keeping Chairman Mao's Little Red Book and *Das Kapital* in the house.'

Whether she'd read them was another matter, but I got the impression she put Mao and Marx on her bookshelf as much to antagonize her dad as to enlighten herself.

'What does your sister think?'

'Lee's my *half*-sister. My mom died before Dad married her mom, who also died. Poor Dad hasn't been so lucky with wives. But Lee can think what she likes. She's a hypocrite like Dad. She says she's for women's liberation – that's why she changed her name to Caraway, for Hattie Wyatt Caraway, the first woman elected to the US Senate. But then Lee joined the blue pigs. Feminism and fascism rolled into one, that's my half-sister for you.'

'So you weren't too happy to see her back in town?'

Stacey made a dismissive shrug. 'This horrible little backwater can hardly get any worse. But as long as she stays out of my way I don't give a shit where she is. Do you mind if I say fuck?'

With a flick of her wrist she looked at her watch and her eyes widened as if she'd lost track of time. 'I need to be someplace else. But let's talk some more. Over a few drinks maybe?'

'Maybe.'

She turned away, walking toward the main house and I pictured her smiling to herself, knowing I'd be watching her. So I looked away. But of course she wouldn't know this, which made the gesture sort of pointless.

I drove home without playing the eight track or the radio. Instead I was thinking about old man Honeysett and his prosthetic legs and paternal take on industrial relations; and about his elder daughter, radical, forthright and every bit of sexy.

Backing into my drive, I locked up the Beetle and started toward my front door.

A rustling noise from the goldenbush shrub by the side of the house made me pause.

Probably a neighbour's cat, maybe a ground squirrel or a lizard.

I carried on.

Stopped again when a twig parted.

Didn't need long range recon savvy to dig that this was no little critter, domesticated or otherwise.

What, then? Had Stokes Honeysett been feeding me bullshit while priming his attack dogs for another gig?

Moving quietly, I pressed my back against the side of the bungalow.

And waited.

Three, four, five seconds.

Approaching footfall was soft and cautious.

The guy stepped around the corner and stood looking at the Bug, his back to me.

Kept my tone even. 'Looking for me?'

THIRTEEN

I learned all I needed to all too fast: the bony frame decked out in an avocado shirt and plum colour corduroy jeans gave me most of the picture. The rest came from a whiff of Hai Karate mixed with the musty odour you get from being around booze without necessarily drinking it.

His voice was anxious. 'Hey, it's me, Wat. Your buddy, Norm.'

He turned slowly, skinny forearms half raised as if I had a gun on him.

'You okay, Norm?'

Small eyes scrutinized me with peculiar intensity. The high and tight haircut was at odds with the flashy garb and I got the impression he was trying to come over as a squared away military type *and* a rock and roll cat without seeing any contradiction. He walked toward me, a little unsteady on big platform shoes. A lot of people put platforms on their feet in 1973 but Norm's two-inch soles and four-inch heels added extra height to an already tenuous physique. Upshot was a body-shape that called to mind a defoliated palm tree.

'You didn't come to the door, man, so I went down the

side.' He seemed agitated. 'Figured you might've been out back. Wasn't poking around or nothing.'

'That's cool, Norm. Didn't imagine you were.' I made a smile designed to put him at ease and mask my irritation. Last person I wanted on my doorstep right then was Norm Dibbitts. On the other hand, I needed to keep him friendly. The death of Marsha Houtrelle was no doubt a tragic accident, but she still had a story and I wanted to tell it. As her former boss and landlord, Norm was a strong source. I kept my voice light. 'So what brings you around here, Norm?'

A knot appeared above the bridge of his nose. 'I know who killed Marsha. And Ray Carmody. And the congressman.'

Now he had my attention. 'Fast work, Norm. So who was it?'

'Richard Milhous Nixon.'

He noticed my sceptical expression. 'Not Tricky Dick himself. But *his* people: CIA, FBI, Cubans, black ops units that ain't even got names – undercover goons who deal with the folks on the Enemies Lists.'

I made an easy-going smile. Nixon's Enemies Lists had caused a stir when they were published in June. But there were only twenty people on the first list and a couple of hundred on the second. These 'enemies' were mainly high-profile figures. They included household names such as Jane Fonda, Andy Warhol and Joe Namath. None of the victims of the Hicks shooting were on either list. Nor would any sane person expect them to be.

Yet this was the America I'd come back to: the land of the freaked and the brazenly corrupt. Guys like Norm were getting pushed nearer the edge by guys like Nixon.

'Did you read the lists, Norm, when they were printed in the *Herald*?'

He nodded with a frustrated frown, as if anticipating my question. 'There's another list, Wat. A super-list. Thousands of people on it. Millions. Including Marsha, Hazeldene and Carmody.'

This was deep serious paranoia. I started to wonder if Norm had smoked too much Maryjane or was jacked on some psychoactive substance. Even so, I wanted to see where this was leading. So I sat on the porch steps and offered him a cigarette. 'I can see how the congressman might have posed a threat. But how come Marsha and Ray Carmody ended up on this super-list?'

Norm placed a Camel between his lips and bathed its tip in the flame of my lighter. 'Like you say, Hazeldene's obvious. Pinko huckster who loved to give out. Loud against Nixon. Loud against nukes. Loud against big business cabals and whatnot. So no surprises the Man wanted *him* dead.'

'And Carmody?'

Norm gave me a sheepish look in the way of a kid who has figured out a tough math question but is too shy to take the credit. 'His daddy was a closet commie. Fred Paulson – guy who owns Fred's Fast Feeder – is fairly sure he was. See, Fred lived opposite the Carmody place ten years and more. Nixon would've hated his son making so much money.'

'So Nixon's stooges shot Carmody on account of Carmody's dad's suspected left wing sympathies?'

Norm sucked in a lungful of smoke, held it, and released slowly. '*Now* can you see how it all stacks up?'

Horseshit for sure. Unusual, not really. You need to remember that this was a time when the hand of conspiracy was seen on the right and on the left and everyplace between. And far out theories were being postulated by people a lot more credible than Norm. The FBI infiltrated the anti-war movement. The CIA used dirty tricks at home like it had in Chile. The Soviets had put Eisenhower in the Whitehouse. Nixon himself was a puppet of the Rockefeller family. The Moonies, the banks, the Symbionese Liberation Army, even UFOs, they all cut a slice of paranoid pie. As the Watergate investigation unfolded on national television, some theories were shown not only to be true, but understated.

I asked, 'What made you think this, Norm?'

'I heard two guys talking.' His eyes narrowed. 'Reckon they was spooks.'

'How could you tell?'

'They was from outta town.'

That sealed it. Anybody from outta town who didn't have an obvious reason for being *in* town could only be CIA hitmen.

'So what did Marsha do to end up on the super-list?'

'Must've said something bad about Nixon. Maybe years back. They'd have wiretapped her phone, or maybe she got taped by a snooper and her name got put on the super-list. Nixon read it and told the CIA to get her too. Makes sense.'

'They don't have those kind of resources, Norm. To wiretap barmaids.'

'The hell they don't. Those bastards killed *three* birds with one stone. And they'll be watching you and me. We're all on that goddamn list, all of us.'

What to say?

Norm's jerky eyes swivelled to a beat-up station wagon that moved slowly along the street. As it rolled by my house, tinny radio music drifted from the rolled-down driver's window.

Norm turned so he had his back to the passing vehicle. 'You see that?'

I glanced again at the station wagon – a Mercury Colony Park, at least ten years old. The sky blue paintwork and faux wooden panelling were shabby and expanses of rust accounted for most of the roof.

Still with his back to the Colony Park, Norm said, 'You know those people?'

I squinted in the direction of the station wagon as it turned right and vanished from view. 'No I don't. But I'm pretty sure they're just neighbours driving by.'

'I don't like the look of that station wagon.'

I gave him a puzzled look. 'It's just an old station wagon. Nothing out of the ordinary. Just the opposite.'

'That's *exactly* what they want us to think. I shouldn't have come. Gotta go.'

He went clomping down my driveway in his platform shoes. A few seconds later I heard an engine start and Norm's maroon Chevy Nova took off fast in the opposite direction to the station wagon.

Crazy or not, Norm was scared shitless and it didn't take a genius to figure out the root of his problem. His experience of the war may have been limited to clerical work in Saigon but he still came home the psychological equivalent of an amputee. This gave me pause for reflection. In his way he served his country every bit as much as I did in my kick-ass Special Forces unit. I did that shit because I was good at it and, if I was honest, it put me in touch with my damped-down emotions. Fuck, I even prospered from it: went in a private, came out a captain. This thought made me feel a little ashamed of my attitude to Norm. Sure, his bullshit bravado and basket-case theories were annoying. But watching him freak out like that made me realize I needed to cut the guy a little slack and quit rolling my eyes every time I saw him.

FOURTEEN

On reflection I should have stayed away from Gary Gerwitz's place, but that was where the music took me.

I started out taking a drive so I could hear some righteous sounds and mull things over. Always did my best mulling when I was driving and listening. The problem was I didn't give too much thought to where I was headed. My soundtrack on this occasion was the Rolling Stones' *Exile on Main Street*. Jagger was laying down *All Down the Line* like only Jagger could as I found myself cruising along the wide and quiet streets of Harrisville, Hicks' most affluent suburb. In fact, Hicks' *only* affluent suburb.

Then it hit me that Gerwitz's house was in the vicinity and the thought occurred that I could swing by. It was late-morning on a Saturday – a good time to catch folks at home. Of course he may well have driven that big Coupe de Ville to the other side of the country by now, but I was in Harrisville anyway so where was the harm?

I wasn't really interested in repaying any of the cash money he'd given me, but this was a good enough excuse for an unannounced visit. What I really wanted to find out was why he checked out in such a hurry one hour before three people got shot to death. This was especially relevant to Gerwitz because one of the dead folks was a politician in town to unionize the factory where Gerwitz was Stokes Honeysett's senior vice president. Somebody rear-ends you, then cops a speeding ticket a few minutes later, his priority is not careful driving. I recalled that pale, fraught face with John Lennon glasses and frizzy red hair tugged back like a slipped hairpiece. I'd seen enough freaked out people not to recognize panic when I saw it. Okay, Caraway hadn't wanted to question him, and that said a lot. But I was still curious.

I parked a couple of hundred yards down the street. Maybe some of Norm's paranoia rubbed off on me, but if Gerwitz wasn't home I wanted to take a look around and wasn't keen on advertising my presence by leaving the Beetle where everybody could see it. I did the Stones the courtesy of waiting till the end of *Soul Survivor*, then killed the engine and ambled down the sidewalk.

The Gerwitz place was a large ranch house with white adobe walls and broad lawns that could have used a mow. A basketball hoop stood on the driveway, though I couldn't imagine a slouchy guy like Gerwitz shooting hoops. Maybe he had kids, though there was no mention of a family in the *Herald* clips file.

I rang the doorbell. No answer. Rang again, same result.

Peering in through one of the big windows, I saw a spacious living room, conservatively furnished. There was a herringbone parquet floor with a three-piece suite in tan leather and a brick-built hearth. Down the side of the house was more evidence of kids: cheap plastic squirt gun half hidden under some shrubs and a bike with a banana seat and ape-hanger handlebars left on its side. As I drew nearer to the back door I heard muted voices. Voices I half recognized, interspersed with incidental jazz music. There was a TV on. Gerwitz must have come back home.

I tapped on the side door. Still nothing.

Tapped louder.

Another gale of television voices and I heard the theme music from the *Flintstones*.

Turning the door handle, I gave it a shove. It swung open.

I shouted his name. Nothing.

I stepped into the kitchen. Dirty dishes filled the sink and pizza boxes littered the counter tops. Flies buzzed over a plate of leftovers that might once have been spaghetti Bolognese. Still calling Gerwitz's name, I went into the living room. The TV set was now blaring the intro music for *The Jetsons*. I flipped the off switch and shouted again, louder. Still no response.

This evidence of a hurried departure chimed with the panicky way he'd bugged out of town.

Quick survey of the three bedrooms showed made-up beds. One room had bunks and kids' stuff on a shelf – Spirograph, Etch-a-Sketch and two Rock 'Em Sock 'Em robots squaring off in a yellow plastic boxing ring.

Last room in the bungalow was Gerwitz's study. Like the kitchen, this was a mess. More pizza and burger boxes, empty soda cans and beer bottles. Candy wrappers scattered about the floor: Atomic Fireballs, Goobers and Zagnut bars seemed to be the favourites.

A desk by the back window was stacked with ring binders and manila file folders, piles of typewritten sheets, spiral-bound booklets and an electronic calculator.

I was checking out the metal file cabinet when I heard the side door being shut.

Whoever had come into the place was moving about freely. Footsteps sounded sharp on the kitchen linoleum, echoey on the parquet floor tiles in the living room, muted on the hallway carpet.

Very probably it was Gerwitz. I considered calling to him, then thought better of it. My presence here wouldn't look so good. Sneaking out undetected, then circling back for a legitimate return seemed a much better option.

But whoever it was headed straight toward the study.

I was trapped.

Pressing my back to the wall near the door, I listened.

Footsteps came closer, closer still.

Then stopped.

I heard breathing just the other side of the plywood door. Soft and even. Inches away.

Then, the sound of a pistol slide being racked, a round slotting into the chamber.

Not what I expected. Not at all.

All I could do, though, was wait. I couldn't figure out my play until I knew who I was dealing with.

A candy wrapper crunched underfoot as the newcomer moved into the study.

I sucked in a long slow breath and...

...Wasn't sure whether I should be relieved or worried.

FIFTEEN

I said, 'You can put the gun away, Sergeant.'

Caraway wheeled around, the Smith & Wesson 9mm levelled at my chest, a faint smile tugging the sides of her mouth.

'I thought I'd find you in here,' she said.

'How so?'

'I saw a '64 Bug with a busted taillight parked along the street. Can't be too many of those in town.'

'Will you please stop pointing that thing at me?' I indicated the pistol.

She kept the gun on me. 'I got you dead to rights this time.'

'You're going to arrest me? I thought we were cooperating now.'

'I'm still a police officer.' She lowered the gun and placed it in a shoulder holster under her buckskin jacket. 'But I accept you're unlikely to resist.'

'What's the rap this time?'

'How does burglary sound?'

'Difficult to make stick. How do you know I don't have Mr Gerwitz's permission to be here?'

'He's outta town.'

'Outta town where exactly?'

She didn't respond, so I pushed on. 'And you're on private property without a warrant.'

'I can show probable cause.'

'That might be tricky. But anyway you won't. You're smart enough to know you'd be wasting time that could be better spent hunting the killer – with me on your side as opposed to in a prison cell.' Cocksure, maybe; accurate, for sure. With Chief Turner and the FBI looking over her shoulder, Caraway needed help any way she could get it. Including from me.

She made a longsuffering sigh. 'So what *are* you doing here?'

I figured there was no point concealing stuff that she could easily find out, and possibly already knew. So I shot her the works about being rear-ended by Gerwitz; the speeding ticket he picked up a few minutes later; and how he didn't look in the least bit like a laid-back guy setting off on vacation – despite what her dad told me.

She said, 'So what do you think happened?'

'I don't know. But I *do* know full-on panic when I see it. Also, when I got here, the door was unlocked and the TV was on. Don't you think that's odd?'

'Odd, how?'

'Gerwitz is your dad's right hand man. The guy in charge of day-to-day operations at Amalgamated Metals – where Hazeldene was trying to unionize the workforce the same afternoon he got hit. And Gerwitz left town in a big hurry less than one hour before Hazeldene died.'

'So you thought you could do your investigative reporter thing here like you did at my crime scene?'

I ignored the jibe and returned her question with one of my own. 'Why are *you* here? You weren't just driving by, were you?'

She gave me an undecided look, as if she was reassessing me. After a few beats she appeared to reach a decision. 'All right, I'm here for personal reasons.'

She walked to the window and looked out at the overgrown lawn. 'I've known Gary and his ex-wife Barbara since I was in high school. They split up five years ago, but I kept in touch with Barbara and the kids. I ran into her in the grocery store yesterday and we got chatting.'

She turned to face me, partly silhouetted against the brightness of the window. 'Seems Gary's been behaving erratically for some time. Forgetful. Short-tempered. Distracted. Prone to mood-swings – and, like you say, freaking out for no apparent reason. According to Barbara, he got so unreliable that she stopped the kids coming over – they used to visit every second weekend.'

That explained the bike and games as well as the candy trash.

I picked up a Kit-Kat wrapper. 'Hope they clean their teeth – if they still have any.'

She shook her head. 'The candy trail is Gary's. He quit smoking a couple of years back and uses this stuff as a substitute. Atomic Fireballs are his main fix. But what concerns me is the mess this place is in. Gary was never the tidiest guy, but he's really let things slide. He used to have a help, but he fired her a few weeks ago. Told Barbara she was spying on him.'

This made me think of Norm Dibbitts and his far out claims. Was everyone in this town so paranoid?

'The kitchen and the study are disaster areas, even by guy standards,' I said. 'But the rest of the place seems okay.'

'Barbara reckons these are the only rooms he's been using – apart from the bathroom. Slept on that thing.' She indicated an army surplus canvas camp bed by the far wall.

'Sounds like he has a problem. Did you ask your dad if he could shed any light?'

'He either doesn't know or won't say. I suspect the latter.'

'Any idea why?'

'Might be to do with all those questions you asked him.'

'Can't I do anything without pissing you off?'

'I didn't say you're not entitled to do your job. But Dad's always been defensive about the company. It's much more his baby than Stacey or I ever were. And when questions are asked, he gets even more protective.'

'I met Stacey also.'

'Poor you.'

'I presume she knows Gerwitz too?'

'She uses him like she uses everybody.'

'And she couldn't help?'

'She wouldn't help *me*, even if she could.'

So the antagonism was mutual.

I moved over to the desk. 'As we're here, we should take a look around. Maybe get some idea of what's been bugging Gary.'

'I'm not sure that's a good idea.'

'Where's the harm? I've come about a road accident and you're here because he's a family friend whose ex-wife told you she was worried about him.'

She looked dubious. 'Okay, but on two conditions: one, we keep it light and tidy. And two, if we do find anything,

I call the shots. I don't want any potential evidence getting contaminated – or worse, appearing in the *Herald*. You got that?'

'I got it.'

I started with the stuff piled on the desk while Caraway got busy with the rest of the study.

The paperwork was disappointingly routine. Delivery notes, purchase order dockets, dense technical memos to Gerwitz's production team. There were half a dozen volumes of Department of Defense specifications for the M60 main battle tank. No surprises there as I knew from Stokes Honeysett that Amalgamated Metals made suspension components. In among it were more candy wrappers and the odd Styrofoam burger box.

'Look what I found.'

Excitement in her voice made me look across the room.

She was holding a narrow cylindrical device, perhaps four inches long, with two yellow electric leads trailing from one end.

She tossed me the bug. Didn't seem especially sophisticated, but then it didn't need to be. Fifty bucks would buy you all the snooping gear you needed for an average size room like this.

'I'm impressed. Where was it?'

She indicated a table light. 'In there. But they'll have fitted these things all over the place.'

'Any idea why he was being spied on?'

'Your guess is as good as mine. Industrial espionage is the most obvious motive, but there may well be others we can't even guess at.' She screwed the bug back into position, presumably so the snoopers wouldn't know she discovered it.

As I turned back to the desktop I noticed a red crayon mark on a sheet of paper half buried under a box file. It was headed *Non-Destructive Test Laboratory Request Form*. The crayon had been used to draw a large ring around the weirdest shopping list I ever saw:

1. *chemical analysis*
2. *light microscopy*
3. *retained austenite*
4. *tensile properties*
5. *impact transition data longitudinal orientation*
6. *toughness (room temperature and -400C)*
7. *carbon and sulphur content*

'Take a look at this.'

She came over and leaned close, brushing her shoulder against mine. When I pushed back, she broke the contact. Message was straightforward enough: *I control this*.

I asked, 'Any idea what any of this means?'

'Clear as Hicks beer. We'd need a metallurgist to make any sense of it. But we can't take it away because I'm not meant to be here, leastways as a cop.'

I wasn't bothered about admissibility in court, but I'd agreed to a deal and had to go along with her.

'This is clearer, though.'

I pointed to the scribbled handwriting on the bottom of the sheet, this time in blue ballpoint ink:

FH, Rich Vein Café – 3.00pm, Thurs Oct 13.

I said what was going through both our minds, 'FH has to be Frank Hazeldene. And Gerwitz bugged out – in a panic – almost exactly two hours before this meeting was scheduled.

He found out what was about to go down, or someone tipped him off. But either way, he made a run for it.'

She said, 'This is a big story, I get that.'

'Damn straight it is.'

'But you can't print it.'

I gave her a disbelieving look. 'You gotta be kidding. Hazeldene told me he was on the verge of getting information that could change the balance of the Cold War. Then someone shut him up before he could get hold of it. And his likely source, Gary Gerwitz, went missing two hours before they were due to meet.'

'But as far as we know, Gary hadn't actually told Hazeldene anything when the congressman died. And we have no idea what Gary knows or – just as importantly – where he got it.'

'It's still a national news story.'

'Is it, though?' She stood right in front of me, pinned me hard. 'You put this in the public domain, you'll jeopardize the whole investigation. You'll alert the people who killed Hazeldene and who may well be trying to silence Gary. Something else to think about: If he *was* tipped off, you might as well publish a death warrant for whoever warned him.'

She'd gotten some solid arguments, I had to admit.

'You still say you're a responsible journalist?'

'Sure I am.'

'Then prove it. Work with me and I'll make certain you get a real exclusive – the whole story – when we catch these bastards.'

I took a few beats to run through my options. I'd gotten a scoop, no argument there. But it was only half the tale – maybe less. It would make a great conspiracy yarn and conspiracy yarns often sold papers better than hard news. But one of the first things my mentor Maggie Call taught me was getting the truth is more important than getting attention. And the deal Caraway was offering made a lotta sense: bide my time and get the bigger prize.

Even so, I was determined to get a little extra out of this. 'One condition.'

'Go on.'

'Dinner.'

She tilted her head and made a suspicious expression.

I gave her a little smile. 'If we're going to work as a team we should act like it.'

'We're not a team. We're cooperating. But okay, I'll pick you up at your place. Seven thirty tomorrow.'

She must have read my expression. 'You got a problem with a woman driving?'

'No I don't. It's not customary is all.'

'*I'm* not customary. If we're going to collaborate, you better get used to that.'

'I got it.'

'Something else you should get, Mr Peasant's Revolt: If there's the slightest hint of any of this appearing in your newspaper, I'll rip your balls off. You dig?'

I kept smiling. 'Language that colourful, Sergeant Caraway, how could I not?'

SIXTEEN

Caraway was late – apparently a woman's prerogative. I wasn't too sure, though, if that applied when she was doing traditional guy-stuff, like picking up and driving.

A glance along the street revealed no sign of her Plymouth Cricket so I went back to thinking about the crazy shit we found at Gary Gerwitz's place. It came down to one question: What did Gerwitz know, or what had he done that could get a congressman assassinated?

When I interviewed Hazeldene on Thursday he'd talked about acquiring information that could alter the balance of world power. But Hazeldene was a pinko polemicist, a self-promoter who courted controversy and was well known for giving out on nuclear Armageddon. He had a vested interest in exaggeration – especially when he was playing to the media.

Maybe Gerwitz had been ready to reveal information about secret activity at Amalgamated Metals. Sure, the firm was in the defence industry. But it made torsion bars – steel rods with grooves at the ends. Not exactly space-age technology. So how could something that basic have anything to do with shifting the balance of power between the USA and Soviet Union? I'd eyeballed one in Honeysett's study and it was plain boring. In fact, my biggest problem writing a feature story about Honeysett's business achievements would be making his product sound halfway interesting.

Maybe Gerwitz kept in touch with leftist academics at Berkeley, particularly in the scientific community. He'd been a professor of applied metallurgy there until '64, when he quit to show solidarity with the Free Speech Movement. That in itself said something about the guy's political sympathies. Maybe a closet commie scientist had fed Gerwitz a line on a new super weapon or quantum leap in technology. As an individual, Gerwitz seemed the most unlikely spy. But the most unlikely spies were sometimes the most effective.

Maybe Gerwitz was a paranoid fantasist like Norm Dibbitts. The state of his house, his ex-wife stopping him seeing their kids, suggested he had problems.

Then again, why was Gerwitz's place bugged? This was suspicious, though not uncommon. In those paranoid days everyone from Nixon down was snooping or being snooped on – or both. Sneaky devices were stock-in-trade for private investigators working for everybody from divorce lawyers to insurance companies.

Maybe Hazeldene wasn't the mark. Maybe Carmody was.

My old pal Finn Sheldon was in town. And my peek into his brief case told me the CIA was investigating the mob's use of LA venture capital funds to wash dirty money, and Carmody had used LA venture capital to get his business off the ground.

Maybe if I thought about it long enough and hard enough I'd end up vanishing up my own ass.

The sound of Caraway's car horn derailed my train of thought. I was glad of the distraction and went out to meet her.

She was wearing an embroidered bell sleeve smock with flared jeans. She looked hot yet elegant with her tawny hair pinned up. I asked if it would be considered sexist to say so.

'Depends how you say it.' She put the car into gear and gave me a sideways glance. 'You look okay too.'

There was gentle mockery in her tone, but I kind of liked it.

'Sorry I'm late,' she said a little later. 'Got held up at the station.'

'Anything interesting?'

'I'm surprised you don't know about it already. Your ears should have been burning.'

'*My* ears?'

'This elderly blind woman who lives across the street from the Desert Diner came in to see me. Said she just listened to your Talking Newspaper tape and wanted to complain about your story. Claimed it was inaccurate.'

'Inaccurate how?'

'She was at home when the shooting started, but claims she heard ten shots, not eight, as you reported.'

'I reported the information you gave me.'

Caraway seemed to find this amusing. 'Didn't seem to matter as far as Mrs Sanchez was concerned. She wanted to have a pop at the *Herald* because it got the Christian name of her late husband wrong. He was voted Employee of the Year at Amalgamated Metals in 1947 and your paper printed Pedro when it should have been Pablo.'

'That shouldn't have happened,' I said. 'And the paper

should have printed a correction. Long time to hold a grudge, though.'

Caraway grinned. 'This is Hicks, remember?'

We drove west toward the cutthroat sunset, a narrowing crimson crack on saw-tooth mountain peaks. Their flanks dimmed to purple-grey, then vanished. The desert at night was a gauzy blindfold that tended to sharpen other senses. You'd hear the rustle and snap of bone dry vegetation as nocturnal predators bushwhacked their prey. Scents came to you clearer too. Sometimes you picked up desert marigold or pygmy cedar; other times, the pungent fishy niff of bractscale.

This started me thinking about what that elderly blind woman told Caraway.

I said, 'You think Mrs Sanchez *could* have heard ten shots? Folks who lose their sight, they get better with other senses.'

Caraway thought about it and shook her head no. 'She'd need exceptional hearing *and* recall. None of the other witnesses could tell how many shots because they were so close together. And ten shots doesn't make any sense. We recovered eight .45 shell casings and eight bullets, all .45 hollow point, all from the three victims.'

She drove to the eastern edge of town where the old state highway was flanked by fuzzy squiggles of neon. The half dozen blocks of gas stations, motels, bars and restaurants was known locally as the Strip, but even Hicks folks used the term with some irony.

The place she had in mind for our dinner date was Florine's Nest, a converted hip-roof barn with maroon walls and white gables.

Wouldn't have been my choice and I was surprised it was

Caraway's. Not at all what you'd expect from an old-money Ivy Leaguer.

Inside, the space was neatly divided into a restaurant, bar and dancefloor. The atmosphere was folksy, respectable and a little stuffy. Uniformed waiters moved between tables. Though the bar was busy, it was hardly boisterous. The dancefloor was squared off and a band was playing country music loud enough to dance to but not so loud you couldn't talk over it. A few couples were up there doing their thing, but they sure weren't Lower East Side punks and the place would never get described as jumping.

We were taken to a table in the centre of the restaurant.

As I sat down I noticed a familiar face across the room: Grover Burdick, my fellow West Virginian. He was with another sergeant from the station and two women I guessed were their wives.

Burdick raised his beer glass and I waved back.

Little farther along the bar I pinned Shane Phillips, the young cop who was first on the murder scene. He was with a halfway attractive girl and two other young couples.

So Florine's Nest was the place off-duty cops brought their wives and girlfriends. That would account for the folksy respectability. And it had to be the reason Caraway brought me here. But I didn't get her logic. Why would she want a bunch of other cops to know she was on a date with a reporter?

I'd find out soon enough.

A waiter arrived at our table. Caraway ordered the Kentucky spinach soup to start and a main of roast Oregon turkey with honeyed biscuits and Idaho cottage fried potatoes. Every item on the menu seemed to be linked to a

US state by a paragraph of florid prose. I just wanted to order some food without having to read about where it came from so I went for the same as Caraway.

As the waiter disappeared my companion leaned forward, placing her elbows on the table and interlocking her fingers to form a platform for her chin. 'I got some interesting information today. I spoke to Hazeldene's secretary in Victorville. She confirmed he was due to attend a confidential meeting with Gary Gerwitz at 3.00pm on Thursday.'

'That *is* interesting. Hazeldene wouldn't sign up to a gig that didn't generate publicity without a good reason.'

'There's more: The appointment was made by Gerwitz the previous afternoon. He called to arrange it less than twenty-four hours before Hazeldene drove from Victorville to Hicks.'

I leaned in close, kept my voice low. 'So two hours before the meeting, Gerwitz freaks out, bugs out, and hasn't been seen since. An hour after *that*, Hazeldene and the two others get shot to death. Someone in Hicks knew what Gerwitz was going to tell Hazeldene and made sure that conversation never happened. Tell me if I'm wrong.'

'You're not wrong.'

We both sat back as the waiter served the Kentucky spinach soup. Tasted good, though I doubted the main ingredient ever grew within fifteen hundred miles of the Bluegrass State.

Without looking up from her soup, Caraway said, 'So, what have you found?'

'What makes you think I found anything?'

'You're compulsively competitive.'

I stirred my soup and made a faint smile. 'You got me pegged.'

Again I leaned forward and spoke quietly. 'I wanted to know more about this big contract your dad told me about – the one to supply M60 suspension parts to the tank plant at Detroit Arsenal. So I called Chrysler's public affairs office. They told me it's subject to a competitive tender process that starts next month. In other words, it's not a done deal as your dad seemed to suggest.'

She looked up quickly, her voice carrying a hint of defensiveness. 'He has a strong relationship with Chrysler going back to World War II. The firm has always won those contracts.'

'And maybe it always will. But Gerwitz's role in drawing up the bid documents will be crucial. As I understand it, he's the head honcho at the factory, the guy who makes it tick while your dad deals with the strategic stuff. So what happens to the bid if Gerwitz doesn't come back?'

'I'm not sure. But I agree it's a concern.'

'Would you say your dad and Gerwitz are close?'

'They're old friends but Dad has always been top dog in the relationship.'

'Like father and son?'

'More big brother and kid brother.'

'So your dad would know if Gerwitz had a problem?'

'What sort of problem?'

'Dunno. The sort everybody gets. We know his marriage broke up, but there could be others: money, health, booze, drugs, gambling, women – men. How long you got?'

'Well, for starters, Gary's not gay.'

'You know that for sure?'

'Well no, but...' She broke off and shrugged. 'Point taken.'

'I just think your dad knows more than he's letting on.

He could be trying to protect Gary. But if that's the case, we need to know.'

'Okay, leave it with me.'

Soon afterward the waiter came to clear the soup bowls and serve the mains.

I looked at her curiously as she speared a slice of turkey with her fork. 'You enjoying life back in your hometown?'

She wrinkled her brow. 'You don't enjoy life in Hicks, you endure it. As you've probably gathered, the place isn't overburdened with free-thinking socialites. But coming here meant getting my sergeant stripes. Couple of years' experience and I'll be gone – San Fran, Vegas, even back to LA.'

I started eating my own food. 'Why did you change your name?'

'Why do you ask?'

'Just wondered. Stacey told me you took the name of Hattie Caraway, the first woman senator.'

She pushed some food to one side of her mouth. 'It was a student thing. When I was at Princeton I considered myself to be a radical feminist. I also wanted to distance myself from my rich parents – like a lot of college kids I guess. When I swapped academia for the real world I lost a lot of the radicalism – much to Stacey's disgust – but kept the feminism.'

'Can't be easy in a job like yours.'

'It isn't. When I get asked if I'm 'liberated' it usually means "Can I fuck you?" But I was warned about so-called traditional attitudes before I joined the LAPD and went ahead anyway, so I just gotta get on with it.'

'That's very stoical. I thought you'd be more angry.'

'What's the point? We are where we are. And at least it's a better place than ten or twenty years ago.'

After a few more mouthfuls of food, she asked, 'What do you think about women in the workplace?'

'They have a right to be there. Don't forget I was taken off the streets and given something of an education by a woman reporter.'

'Your friend Maggie Call? I checked her out with some of my New York contacts. She's a righteous sister. But you're not a right-on radical sort.'

'Maggie didn't do such a bad job. I have a fairly open mind. And Vietnam wasn't exactly a liberal arts college.'

'I didn't mean to criticize.'

I waved her hasty qualification aside. 'You got a fair point. Seven years in the green machine meant I missed all the big changes in the sixties. Still not caught up in lots of ways.'

She asked me if it had been tough coming out of the combat zone and I said sure, but not nearly so tough as going in. That made her laugh and I found myself thinking how much sexier she looked when she was smiling.

Later, after the waiter cleared the table, she indicated the half-full dance floor. 'You wanna boogie?'

'Why not?'

We were ten feet from the dancefloor and passing through a chicane of close-together tables when a guy pushed back his chair, blocking our path.

SEVENTEEN

He came to his feet: an athletic-looking guy with a V-shaped torso and short dark hair, not high and tight military like Norm's, but neat and tidy respectable. And absolutely not rock and roll. His face was rectangular, clean cut and clean-shaven. Late-thirties I guessed. I'd seen him before, though I couldn't immediately recall where.

'If it ain't Calamity Jane.' Accent was local.

Caraway kept her voice level. 'Excuse us, Bobby, we need to get by.'

Mention of his name gave my memory a poke. This was Bobby Peeples, a sergeant in Bull Turner's office. I'd seen him a few times when I went to see the chief, but we'd not been introduced.

'You solved your triple homicide yet, sweetheart?'

'Get out of my way.' Caraway's tone was less accommodating.

'I'll take that as a negative. But that's a chick cop for you. You should stick to what you're good at: cooking in the kitchen and whoring in the bedroom – '

'For Chrissakes, Bobby, sit down!' The guy who had been sitting next to Peeples tugged at his jacket sleeve, but Peeples was having none of it. He shrugged his arm free, moving toward Caraway. Up close he towered over her – perhaps six-one to her five-six.

She placed one hand on her hip. 'Let's speak another time, Bobby. Right now you need to calm down and sober up.'

'You ain't gonna fob me off, rich bitch.' Peeples had been drinking, though he was a way off being drunk. 'You took my job.'

A hush started to fall across the room. Table by table, folks stopped chattering and began listening.

'A man has no more right to a job than an equally qualified woman.' Caraway spoke with the calm assurance of someone who had been here plenty times before.

'That's bra-burner horseshit. But it ain't my beef with you.'

Caraway tilted her head, frowning. 'So tell me what is.'

'*I* should've been chief of detectives.' Flecks of spittle fountained from Peeples' lower lip. 'Bull Turner all but promised me. But I didn't get the job. You wanna know why?'

'Go on.'

I sucked in a lungful of warm boozy air. This was what Grover Burdick told me when I spoke to him at the Say When. Problem was I couldn't do or say anything without betraying Burdick's confidence – and destroying any that Caraway had in me.

Peeples was warming to his big moment. Must've been planning it since he saw us walk in. He made a leery grin. 'I didn't get the job because your daddy leaned on the mayor. And the mayor leaned on the chief.'

'That's nonsense.' First time I ever saw Caraway on the

back foot. 'I filled out the application form just like everybody else.'

'Don't believe me, ask your daddy.'

Peeples' pal was tugging his sleeve again, but Peeples was laying down some hot jive and was not about to give it up.

'Don't matter anyhow. Rich bitch gonna find out soon enough how out of her depth she really is.' Peeples' voice took on a patronising air. 'Then, when she goes scooting back to daddy, the job'll be mine.'

The guy rocked back on his heels, hitching his thumbs into his belt, cocking his head so he was looking down on Caraway through one eye.

I'd had enough of this. If Peeples wouldn't sit down, I'd put him down. Took half a step forward, but a restraining hand rested on my shoulder.

I wasn't surprised to hear Grover Burdick's voice close to my ear. 'You gotta let her handle this herself, Wat. You can't help her, you can only make it worse.'

I halted. He was right.

Peeples' eyes widened, like he'd hit on some far-out idea. 'You couldn't make an arrest to save your life, could you? Hey, why don't you try? Go on, sweetheart, arrest *me*.'

He reached out and shoved her shoulder with the heel of his palm.

'C'mon, little missy, let's see what you got.'

If Caraway was still flustered, she hid it well. 'You're juiced, Bobby, and you're way out of order.'

But Peeples was not going to let this go. He was totally getting his rocks off. Quick glance sideways to check his audience was paying attention, then he reached out to shove her again.

Caraway moved fast and smart, gripped his wrist and rotated his arm clockwise 180 degrees. Peeples snapped forward at the waist as she wrenched his arm behind his shoulder and levered his face downward so his left cheek was pressed on the chequered table linen.

'Consider yourself arrested now, Bobby?'

'Bra burner bitch. I'm gonna – '

Rest was lost in a falsetto yowl as she cranked his arm still further around.

'Question's simple enough, Bobby? Have I arrested you? Or have I not?'

'Yeah, yeah, yeah, you got me! Now let go for Chrissakes!'

Caraway released her hold and Peeples stood up, wincing as he nursed his arm. Shielded by his buddy, he was ushered from the room while embarrassed spectators resumed polite conversation in that phoney sort of way you often saw after a bar fight.

I turned to Caraway. 'You okay?'

'Why shouldn't I be?' Her voice was defiant but not entirely convincing.

'Maybe we should leave too.'

'No way.' She gave me a determined glance. 'We said we were going to dance and that gorilla isn't going to stop us.'

She grabbed my hand and led me to the dancefloor. The band had started up again by the time we arrived. At first other folks cut us a wide berth, but the awkwardness vanished after a couple of lively numbers.

Toward the end of the evening, the band went into a smoochy sequence and Caraway pushed her body close to mine, looping her arms over my shoulders. Later she rested her chin on my shoulder, nestling her head against my neck.

Her hair felt smooth on my skin and smelled of smoky vanilla. My pulse went up a gear when she moved one leg inside mine and pressed her breasts against my chest.

When the singer began announcing the last number, Caraway drew her head back and placed her lips on mine. At first, a soft glide, then a full-on mouth massage. It was true that adrenalin could be a powerful turn-on and she'd have gotten a real hit from the action with Peeples. Was I surprised? Well, I guess. Complaining? Fuck, no.

Eventually the music stopped and so did the kissing.

She took a step backward and smiled up at me. '*Now* I'm ready to leave.'

The place was half-empty as we headed for the exit. I saw Grover Burdick watching from the bar but it was impossible to read his expression.

In the parking lot, she linked her arm through mine as we walked toward her car.

'Before you ask,' she said, 'I have no idea where Peeples got that stuff about my dad leaning on the mayor.'

Knowing what had gone down before she did was not good, but I had to play dumb. 'It'll be locker room scuttlebutt,' I said. This at least was true.

We didn't say much on the drive back. She played Carly Simon's *No Secrets* on her eight track and that was fine by me. The musical interlude gave me time to think what I should do next. When she picked me up three hours earlier, getting into bed with Caraway was not at the front of my mind. It was now though.

When she pulled over outside my place I craned across the small gap between us and kissed her again.

I knew immediately something was wrong.

She didn't resist, but she didn't kiss back.

I pulled away, took out a Camel.

As awkward silences went, I struggled to recall an awkwarder one. But I let it play, waited for her to say something.

'It's not that I don't like you, Wat. But we need to keep this professional. Leastways for now.'

'I'm cool with that.'

Another difficult silence.

After some while, she said, '*But*?'

I removed the unlit cigarette from my mouth. 'That's not the way I read the situation back there on the dancefloor.'

'I'm sorry about that. I guess I wanted to make a point. I guess I went too far. It's not that I regret it, but – '

'What sort of point, Lee?'

'What sort of point do you think?'

I made a knowing nodded. 'Take down a shitbird like Bobby Peeples, he's gonna harbour the grudge. He'll put it about that you're a dyke, which wouldn't help your career in a conservative place like this. So the smart play was to put the rumour mill out of action before it could get cranked up.'

Another puzzle piece slotted into place and I made a heavy sigh in the way of a sucker who realizes he's been comprehensively had. 'In fact, that was why you took me to that stuffy cops and wives joint in the first place, wasn't it? To show all those officers – and their womenfolk – that you're not a sister.'

She made a smile that was somehow apologetic and ironic and sexy. 'That's why I like you, Wat. You got a magnificent mind.'

I couldn't help but return her grin. 'You can't imagine

how good it makes a guy feel when a girl says she digs him for his brain not his body.'

She eyed me up and down with mischievous expression and kissed me quickly on the mouth. 'I never said there was anything wrong with your body.'

She pushed the shift stick into gear.

'Now get out of my car – I gotta have a late-night conversation with my dad.'

EIGHTEEN

With the first edition of Monday's paper ready to hit the presses, I sat in my office and thought again about the wisdom of the deal I cut with Caraway. Today's page one lead could have been about Gary Gerwitz going missing two hours before a secret meeting he'd arranged with Frank Hazeldene, and one hour before the triple killing. Story like that would have been national news – second time in five days my tinpot paper would have sent the big hitters scurrying to re-plate their front pages. Instead we were leading with a piece on the chamber of commerce calling for state investment in a half-built business park that had run out of development funding.

Again, I asked myself if I'd agreed to the deal because I liked Caraway, and again I came back with the answer that I'd made a sound decision based on solid journalistic logic. Doubts persisted, though.

Jacinta Vasquez, the city editor, tapped on my door and came in looking down at the spiral-bound notebook in her hand.

'We just received an odd request,' she said. 'There's a short piece in today's paper about plans for a new rackets club and gym over in Harrisville. But the councilman who owns the business behind the project wants it kept out.'

This *was* unusual. A commercial real estate developer would normally chew his arm off to get editorial coverage. 'What's his reason?'

'Says it could be seen as competing against the city council's fitness centre. It provides similar facilities.'

I leaned back in my chair. 'Still a legitimate business venture. So why doesn't he want the free advertising?'

'Place he's planning is billed as 'exclusive'. I don't think he wants ordinary folks through his doors.'

'But he wants them to vote for him come election-time and thinks our story would paint him in a bad light?'

'That's the impression I got.'

'What's the councilman's name?'

'Chester Peeples – and yes, he *is* related to Bobby Peeples who your friend Lee Caraway had the altercation with last night. Chester is Bobby's pop.'

'News travels fast.'

'You pay me to know this shit.'

I gave Jacinta a hard look. The woman was a puzzle. At thirty-nine she was still attractive and could have cut it on a big city paper. Instead she chose to stay in Hicks where her husband ran a modest family business. The reporters she managed were early twenties and ambitious for the high-flying jobs she'd never had a shot at. Sometimes I got the impression she resented them, but they sure respected her. Sometimes I got the impression she resented me, but in the role of city editor she was right on the beam.

'Tell me about Pop Peeples.'

'Big fish, little pond businessman. Almost every pie in this town has his finger in it. As well as the real estate company, he manufactures plastic products in a factory on the edge of town. They make cheap, low-margin stuff. Pay and conditions are third world. Most of his workers get significantly less than the minimum wage but nobody complains. Any hint of union activity is dealt with by way of immediate dismissal.'

This was interesting. So Stokes Honeysett wasn't the only employer in Hicks who would have seen Frank Hazeldene's visit as a threat.

I stood up and looked out the window at the fractured peaks. 'How are we planning to use this piece he wants us to pull?'

'It's a 150 word news story. We wrote it from an investment brochure circulated in the local business community. Single column, page nine.'

'Okay, put it on the front, above the fold. And get as many extra words as you can. Tell the copy chief to do a straight swap with the piece on the new speed restriction on Third Avenue.'

She wrote some notes on her pad.

'I presume we got a picture of Councilman Peeples?'

She nodded yes.

'I want it across two columns.'

She gave me a questioning look. 'You sure this is a good idea?'

I shrugged. 'You let these people push you around, they end up running the paper.'

'You sound like someone from the nationals.'

I knew what she was driving at – and I had some sympathy. The nationals didn't care about pissing off local folks. They came to town for one story and cut out when they got it. Regional reporters resented this. They got tarred by the same brush but still had to work their beat.

'You mean you'll have to deal with the Peeples long after I move on?'

'You got it.'

'Even more reason to let him know he can't push you around.'

Jacinta stood her ground – a quality I liked. 'There's another reason it might not be a good idea.'

'Go on.'

'Folks will think you did it because of what Bobby Peeples did to Lee Caraway last night.'

'Should I be worried about the Peeples family?'

'They aren't as powerful as the Honeysetts but they're a hell of a lot meaner. A lot of folks in this town are in hock to Chester Peeples – some of them in positions of authority. And bad stuff has happened to individuals who crossed him. Beatings, suspicious fires, vandalism, that sort of thing. Very little reported to the cops, even less action taken.'

I shrugged. 'I still want the story on the front page. Big picture too. Folks living near that construction site have a right to know what's going down and I won't suppress a valid news story to protect some councilman's political position.'

'You're the boss.' She wheeled away and headed for the door.

'Hey, Jacinta.'

She turned. 'Yeah?'

'Thanks for your advice. Fact I didn't take it doesn't mean I don't value it.'

She nodded and left.

Sometime later I was looking through the obituary

notices when my eyes snagged on a quarter-page display ad with Marsha Houtrelle's picture at the top.

There was no text as such, just some lines from Paul Simon's song *Bridge Over Troubled Water*. That bit about the silver girl sailing on by. Nice touch, I thought. Ad that size wouldn't have come cheap, though, and the information I'd gathered on Marsha didn't suggest wealthy pals.

I called Sheila on the front desk and asked her to find out who placed the ad.

She came back a few minutes later: Stacey Honeysett.

I picked up the phone again and dialled number I had for the Honeysett place.

*

The Say When was almost empty when I met Grover Burdick for a drink after work.

He took a bourbon and a cigarette before revealing he had nothing for me. This was fine. Burdick was as valuable a source as they came and it paid to keep him sweet. Even so, I was pretty certain the skinny he gave me was the kind Chief Turner wanted me to get.

He drained his whiskey glass and continued to stare at his image in the smoky mirror behind the bar. 'I saw one of them Peace Committee fellas on the TV with Jane Fonda, giving out on the Hanoi Hilton officers. You're a vet. What's your take?'

I gave him a wry glance. Burdick liked to sound me out on Vietnam as well as political stuff. This latest poser was about Nixon's attempt to turn the homecoming of prisoners of war into a public relations victory. The plans turned sour, though, due to bitter divisions between officer pilots held at the 'Hanoi Hilton' POW camp in north Vietnam, and enlisted grunts imprisoned in the jungle. This came to a head when Theodore Guy, an air force colonel from the Hanoi Hilton contingent, accused eight enlisted men – all ground troops – of collaborating with the enemy. Ultimately the Pentagon refused to prosecute the men, known as the Peace Committee. But that didn't stop one of them, Sergeant Larry Kavanaugh, shooting himself dead. Kavanaugh left a pregnant widow, who was suing Colonel Guy and the Pentagon.

I took a mouthful of whiskey. 'Vietnam was a different war for different folks. Air force types like Theodore Guy are career officers. They fought the war from twenty thousand feet. Enlisted grunts, they fought Victor Charles close up and that was a whole other deal.'

This was the mother of understatements. Theodore Guy never experienced the effect of heavy ordnance at ground level. Foot soldiers did. They didn't get hit so much by bombs but they knew plenty about shellfire. And sometimes we died at the hands of our own air force. One time a strafing run took out the wrong side. One time I saw a pair of legs standing sheared at the knees in a rice paddy. The grunt they were part of few seconds earlier was someplace else. We never found him. On another occasion, a napalm attack went wrong, burning an infantry platoon beyond recognition. We had to ID dead guys using mine detectors to find their dog tags. I could go on.

Burdick signalled the bartender for another bourbon. 'So where do your sympathies lie?'

'I can see it from both sides.' The bartender came over and I indicated that I'd have the same as my buddy. 'Guys who went to officer school, they drank in the military code of conduct like their mama's milk. So they knew how to conduct themselves as prisoners, even under torture. Kids who grew up in the projects and got drafted at eighteen, they weren't so hip to the code and didn't cope too well in Charlie's prison camps.'

I looked sideways. 'Anyways, what do *you* think?'

Burdick heaved his big shoulders in a what-do-I-know? shrug then switched the subject. 'So what's the latest on the White House shenanigans?'

'I only know what I read in the news.'

'The hell you do.' He drank some whiskey. 'What are your sources in Washington saying?'

I didn't have any sources in DC, but I did have pals in the White House press corps and sometimes they told me stuff. So I played along.

'Nothing new on Nixon, but Agnew is dead meat. Seems they got him dead to rights on tax fraud. We'll be looking for a new vice president very soon – maybe even this month.'

'Who's your tip?'

I took a mouthful of whiskey. 'Best information I got is Gerald Ford, House minority leader.'

'Worth a bet?'

'If you can get the odds. Word is it'll be a one-horse race.'

A group of people came into the bar and he lowered his voice. 'Okay, *I* got a tip for *you*: Don't make enemies when you don't need to.'

'Sorry, Grover, no comprendo.'

'You will in a minute.' He knocked back his whiskey and slid off the bar stool. 'Last night you played it right with Lee Caraway. Bobby Peeples was her problem and she had to deal with it. Scuttlebutt I picked up today, though, says you pissed off his old man big time with that front page story you ran.'

'He tried to get it pulled. I won't be pushed around by anybody.'

'Yeah, well Chester Peeples ain't anybody. Lotta places in Hicks, he's the motherfucker. My advice? Use this opportunity to mend your fences.' He slapped me on the shoulder and left.

It was then that I realized he was talking about Chester Peeples. I recognized him from the photograph in that day's paper. He was with the group that just came into the bar. He detached himself when he saw me.

I was looking at a tall, wide-shouldered man, maybe six-two and north of 250 pounds. I pegged him as late forties, early fifties. Sometime gone he'd have been a bruiser. Maybe still was. Decked out in an expensive-looking suit with a maroon silk tie and patent leather shoes. His face was deeply suntanned, rugged.

'Mr Tyler, I presume.'

'And you must be Councilman Peeples.' I took the hand he extended.

He perched one butt cheek on the stool Burdick just vacated and went straight to it. 'I was real unhappy with your page-one story.'

'Which one would that be? I counted five on today's front page.'

'You know which one. The one I asked you not to use.'

'That's what can happen when folks ask me not to print a piece because it doesn't fit their political agenda.'

'But my rackets club project isn't political. I'm not competing against the city council's fitness centre.'

'That's what the story said.'

'The way you wrote it suggests the opposite. You slanted it like I was responding to criticism.'

'*You* called the paper. *You* said there was no conflict of interest.' I grinned, knowing it would piss him off. 'Or are you now saying the story is incorrect? That there *is* a conflict?'

He leaned close, his voice a bass growl. 'There's a conflict all right, you piece of hillbilly shit. Between you and me. And you won't fucking win.'

I raised my glass in a mock toast. 'Here's to it, Councilman.'

Peeples turned away and moved slowly back to the folks he came in with.

Should I have taken Burdick's advice and made peace? Probably. Did I enjoy sticking it to the Man? Well, I guess.

NINETEEN

Later that morning I drove over to the greasy spoon café where Stacey wanted to meet. It was an unusual location, but then Stacey was an unusual woman.

She wasn't there yet so I used the pay phone to make an appointment for later that day. I made a note of the details and called Jacinta on the city desk so she was aware of my movements. Then I took a table by the window.

Hicks didn't have the sort of deprivation you saw in big cities, but the area around Third and Congress streets had a remote despondency all of its own. There was a liquor store with a cash loans company right next door; an auto repair shop with rusted engine parts out front; a butcher shop selling hog maw and ham knuckle and chitterlings. Between them, abandoned lots were overrun by mesquite and creosote bush. Half hidden in the weeds you could see busted couches, fridges, other domestic junk. Residents were mainly Hispanics and blacks, old already in their forties and fifties. Most lived in small houses with wood-slat walls and rusty tin roofs with mud yards fenced off by chicken-wire. Nearly every place displayed the Stars and Stripes, though this was not so much about making patriotic statements as circling the wagons. *We're Americans*, they said, *just like everybody else*. But they weren't like everybody else. If you needed reminding why, you could listen to the never-ending freight trains rumbling and squealing along tracks that cut a solid demarcation line between the respectable side of town and here. I say 'here' because the locality didn't have a name. Maybe the city council didn't think it deserved one. Maybe you don't have a problem if it doesn't have a name. Third and Congress was the only identity this place ever had.

The café was opposite the homeless shelter, a disused timber frame warehouse with boarded-over windows and flaking paintwork. A wino sucked on a muscatel short dog, ditched the empty bottle and moved on in his endless quest for more booze. This made me think of my mom and I was glad of the distraction when Stacey stepped out the front door and crossed the street toward me.

Blonde hair spilled out from a Che Guevara-style beret and she wore an olive drab jacket with a short denim skirt. As she got closer I made out shiny lipstick and heavy eye make-up. Overall effect was a clash of military grunge and glitzy swank. If nothing else it would get her noticed, which I suspected was what she wanted.

'I wouldn't have expected to find you in this part of town,' I said.

She took a seat opposite. 'It's the only part of town where people aren't hollow, plastic, pretentious, or on the make.'

I was tempted to ask why she didn't live here if the folks were so great, but I wanted information not confrontation.

I said, 'Drink? Bite to eat?'

'I could use a coffee. Black, no sugar.'

She waited until I'd ordered two black coffees, then gave me a pensive look. 'What did you want to talk to me about?'

'That ad you placed for Marsha. It was a nice gesture.'

'It was the least she deserved. No family, at least not in these parts. So I figured it was important to show some respect, that somebody in this horrible little town gives a shit.'

I was impressed by her generosity of spirit, if a little bemused that both Stokes Honeysett's daughters despised their home town. Difference was Lee had an obvious reason for being here, Stacey didn't.

'Speaking of Marsha's family, do you know where she's from?'

She gave me a suspicious glance. 'Why do you want to know?'

'I'd like to write something about her – a proper obituary. Everybody's talking about Hazeldene and Carmody. Marsha's already a footnote and I don't think that's right. If could find out where her folks live, maybe I could speak to them, get some quotes and a little background.'

Stacey made a point of thanking the waitress who brought the coffee, then returned her attention to me. 'A story like that would be cool, but I can't help you much. She mentioned that she'd had previous jobs in San Jose and the San Fran Bay area, but nowhere specific. Never wanted to talk about home and always changed the subject.'

I scribbled some shorthand in my notebook.

'I hope you're not going to quote me.'

I laughed. 'You haven't said anything quotable. Just background information.'

I took a sip of coffee. It wasn't bad and certainly better than the muck we got at the *Herald* office. 'You must have known her quite well, though – I mean, to dig that she liked *Bridge Over Troubled Water*.'

'It was her favourite song.'

I made more notes. She didn't raise any objections. 'How did the two of you meet?'

Stacey glanced back at the street she'd just crossed. 'She turned up at the homeless shelter one night about six months ago. I was working a voluntary shift and helped her get settled in. Couple of days later, she got the job at the Million Dollar Nugget. I swung by a few times to make sure she was okay and pretty soon *she* was listening to *me* pouring out my woes. That was what was so special about her: She listened and didn't judge.'

'Sounds like my kind of person.'

'Is that so?' She took a cigarette from a pack of Gitanes and examined me a little closer. 'And exactly what kind of a person is Wat Tyler?'

I flipped my Zippo and offered her a light. 'Ordinary joe, that's me.'

She laughed. 'I've met a lot of far-out guys, but not one who talks like Jed Clampett and writes like Ernest Hemingway. How'd that happen?'

I made a resigned sigh. There had to be give and take in this conversation and I figured it was time to do a little giving. So I told her how my dad got laid off and starting hitting the hard stuff and my mom, usually in that order; how she took me to New York, where she hit the hard stuff even harder; and how I ended up on the street with no proper schooling and no discernible prospects.

I took one of her French cigarettes and sucked in the powerful fumes.

She sensed my reticence and pinned me with a hard, 'go on then' stare.

'I met Maggie Call when I was out one night in a district of Brooklyn that was mean, even by local standards. Street gang had gotten this woman cornered and it looked like she was in for a deep serious beating, maybe rape. Word was she was a reporter. Anyways, I barged through the crowd and got her out. No idea how I did it. I was a tough kid with a reputation, but it was more to do with brass neck. I also have no idea *why* I did it. Maybe, deep down, I thought I was saving my mom. And in a weird way, that's how it played out.'

She took a sip of coffee, leaving a vivid lipstick imprint on the rim of the cup. 'You got me captivated.'

'After that sort of ordeal, most reporters would have bugged out and stayed out. But Maggie was different. She wouldn't give up on her story and that made me respect her. So we did a deal: She paid me five bucks a day and I got her into the places she needed to go. We worked well together. I became fascinated by the way she got folks to talk to her, even when they said they didn't want to. I was even more fascinated by the stories she wrote, the way she explained my fucked-over neighbourhood and how it got to be like it was. You mentioned Hemingway. Maggie could out-write him and then some. Still can.'

'Must be one cool lady.'

I nodded. 'Later, she took me on as an unofficial apprentice. I'd go around to her place in the evenings and she taught me how to write a news story, how to put together a feature, what reporters need to know about the law. Eventually, she had me reading novels, poetry. And suddenly I couldn't get enough of the stuff. After a couple of years she swung me some freelance shifts on the *New York Examiner*. Frank Esposito, the city editor, liked my stuff and gave me a training contract.'

'That must have been unusual for a kid with no formal education.'

'It was. But Frank was more interested in clips than journalism school – especially since most of my clips were pieces from his paper that I'd gotten from my own sources. And there you have it: from gutter mutt to pedigree newshound in a single bound.'

I took another pull on my cigarette, jetted the smoke through my nostrils. 'Of course it was more complicated than that. A shrink friend of Maggie's said my problems were rooted in the way I never bonded with my mom when I was small and all I knew was violence and chaos. Never mind eighteen years, I was in a combat zone at eighteen months. These days they call it attachment disorder. Maggie paid for the shrink and part of our deal was that I undertook therapy.'

She looked genuinely concerned. 'And that worked, right? You're okay now?'

I made a maybe/maybe-not expression. 'I still struggle with feelings. That's where music and literature come in. They help to tap into emotions I sealed off as a survival instinct when I was very small. Well, sometimes they do.'

She tilted her head to one side and made a benevolent smile that I sensed was reserved for working class heroes. 'That's such an uplifting story.'

'Don't get carried away.' I drained my coffee cup. 'Those are the highlights. I got plenty low ones.'

Time to get back to my news agenda. I turned over a fresh page in my notebook.

'Now,' I said, 'can we talk about your friend Gary Gerwitz?'

TWENTY

Suspicion returned to her voice. 'Why Gary?'

I shrugged. Couldn't afford to give too much away, but Stacey wouldn't talk unless I gave her a reason. 'I'm chasing down a lead. Probably one of those that goes nowhere, but Gary left town a couple of hours before he was due to meet with Frank Hazeldene. And according to your dad Gary is now on vacation, so I can't ask him direct.'

She made an incredulous expression. 'You think Gary's involved in that triple killing?'

'He ran into the back of me on his way out of town. We only talked briefly but the guy was real antsy, no doubt about it.'

'Gary's not a violent guy. He's incapable of violence.'

'I'm not suggesting he did anything wrong. I just wonder what that meeting with the congressman might have been about.'

She ordered more coffee. 'Maybe Gary thought he could persuade the congressman to call off his union meeting.'

I frowned. That sounded odd in light of Gerwitz's left-leaning history. 'I thought he'd sympathize with organized labour.'

She seemed lost for a moment but recovered quickly. 'He does. He's your quintessential hippie. Been trying for years to persuade Dad to allow unions into the factory. But he wouldn't want the company getting destabilized with this big tender coming up. Knowing Gary, he probably lost his nerve and pulled out of that meeting. He's not good with people in difficult situations – especially firebrands like Frank Hazeldene. And anyway, I'm sure none of it had anything to do with the horrible shit that went down outside the Desert Diner.'

'I'm sure you're right.' I made a reassuring smile. 'When did you see him last?'

There was more outpouring of gratitude as the waitress served the fresh coffee. Stacey took a sip and placed it in the saucer. 'We talked on the phone. Would have been Saturday last week. Soon after nine. *M*A*S*H* had just finished and we'd both watched it.'

'Did he sound nervous, uptight?'

'He was a little agitated, but that's not unusual for Gary.'

'Did you talk about anything that might have had a bearing on his absence?'

'Not that I was aware of. It was just a friendly chat after dinner.'

'And you didn't hear from him since?'

She shook her head no.

'You and Gary are close, right?'

'You could say that. Known him since '59 when he spent a year on a research project at the factory and lived at our house. I was only seventeen but we hit it off straight away. Gary was a liberal, even a radical. Had principles and five years later he quit his job as a Berkeley professor because of them. I always admired that.'

'Your dad stuck by him, though. Gave him a top job in the company.'

She made a dubious expression. 'Dad got more out of that deal than Gary ever did. Gary's one of the country's finest metallurgists and getting him on board was a great move for the business. But Gary's not cut out for management and his wife Barbara always resented trading Berkeley for Hicks. Who wouldn't? I guess that's what eventually wrecked their marriage. Gary copped a lot of grief running that factory and he'd tell me stuff, offload, especially after Barbara left him.'

I made more notes and she watched, apparently fascinated. 'What type of stuff did he tell you?'

She tapped the side of her nose. 'No industrial secrets if that's what you mean. Just boring, shitty work stuff that everybody talks about.'

'Anybody named Tyler here?'

I looked over my shoulder and saw the café manager standing by the payphone, holding out the receiver.

'I'm Tyler,' I said.

The manger thrust the receiver in my direction. 'Call for you.'

It was Jacinta. We'd gotten a call from Chester Peeples' attorney. He said we could expect a libel writ on account of our piece about his client's exclusive fitness centre. If Peeples wanted to waste money on lawyer bills, that was fine. I knew our story was watertight because it was based entirely on information Peeples had published in his own investment brochure and a quote from the big man himself asserting that it would not compete with the city council's facility. Even so, Peeples was clearly making a statement and I had no doubt it would be the first of many.

I hung up with Jacinta and returned to the table to find Stacey looking through my notebook.

'This is weird shit you write.' She didn't look up from my shorthand outlines as I sat back down. 'Looks like Sanskrit or Arabic.'

'It's Pitman shorthand.'

'How fast can you go?'

'On a good day, one hundred and twenty words a minute. Most folks talk at around one hundred so I can usually get everything anybody has to say.'

She pushed my notebook back across the table. 'Is it tough to learn?'

'Not tough so much as time-consuming.'

'Time's a scarce commodity.'

'Sure is.' I waited a beat, then gave her a curious look. 'So why are you spending yours here? In Hicks?'

She seemed puzzled, as if my question didn't make sense.

'I thought you were a radical,' I said. 'The revolution won't happen in Hicks.'

'But if capitalism can reform itself sufficiently, maybe we don't need a revolution.' She sounded as if she'd thought this through, reached a pragmatic conclusion. 'One place to start is Amalgamated Metals.'

'I didn't know you worked there.'

'I don't. Dad won't let me anywhere near the place on account of my leftist principles.'

I made an amiable expression. 'Let me guess: You've been working on your dad and Gary's been helping you?'

'Why not? Dad's seventy-seven. He'll have to retire soon – maybe very soon. Gary's his natural successor. He wants to give me a junior job now so I'll be ready for something more senior when the time comes.'

'You reckon your dad's gonna agree to that?'

'Participatory democracy has been successful in German companies. No reason we can't do the same here.'

The revelation of Stacey's agenda made me re-evaluate her. For all her textbook idealism, she was no armchair revolutionary. She got things done, putting in shifts at the homeless shelter and befriending working people like Marsha. If she ever did get into her dad's board room, though, I had no doubt she'd wind up running the place on her terms and nobody else's.

*

I left the office late that afternoon for the appointment I'd arranged on the pay phone at the greasy spoon. This was with Tab Thornley, a former editor of the *Herald*, who still held some shares in the business and had to be kept sweet while my pal, Dave Tomaszewski, was on his "sabbatical" in a rehab clinic. I didn't mind chatting to old journalists, though I had an editorial to write that evening and Tab's house was out near Newberry Springs, which was a half-hour drive.

I was on Franklin Avenue, headed toward South Constitution Road, when I first clocked the mint green Oldsmobile Starfire. Still there as I left South Constitution in the direction of the interstate. I took the on-ramp and the Starfire did likewise.

Easy way to spot a tail on a freeway is to slow right down. If they do the same, they give themselves away; if they pass you, you've shaken them. Or a second car has picked up the tail.

I took my foot off the gas and watched my speed drop to fifty, forty, thirty. The Starfire's seven litre V-8 motor roared by. In my rear-view the interstate was empty. No second car.

Three miles up the road, though, the Starfire was on the shoulder with the hood up, as if the driver was checking his engine.

I watched in my rear-view as he dropped the hood, hurried around to the driver's seat and accelerated after me. I left the interstate at Harvard Road. He followed suit. I turned into the parking lot of a burger joint at the end of the off-ramp, stopped for ten seconds and drove back to the road. So did he.

It was obvious that he wanted me to know I was being tailed.

TWENTY-ONE

I drove south on Harvard Road toward Newberry Springs. Directly ahead, the Rodman Mountains reared from the desert floor. Either side were flats of dirt and dust, stained dark by outcrops of sagebrush and mesquite. And someplace hidden, the upside-down Mojave River wrestled east beneath its cover of gritty alluvium. Occasionally it was forced above ground by dikes and stubborn rock formations, but this time of year there was very little water to be seen.

Behind me the Starfire maintained a set distance. This was a remote stretch of road and I half expected the driver to ram me, or maybe try to pass and force me off the road. He did neither. When I let my speed drop to twenty, so did he; when I went up to fifty, there he was keeping that same measured gap.

I thought hard about who those guys might be.

The obvious answer was Chester Peeples' hired muscle.

But going from lawyer letter to physical intimidation in the space of a few hours was unlikely.

There were other possibilities.

Those boys who attacked me outside the *Herald* office made it plain they considered the business to be unfinished.

What was it they shouted as they drove off? *This ain't over, newspaperman.* Was this Round Two?

Then there was the FBI. Special Agent Schwenk laid it down in the frankest possible way that he wouldn't tolerate me getting involved in his investigation. Maybe this was a second warning, a sterner one.

The road descended into the desert basin in a series of straight dips. A quarter mile ahead, a red-brown tow-truck moved along a dirt track and turned onto Harvard Road, headed in my direction. As it came closer, I made out a flashing amber light on the cab roof and a hydraulic boom mounted on the back.

Seemed like somebody was in trouble.

I glanced in my rear-view to check on the Starfire. Right there where I expected it to be.

Or was it?

Difficult to be certain, but it seemed to have edged a little closer.

Up ahead the tow truck was approaching fast, churning a plume of dust.

My eyes returned to the rear-view. The Starfire was right on my tail now. Maybe twenty yards separated us.

I refocused on the scene upfront and realized the dude in trouble was me.

The tow truck driver floored his brakes and swung the vehicle around so it straddled the road. I hit my own brake pedal. The tow-truck was suddenly massive, filling my windshield.

The Bug's wheels locked. I skidded to a stop on the dirt shoulder.

Time to make some choices.

The Starfire had also stopped. Doors came open. Two guys were getting out.

Ahead, the tow truck driver's door had also been thrown open and he was climbing down onto the road. I guessed he'd have at least one passenger debarking from the opposite side. Ten yards separated me from the tow truck, twenty from the Starfire.

Option one was to go off road, try to drive around the tow truck. But the Beetle wouldn't get far in the rocky desert. More important, driving on rough terrain might damage the eight-track. And if the car was expendable, the sound system wasn't.

This left option two. I got out the car and faced my opponents.

From the Starfire came a stocky fellow with a porkpie hat and purple spoon-collared shirt, rolled up at the sleeves. At his side was a Hell's Angel-type with long hair, mirror shades, and studded leather vest.

The tow truck driver was a muscle-builder with armour plate pecs and huge traps that turned his neck into a cone of fortified flesh. Alongside him was a whippety guy, unremarkable, unthreatening, and probably the most dangerous. I'd seen that relaxed attitude and don't-look-like-much appearance before and pegged him as ex-Rangers or Special Forces. That would almost certainly make him the leader.

They were a motley crew for sure, which could mean they were recruited in a hurry. Having said that, some of the best units I worked with comprised diverse individuals and I had no doubt each one of these guys could handle himself. This wasn't another encounter with out-of-shape factory boys after a few beers.

Same tactics applied, though. Find yourself outnumbered, engage the enemy in a series of small actions that stops him concentrating his full strength at any one time. And don't let him get behind you. That happens, you're probably fucked.

Also I could count on an important ally: surprise. Four-on-one, last thing they expected was me attacking them.

Porkpie was the first item on my agenda. I stepped forward and threw a two-fingered eye-jab. His guard came up too late. One of my fingertips struck his cheekbone but the other stabbed his eye. He stumbled sideways clutching it.

This bought me the two seconds I needed to see Muscle Man winding up a roundhouse kick to my head. Swivelling on my heel, I slipped outside the arc of his foot and caught his boot in both hands, jerking it counterclockwise with massive torque. Bone and tendon crackled and Muscle Man yowled as his ankle shattered. I pushed him away, blocking off the Hell's Angel, and moved a few steps back from the Beetle so they couldn't go around me. With the advantage of surprise gone, the trick was to stay mobile: hit and move and not get outflanked.

Immediate threat now was the Hell's Angel. Regular Joe was hanging back, looking for an opportunity to move in behind.

Hell's Angel came in from the left. I ducked his jab and drove my elbow into his abdomen. His head snapped down; my knee came up. Caught him flush in the mouth and felt him go limp as the shock transmitted to his brain. Wasn't sure whether the blood on my pants was his or mine. The broken teeth were definitely his.

Problem now was that Regular Joe had flanked me. I sensed his kidney kick before I felt it. Fiery pain scorched my lumbar region and I fell sideways, away from the blow. I knew how to live with pain, though. I didn't get distracted. Snatching the hot dust with one hand, I levered myself around and stood facing him. He was the leader, no argument there. Seeing what I just did to the others, anybody not totally committed would have checked out already.

Adopting a martial arts stance, Regular Joe wove his open hands this way and that, slowly circling me. The desert wind wasn't very strong, but strong enough to affect my plan. Right now it was blowing between us, so I shifted sideways and watched Regular Joe follow me around until he was downwind. Then I flung my arm out and opened my fingers. My fistful of grit sprayed in his face. Eyes clamped shut. Guard went to shit. I punched him hard in the head three, four, five times before he keeled over.

This left Porkpie.

He was fifteen feet away, still covering his injured eye with his palm. The other eye, though, was locked on a knife shimmering in the sand near his feet. He, or one of his compadres, must have dropped it. Either way the blade represented a fresh threat. No way I could reach it before he did, which would give him the option of throwing it or trying to stab me.

The problem was removed by the crack of a gunshot that sent the knife spinning away, out of reach.

I looked back along the road to the crest of a shallow slope, where my ally was looking down the sights of an M1 carbine.

Not who I expected: not Caraway or Sheldon. Not even Schwenk.

TWENTY-TWO

Norm Dibbitts kept his carbine on Porkpie. 'You okay, Wat?'

'Fine, thanks, Norm. Mighty grateful for your help, though.'

Could I have managed Porkpie with the knife? Probably. Was I happy not to risk it? Damn right. More interesting, though, was the revelation that Norm's time on Uncle Sam's firing range hadn't been wasted after all.

Back at the interstate burger joint, I swallowed some aspirin to dull the pain in my kidney and used the pay phone to call the county sheriff's department in Hicks. I'd left Regular Joe and the Hell's Angel unconscious, and although I didn't expect either to die, nor did I want to risk a manslaughter rap.

Neither of the two who stayed conscious had been very talkative. To be fair, Muscle Man was in some pain on account of his broken ankle so I understood his reluctance to chat. Porkpie was less debilitated. Threatened with a poke in his other eye, he said they'd been offered a hundred bucks apiece from a contact of Regular Joe's. Regular Joe – known to his buddies as Duane – had contacted them by phone and told them to meet up outside the *Herald* office in the Starfire and at Newberry Springs in the tow truck. The idea was to put me in the hospital rather than the grave, which tallied with the absence of firearms. Porkpie insisted he had no idea who Regular Joe's contact was and this was probably true. Of course Regular Joe would know, but he was out cold and I couldn't hang around.

What bothered me was that whoever ordered the attack knew exactly where I'd be and when. Only people with that information were the former *Herald* editor Tab Thornley, who I'd been on my way to visit; and anyone with access to the newsroom diary. I'd arranged to see Tab that morning, so it was possible that he or someone in the newsroom mentioned it innocently to a third party or was overheard doing so. I'd call Tab later and have a word with Jacinta when I got back to the office.

I hung up with the sheriff's dispatcher and called Caraway. The attack had taken place outside Hicks city limits, though the guys in the Starfire started tailing me right outside the *Herald* office, which was well within her jurisdiction. She wasn't available, so I left a message and went back to the table Norm had taken near the front window.

He was chatting to a skinny girl with pale skin and mousy hair so thin you could see her scalp. She wore a mustard nylon dress that did nothing for her meagre figure, and open-toe platform shoes.

Norm introduced her as Lucinda Hannity and explained that she worked as a part-time waitress at the burger joint and part-time barmaid at his bar.

'Norm told me how you beat up four bad guys who attacked you there on Harvard Road,' she said. 'I'm mighty impressed. You gonna write about it in the *Herald*?'

'Maybe,' I said. 'Depends how the deputies decide to deal with those guys.'

Lucinda returned to her waitressing duties and Norm watched her go with an appreciative smirk. 'Ain't she a doll?'

'Sure is.' I couldn't see it myself, but they said there was a lid for every pot and it seemed Lucinda was Norm's. I wasn't happy that he'd shot the works about what happened with Regular Joe and his boys, but after what Norm had done for me it was difficult to be pissed off with him.

'I only come here to see Lucinda.' Norm was still watching Lucinda. 'Been trying to persuade her to work full time at my place, but her cousin's the owner here and she's loyaler than Old Yeller.'

'Is that how you knew I was in trouble, Norm?'

Lucinda finally disappeared and I got Norm's full attention. 'Sure is, pal. Here I was, right by the window, eating a burger and chatting to Lucinda, when I saw your Bug come down the off-ramp with that big old Starfire on your tail. Figured there was something wrong when you pulled into the parking lot just opposite and stopped awhile, then drove off – with that guy still following.'

'That was quick thinking, Norm.'

'That's what buddies is for, ain't it, Wat? You and me, we gotta watch each other's back.'

'We sure do. But I didn't realize you were such a good shot.'

Instead of the comradely grin I was expecting, he banged the Formica tabletop with his fist. 'Too fucking slow. When I saw what was going down I pulled over and went to my trunk for the carbine. But the ammo wasn't with the gun where I normally keep it. It was in the glove compartment. Time I got a clip into the carbine, it was all over. Well, nearly.'

I nodded. The fight did happen fast – two minutes tops. And Norm wouldn't have made the scene until the action was underway.

'You did good, Norm.' I clapped him on the shoulder and this time he gave me a sheepish smile.

*

I was still going through my messages when Sheila on the front desk buzzed through to my office: Special Agent Schwenk was here to see me. My back was hurting real bad and more grief from the Bureau was not what I needed. But I thought, what the hell.

Two minutes later the cuboid G-man was gazing across my desk from the outer limits of the generation gap. In his heavy gabardine suit, he was overcooked and took out a handkerchief to dab sweat from his brow. His tone was stiff. 'We got a problem, Tyler.'

I made a small smile. 'Let me guess. Those guys claim I started it.'

'*Which* guys?'

'The guys who attacked me out on Harvard Road.'

He tugged at his shirt collar but stopped short of loosening his tie. 'There weren't any guys. Place was deserted.'

I lit a cigarette and waited for him to continue.

'I went out with the sheriff's deputies and we took a good look around. But there was no Oldsmobile Starfire; no red tow truck; and no evidence of any sort of violent struggle.' He smoothed the short, slicked back hair that belonged in some scene from World War II. 'Which makes me wonder what you're trying to pull here.'

I took a few beats to consider the implications. State I left them in, none of those men was capable of driving off in the tow truck or the Starfire. And certainly not in the twenty minutes it took the deputies to drive out from the sheriff's office in Hicks. Either Schwenk was part of some bullshit conspiracy or someone had gone out there and cleaned up the scene before the deputies arrived.

'Did you speak to Norm Dibbitts over at the Million Dollar Nugget Bar? He saw it too.'

Schwenk made a dismissive expression. 'Dibbitts is an unreliable screwball and probably a deviant.'

'A deviant being what? Anybody you don't like the look of?'

'You made up this whole situation, didn't you?'

'If I did, I'd never work on a newspaper again.'

'Only if you got caught. If you didn't, you'd have a front page story that would make you look real good – along with that retard Dibbitts. You could link it to the triple homicide and give that pot a good stir. Sure wouldn't harm your circulation numbers either, would it?'

I made a couldn't-give-a-shit shrug. 'I'd also be guilty of reporting a false emergency. So why don't you arrest me?'

Schwenk's razor-slash eyes narrowed a little farther. The square shoulders pushed back into his chair. 'Don't think I don't want to.'

'But, let me guess: You'd piss off local law enforcement and shut down access to every household in a thirty mile radius?'

'You're too smart for your own good, Tyler.'

'More like too smart for your own good, Schwenk.'

The G-man levered his boxy frame out of the chair and headed for the door.

'You should watch your step.'
I called after him. 'That an official warning?'
He didn't look back. 'Sure is.'

TWENTY-THREE

Want some real gone Mojave jive, take Interstate 15 to Baker and head north on Death Valley Road – but make sure you got a four-wheel drive vehicle. After twenty miles or so, turn right off the road and go east across Silurian dry lake. Its grey fractured surface makes you think of rhino hide or shattered ceramic and all sorts of crazy shit. Even in 110 degrees of heat, creosote bush somehow stays alive. Wild burros browse the edges of the lakebed as if they've strayed from a petting zoo. And in the middle distance the Silurian hills call to mind grocery store wrapping paper, crumpled and discarded.

Finn Sheldon drove out here because he reckoned we couldn't be bugged or snooped on and were unlikely to be followed.

He started eating as we left Hicks and didn't say much as he drove. Now, with the contents of a burger box transferred to his belly, he was munching artificial bacon bits from a plastic tub on his lap.

The Jeep Wagoneer bounced off the dry playa's edge and onto a dirt track that took us toward the three hills. The ride was bumpy and made my back ache where Regular Joe landed his blow.

'Got a cigarette?'

Never did understand how folks could eat and smoke at the same time, but I said nothing and offered him a Camel from my pack.

The wheels spun occasionally as the Wagoneer worked its way up through a pass between the middle peak and the southernmost one.

Sheldon had not been enthusiastic about this meeting and insisted we didn't discuss anything sensitive until he gave the all-clear.

Finally, he pulled over near a solitary stone-built fireplace, complete with mantelpiece and chimney. Difficult to tell whether this was the start of a new building or the remnants of an old one, though a rusted tin privy and busted mineshaft headframe suggested the latter.

Clambering out of the Wagoneer he manoeuvred his substantial bulk toward the fireplace and took a seat on the hearth. 'What is it you want to talk about?'

I took off my sunglasses so I could look him in the eye. 'You have any clue why I got attacked yesterday?'

'I had no clue you *were* attacked.'

'Of course you didn't.' I massaged my back to stop the burning sensation in the muscle.

He made an indulgent smile. For a moment I saw handsome features in the massif of flesh. 'Okay, officially I didn't know. *Un*officially I heard you ran into severe opposition but handled it with your customary efficiency.'

'Any skinny on why those guys were sent after me? Unofficial skinny, I mean.'

He shook his head. 'Nor do I know why someone busted a gut to clean up the mess before the sheriff's deputies arrived, along with Schwenk.'

'You know an awful lot for someone who's not supposed to know anything at all.'

He examined his cigarette. It was almost down to the filter, but he took one last, long pull before flicking it into the dust. 'Isn't that why you wanted this conversation?'

'It's a big part of the reason.'

'That's all I heard. But here's some free advice: Watch out for Schwenk. He comes over like a D-Day throwback, but he's smart and he's mean – and more J Edgar Hoover than J Edgar Hoover.'

He turned away, looked across the desert's violent chaos. From up here, the dry lake gave off a pale shimmer, like a misty mirror. The main road threaded north between uplifts of black rock that stood out like old bruises on the dusty land.

He used a red handkerchief to wipe sweat from the flesh cushioning the back of his neck. 'So what else do you want to talk about?'

Sheldon never appreciated indirectness so I went right to it. 'You're not in town to debrief a NATO general, are you? You could do that at the Pentagon. And it would take a few hours, not a few days.'

'What do you expect me to say? You know the rules.' From inside his cotton jacket he produced a pack of Oreo chocolate cream cookies. Opening the heat-sealed plastic was a problem and he fumbled with the pack until he dropped it.

I picked it up and slit the end with my fingernail then handed him the pack. 'And you know the rules can be bent.'

He picked out an Oreo. The cream filling was gooey

liquid in this heat. It oozed out from between the two cookie layers but he ran his tongue around their circumference so nothing escaped. 'Okay, we'll play the game.'

The 'game' involved me telling him what I knew, or suspected, and him letting me know if I was on the right tracks.

I put my sunglasses back on. 'Deal like this, FBI involvement is a given. What isn't is Schwenk paying me not one, but two personal visits. That tells me this is deep serious shit at a deep serious level.'

He bit into the cookie. 'Can't fault your logic.'

I stepped from the lee of the fireplace and the buckshot wind scraped my face. 'That reinforces Lee Caraway's thinking that the mark was either Hazeldene or Carmody. They were two big hitters from different worlds, placed by happenstance in the same spot at the same time.'

Sheldon pushed the rest of the cookie into his mouth and prepared to load another. 'Makes sense.'

'Except Hazeldene *wasn't* there by chance.'

'Go on.'

'His schedule was publicized well in advance. Whoever organized this hit would have known his itinerary. Carmody, though, was a wildcard. Word is he sometimes ate at the Desert Diner, sometimes at a half dozen other places. Nobody – including Carmody – knew from one day to the next where he was going to eat his lunch, or when.'

'Your point being?'

'Hazeldene's movements were predictable, Carmody's weren't. So you could hit Carmody and make it look like Hazeldene was the target, but you couldn't do it the other way around.'

Sheldon crunched into another Oreo. 'That's a credible hypothesis.'

'Thing is, the cops are sidelining Carmody to focus on Hazeldene. I can understand why because the congressman represented a much more obvious target. He was, after all, corporate America's number-one pain in the ass. Also anti-nuke and pro-choice. Anything controversial, he'd have some provocative shit to shoot. And, like any politician, he was accessible and therefore vulnerable.'

I gave Sheldon a sideways look, tried to gauge his reaction. 'When you think about it, though, Carmody must have had enemies too. You don't make that much money that fast without pissing off somebody somewhere.'

He said nothing. The silence hung strange in the dusty air.

'Am I way off the mark?'

'No, you're not.'

'Carmody was the reason you came to Hicks, wasn't he?' I tried to make my words sound like I was playing a hunch.

My old buddy gazed at me long and hard, as if to say: *I know exactly what you did. I know you rooted through my briefcase.* But then he looked away and popped another Oreo.

'What I tell you is strictly non-attributable background. You can't use anything unless you can make it stand up from separate sources. That clear?'

'Totally.'

'Okay.' He paused to finish chewing the Oreo. 'The CIA is investigating Carmody's funding sources. We know the mob has a glut of dirty money in offshore accounts that it's desperate to bring back to the US. We also know there's been a lot of unusual activity involving LA venture capital funds. And we suspect the cash they're investing in local firms is being moved from offshore mob accounts. It's a sound strategy because it doesn't set off any trip wires. Big money injections help local entrepreneurs to expand their businesses and create jobs. Everybody's a winner. Nobody wants to rock the boat.'

He turned to look at me, squinting in the sharp sunlight. 'Problem from the mob's point of view is that putting money into privately owned or penny stock companies is a slow and risky way of getting your cash. If it's a private firm you have to wait until the company gets sold. That takes time. If it's a penny stock business, the value of your shares can fall as easily as they can rise. So you have to be very careful where you invest and when you sell.'

He offered me an Oreo, I shook my head no. 'All that changed when Ray Carmody bought High Rock Mine outright with cash from a venture capital outfit we were investigating. The deal didn't generate much interest. Carmody's tourist attraction idea wasn't going to be a fast growth business and Carmody wasn't expected to sell up any time soon. That meant the mob's money would be tied up long term without creating much value. In fact, we read it as a sign that the mob had too much money chasing too few investment opportunities.'

I stepped out of the gritty wind. 'So when Carmody hit pay dirt the mob got a very pleasant surprise. Only they had to figure out how to get their cash out.'

My buddy nodded yes.

'Where's your investigation at now?'

He shrugged. 'Hit the buffers when Carmody got shot. We still need to link the venture capital fund in LA to the mob's laundering operation. Carmody owned fifty-one per cent of the business but died without a will. The venture capital investors own forty-nine per cent and there's a shareholder agreement giving them a right to buy the entire stock in the event of Carmody's death. But Carmody's widow is disputing the legality of the agreement. There's also a dispute over what the mine is actually worth. So nobody knows who owns what.'

'And all you can do is wait for the dust to settle?'

The last Oreo vanished. 'That's about the size of it.'

TWENTY-FOUR

Early evening back at my place and I was sipping a beer when Caraway's Plymouth Cricket pulled up outside.

I hadn't seen her since Sunday evening and she hadn't responded to the message I left at the police station after I got attacked the previous afternoon. That annoyed me a little, though I knew she was busy. I showed her into the living room.

'Sorry I never got back to you.' At least she was tuned into my wavelength. She made a righteous smile and squeezed my forearm. It felt good, even if I wasn't sure if she liked me or was playing me or both. 'I heard about what happened on Harvard Road and I knew you were safe. How's your back?'

'Painful, but I've had worse. Doc says my ribs are bruised.'

I offered her a drink and she asked for a beer the same as mine.

I went into the kitchen and came back with a cold one. 'So you believe it happened?'

She made a curious expression. 'Believe what happened?'

'That I was attacked.'

'Why shouldn't I?'

'Schwenk thinks I cooked it up to make myself look good.'

'Schwenk's paranoid. He thinks everything's a conspiracy.'

'Maybe everything is.' I swallowed some beer. 'What do you think?'

She shrugged. 'It's conceivable that Chester Peeples hired those heavies. But I'm not so sure he'd have the resources for the clean-up. From what I heard, those boys needed urgent medical attention. I tried all the hospitals in the county and none has any record of treating any such injuries.'

'Where'd they go then?'

She drank some beer. 'LA or Vegas, or more likely across the Mexican border. They could've been in Mexicali before sundown. Anyways, I don't think they'll trouble you again.'

'What about the vehicles?'

She produced a pack of Belair menthol filter cigarettes. 'Without plate numbers it's obviously tough. Having said that, a big red tow-truck and a mint green Starfire aren't exactly inconspicuous. But nobody at Hicks PD or any of the county deputies knows anything about those vehicles. All points to outta town. And outta town means outta the sphere of Chester Peeples' influence.'

I flipped my Zippo and offered a light for her Belair. 'What about for those guys who came at me outside the *Herald* office? They said in no uncertain terms that they weren't through with me.'

'You didn't seriously believe that, though, did you?' She made a faint smile. 'From what you told me they're simple Hicks boys. The kind who like to run their mouths after a few drinks but not so much when they're sober.'

I took a pull on my beer. 'Maybe. At first I assumed they were from your dad's factory. Then I discovered Chester Peeples owns a plastics manufacturing operation where pay and conditions are 19th Century. So Hazeldene rolling into town and preaching unionisation would have antagonized Peeples as much as anyone at Amalgamated Metals.'

She said nothing for a while. 'Peeples is a ruthless bastard with a reputation for taking things into his own hands.'

'So it's possible that he sent the Hicks boys after me, realized they weren't up to the job, then went outta town to hire the Harvard Road crew.'

'It's possible,' she said. 'I'll look into it.'

I gave her a searching look. 'Then there's Schwenk.'

She took a pull on her Belair. 'And I thought *he* was paranoid?'

'He's pissed off with me, that's for sure. He's now paid two visits to my office, telling me to butt out, or else.'

She peered through the menthol cigarette fug. 'Okay, Schwenk resents you getting information from me and your other sources – even though you've helped more than you've hindered. In fact, that's probably his problem. But, like me, he's under a lot of pressure to make an arrest. He simply wouldn't have had the time or resources to arrange something like this.'

This was a fair point, I had to admit. Even so I was convinced Schwenk was party to a crock of off-the-books shit.

Time for my side of the quid pro quo deal. I told Caraway what I found out about Carmody – without revealing my source.

She took a swallow of beer. 'Spooks as well as G-men in a little old town like Hicks. Now that's really interesting. But there's not much I can do about Carmody right now. Chief Turner wants one hundred per cent focus on Hazeldene. Besides, there is no mob connection in Hicks – only crime we get is *dis*organized. And from what you told me, taking out Ray Carmody would be counter to the mob bosses' interests. He was the goose laying their golden egg.'

'Silver egg.'

She made a sarcastic smile. 'Whatever, but the upshot is their goose is cooked and that's not what they would have wanted.'

I leaned forward. 'I still think there's more to this. Could you have a word with some of your old LAPD contacts?'

'Not unless we get something more concrete.' She made a teasing grin. 'You could always ask Schwenk. He's based out of the feds' field office in LA.'

I returned her smile. 'You are joking?'

'Not entirely.'

But we both knew I wasn't going to go to Schwenk.

'I could use another of these.' She held out her empty beer bottle.

I went to the refrigerator for two more bottles. When I returned she was thumbing through one of two cardboard boxes of vinyl LPs.

'Alphabetically filed by artist from the Allman Brothers to the Zombies.' She smiled. 'So you're not as laid back as you seem.'

I grinned at the dig. 'No point having records if you can't find the one you want.'

'You got taste, though.' She scrunched her brow as she moved onto the second box. 'This is quite a collection.'

'That's only my travel version. The main one is back in New York.' It was the sort of shit you talk to look cool then realize you just did the opposite. She already thought I had librarian tendencies. Now I'd confirmed it.

She gave me a come-again look. 'How many do you own?'

'Too many.' I wanted to explain that no one can own music. It belongs to anyone with a functioning pair of ears. But that would have sounded even more goofy. And anyways it wasn't true. I collected records specifically to possess them. With some artists – Little Richard, Chuck Berry, Bob Dylan, the Velvets, the Stones – I had everything they ever released, along with every bootleg I could lay my hands on. I guess it went back to my childhood, when I never possessed anything my dad couldn't trash. When I had money of my own, I bought records of my own so that no one could ever take them away. Perhaps it was an unhealthy compulsion. Having said that, there were worse things to get hung up on.

I handed her the beer and we went back to the couch.

We smiled at one another but said nothing in the way of two people weighing up how to broach a difficult topic. The silence started out okay, then turned into an awkward hiatus.

I wanted to ask if she'd talked to her dad. Something held me back though. I guessed she too had been avoiding the subject. But now it was hanging there between us like a solid object.

We looked at one another straight.

I said, 'Did you ask your dad yet – '

At the same moment she said, 'My dad is dying.'

I could find words for most situations, but this was not one of them. What to say? What not to say?

She picked up on my uncertainty. 'He has a critical heart condition. The doctors give him six months, maybe a year.'

'I'm so sorry, Lee.'

'He was fine about it. Really. Totally at peace. Said he was ready to go and just hoped it wouldn't be too uncomfortable.

As if he was having a tooth pulled.' Her attempt to sound upbeat fooled neither of us.

I took her hand. 'How do *you* feel?'

'I can't say.' She looked at me hard. 'You know what? I'm not even sure I love him.'

This was something I could relate to, but now wasn't the time to give out on attachment disorder. So I asked, 'Why do you say that?'

She took a moment to think this through. 'He was never a bad father. Never neglectful or mean. But he was always more of a supervisor than a parent. More like a concerned sergeant or lieutenant to a rookie cop. That sounds awful. But my dad didn't love me in the conventional sense. He managed me. Managed my upbringing, my education and, yep, my career.'

'Meaning your job at Hicks PD?'

She made a short, bitter laugh. 'Meaning the job *he arranged for me* at Hicks PD.'

She chugged the rest of her beer and set down the empty glass with a bang. 'I wanted to be angry with him. He even said I could be – that I had every right. But how can you be angry with your dad when he tells you he's dying?'

I sipped my beer and thought about what I should say next. 'I only met your dad once, but I liked what I saw. He struck me as a genuine man who does right as he sees it.'

'That just makes it worse. I got all this anger and he's even managing that. He doesn't mean to, but he's still doing it.'

After a while she said, 'He asked me to forgive him for fixing my appointment at Hicks PD.'

'What did you say?'

'I said I couldn't. Not yet.'

'You don't have a whole lot of time, Lee.'

'I know that, dammit.' Her grip on my hand tightened. 'But first I need to prove I'm up to the job he fixed for me. Until that happens, I'll feel like a fraud in my hometown.'

I had no doubt Caraway would prove herself. This wasn't the problem though. The problem was doing it while her dad was still alive.

TWENTY-FIVE

High Rock Mine was the weirdest industrial plant I ever saw – somewhere between the visitor attraction it had been built as and the functioning mine it later became. The complex was strung out across a broad area of desert with a sheer canyon wall at its back.

The main processing plant was a grey sheet metal structure that resembled an aircraft hangar. Directly in front of it, replica frontier buildings flanked a main street. This area had the feel of a movie set – not surprising as it had been erected to recreate a silver rush mining settlement of the 1870s. When Ray Carmody struck it rich, the Wild West real estate was hurriedly converted to support the needs of a modern mining operation. I saw signs denoting an electricity station, machine shop and drill store in buildings that looked more like 19th Century saloon bars, hotels, and livery stables. Even the whitewashed fake church had been pressed into service as a canteen.

Surrounding the entire facility was a fifteen foot high fence, topped with razor wire. It gave the impression of a prisoner of war camp, except this wire was in place to stop folks getting in, not out. With large quantities of high grade silver ore on site, it wasn't difficult to understand the need for security.

I parked the Beetle near a prefabricated office block and turned to Suze Carter. 'You okay?'

She gave me a slightly freaked out smile. 'I guess.'

The kid was tough – not surprising as she'd been raised in the Third and Congress neighbourhood – but going down a mineshaft required a different type of nerve. Suze hadn't seemed overly enthusiastic when I told her what the job entailed and on the drive over she confessed to being claustrophobic. 'You'll be fine,' I told her. 'Concentrate on getting your pictures. Don't think about anything else.'

Easier said than done for sure. But if Suze wanted to be a photojournalist she'd have to handle tougher assignments than this.

'Mr Tyler?' A slouchy fellow in a rumpled earth-tone safari jacket approached from the office block. Dark sweat patches spread out from under his arms and a paunch sagged over the waistband of his nylon pants. Hair was thin and frowzy, too long to be smart, too short to be cool. Round face was pale and beaded in sweat, jowls peppered with grey stubble – a five o'clock shadow at ten in the morning. I guessed he'd be late thirties or early forties.

'I'm Rex Hambly, the general manager. We spoke on the phone.' The accent was Australian, the whiff on his breath, whiskey. Experience taught me never to read too much into first impressions, but Hambly didn't look much like a mining industry type or a corporate guy.

I shook his hand and introduced Suze.

'Good of you to do this for us, Mr Hambly,' I said. 'Especially in such difficult circumstances.'

After what Sheldon told me I wanted to get a closer look at fifty million dollars' worth of mob investment and managed to swing the press facility tour by suggesting to Hambly that the mine needed to show the outside world it was doing business as usual.

'Always happy to help the press.' His smile revealed nicotine-tinged teeth. 'Although I'm afraid it'll have to be a whistle-stop tour. Like you say, these are tough times. Ray used to do so much. We're only beginning to realize just how much now he's gone.'

'So he was a dynamic sort of boss?' I started making notes.

'Absolutely. Nothing happened here without him knowing. He'd get involved in everything, everywhere.'

'Even so, you're still operating normally?'

'Absolutely. It's what Ray would've wanted – demanded.'

I looked up from my notebook. 'How long you been here, Mr Hambly?'

'Rex, call me Rex.' Again the yellow-brown grin. 'Two years. Ray brought me in as a consultant engineer after they found the tetrahedrite deposit.'

I gave him a puzzled look. 'Tetra what?'

'Tetrahedrite. It's a superior silver ore – what made the strike so special.'

'And before that?'

'I've been all over.'

'All over the USA, the world?'

The man from Down Under seemed a little off-balance. 'This article you're writing, it's about the mine, isn't it, not me?'

I made a reassuring smile. 'Sure it's about the mine, Rex. But you're the guy in charge now. Our readers will want to know something about your background. A thumbnail sketch is all, though.'

He shrugged. 'I worked at silver mines in Queensland, Australia, then I moved to Argentina, Peru, and Mexico.'

'You really been around, then.'

'You could say that.'

We were walking close to the hangar-like building where the ore processing operations took place. 'That where all the topside stuff gets done?'

'Certainly is.'

I glanced at Suze. 'You should be able to get some nice shots in there.'

Hambly cleared his throat as if embarrassed. 'I'm sorry, but you can't go in there. It's strictly out of bounds for visitors. Lots of hazardous processes. Safety regulations and all that.'

I gave him a baffled look. 'But we're allowed down the mineshaft aren't we? Surely that's at least as hazardous?'

He hesitated as a half dozen muck-filled carts rattled past us on a track running into the processing plant. Then he made a slightly abashed expression. 'Okay, you got me. Truth is there are chemical engineering processes going on in there that we don't want our competitors to find out about. Industrial secrets. Even some of our own workers don't have access to the main plant.'

He made another toothy grin. 'But you're quite right – you can go down the mineshaft. That's not a problem.'

I made a sideways glance and Suze. Didn't take a mind reader to dig that this was the exact opposite of what she wanted to hear.

*

Riding the cage down to the thousand foot level was like freefalling into hell. The deeper we went, the hotter it got. By the time we reached our destination, humidity was more than eighty per cent.

I knew this because I wrote it in my notebook during a briefing by Jimmy Lefroy, the supervisor conducting our underground tour. Lefroy sure looked the part. A veteran of the Coeur d'Alene mining district, his face was as pitted and chiselled as the rock faces he worked. Ore grit and drill oil were ingrained so deep in his coveralls you got the impression they'd stand rigid when he took them off.

We stepped out of the cage and Suze slotted a flashgun into place. I was glad she was getting to grips with doing the job.

We found ourselves in a well-lit cavern that contained stacks of wooden boxes, steel pipes, and machine parts. Whiffs of engine exhaust, ammonium nitrate and nitroglycerine fumes hung heavy in the air. I also picked up fainter odours of methane gas and tobacco smoke. That whole olfactory deal reminded me of the coal shafts in West Virginia that my dad showed me back when he thought I'd follow him down the mines.

Lefroy led us to the centre of the storage area and pushed back his hardhat. 'Either of you been in a mine before?'

Suze shook her head and I followed suit. I wasn't sure exactly what I was looking for at High Rock but didn't want Lefroy to put up his guard because he thought I might know about mining – even coal mining.

'The shaft we just came down – the Carthage shaft – that's the main access point to the entire mine,' he said. 'It's a regular rat-nest of drifts, stopes and raises. Drifts are what miners call tunnels, stopes are ore excavations, and raises are the vertical cuts you'll see between working levels.'

Suze looked up at the high rock ceiling, her rounded features sheathed in moisture. 'What's this place called?'

Lefroy chuckled. 'This is just a room. There are a few scattered around the mine. We use 'em for all sorts: hoist spaces, machine shops, and supply dumps like this one.'

He set off towards a tunnel entrance. 'C'mon, I'll show you some stuff that'll blow your minds.'

What he had to show was certainly impressive. To begin with the tunnel was big enough to drive a car through; a hundred yards farther there was barely enough room for a steel cart. Bulkheads were patched with metal plates and plastic sheets; cross-drifts shored up with huge timber frames that looked as if they'd been there since the shaft was sunk. Every couple of hundred feet, the vertical raises Lefroy had told us about led to other areas above or below. Underfoot the ground was mucky; every so often our boots splashed through pools of muddy water. And the humidity got worse. Felt as if a kettle was boiling close to your face.

After a few hundred yards, Lefroy stopped to give out more information. 'Look at an engineer's design, you'll see straight lines coming together at various intervals – like the New York City Subway map. Down here, though, the drifts follow the ore, and ore never runs very far in straight lines, or stays level over any distance. So the mine you see down here don't look much like the neat and tidy lines on the plans.'

Suze's flash gun fired, illuminating a wall of rubble built into the side of the tunnel. 'What are these things? They seem to be around every corner.'

'Old stopes. All the ore's been taken out and they've been

gobbed-up with waste rock and trash to stop 'em collapsing. This one's pretty small. Back end might be just five or six feet high, so a tight squeeze.'

Not nearly so tight as the coal stopes my dad used to work. He'd wriggle and crawl through a world of shit to chase a vein, then show off the gashes and bruises – usually after sinking a half pint of whiskey.

Around the next bend we got our first sight of activity – a group of miners adjusting a twenty foot coring rig in the middle of a big stope. The rig called to mind an artillery piece, except the business end was pointing at the earth instead of the sky. At the back end of the stope other miners were operating jackleg drills that looked like heavy machineguns with the front tripod leg missing.

'How about a group shot?' Suze said.

It was a good idea – the kid was getting the hang of this. I turned to Lefroy. 'Could we do that?'

Lefroy looked dubious. 'They'd need to stop work.'

'Five minutes tops,' I said.

He agreed and went to speak to the miners. I left Suze to set up her shot.

It was a decent one: a dozen miners standing, leaning and sitting on the big coring rig. Suze did a few extra shots of individual miners working the stope and seemed happy with her haul.

I was too, but not for the same reasons.

Back on the surface, Lefroy handed us back to Rex Hambly. This was the end of our tour and Hambly asked if there was anything else we needed.

I asked for a shot of him, with some mining buildings in the background.

He didn't seem too keen but went along with my request on the condition that the processing plant was well out of shot. Also, he needed to go put on a tie.

As he went into the office block, I spoke to Suze.

'While you're getting your pictures of this guy, I need some close-up shots of the canyon wall. You'll have to shoot over his shoulder, without him knowing.' I pointed to the cliff face behind the camp. 'From just below the highest point to where the rock face meets the ground. Can you do that?'

She gave me an odd look.

Hambly was shambling back toward us, knotting a stringy tie.

'Can you do it, Suze?'

She tuned into the urgency in my voice and nodded yes.

*

Back in the office I wrote up my story and started working my way through the photos Suze brought through. She'd done a good job and I told her so. No doubt the praise put a smile on the kid's face, though I sensed she was also baffled as to why I asked for those sneaky pics right at the end, and why I wanted the prints blown up.

I'll come to that shortly.

First I studied the group shot of the miners.

The suspicions I had down in the mine sharpened as I stared at the enlarged image. The faces were dirty but not weathered. Physiques honed but not hard and scarred in the way of my dad's. And there were no fuck-you expressions. Many were grinning, their teeth white and even. Some had removed their hardhats, showing off fashionable haircuts.

It looked more like a college football team shot than a bunch of bad-ass miners.

An individual picture of one guy was just as peculiar: with his protective gloves tossed to one side, he was gripping a jackleg drill with uncalloused hands. I could even make out the fingernails – unsplit, not a trace of dirt under them.

Jimmy-Joe Lefroy might have been a regular Coeur d'Alene rock-buster, but not these guys. Where I came from, it was said with some truth that miners worked hard, played hard and fucked hard. They did stuff hard when they could do it easy because hard was their thing. They resented authority and considered rules there for the breaking. And they hated outsiders poking around their underground world like Suze and I just did. Miners had a lot in common with the military. Their communities were isolated and conditions were harsh, but they endured with sullen resolve, and more than anything, hardness. Of course I'd only known West Virginia coalminers, and only as a kid at that. But I couldn't imagine hard rock miners were so different. Those guys staring back at me from Suze's picture weren't soldiers, they were civilians. They were there to look the part. Whatever muck got hauled out of that shaft wasn't by them. And whatever processing went on in that off-limits building, it wasn't ordinary. I'd been shown around more industrial plants than I cared to admit, but none had been as paranoid about industrial secrets as Rex Hambly. And the oddball Aussie seemed to have worked at silver mines everyplace in the world – except the USA.

I needed to find out what was going on at High Rock. So I turned to the close-up shots of the canyon wall. It fell sheer 150 feet, providing far better security than any razor wire fence.

Leastways, that was how it looked at first glance.

TWENTY-SIX

A little after 1.00am I was standing atop the canyon wall, high above High Rock Mine. Full moon hung pale and pockmarked in the grainy sky. I was wearing a black turtleneck sweater and the darkest pair of jeans I could find. Small backpack contained an SLR camera, zoom lens, extra rolls of film, set of lock picks, and a plastic bottle of water. I'd blackened my face and used black duct tape to secured everything that might rattle or reflect light. Shifting a little closer to the edge, I jumped up and down a few times to make sure I didn't make any noise. Just like preparing for an in-country operation in the Nasty – except I had no weapons.

My plan involved climbing unaided down the canyon wall – which was not as crazy as it might sound. See, when most folk see a steep drop they tend to assume it's more vertical than it actually is. That was what the security people at High Rock did. Me, I'd scaled enough genuinely perpendicular cliff faces in my Special Forces days to know this wasn't one. That was why I asked Suze to shoot over Rex Hambly's shoulder and print out some blow-ups of the canyon wall.

Looking at those photos real close, I picked out a

natural three-sided chimney in the rock with recesses and projections and fractures. It wasn't continuous, but two ledges – possibly even narrow pathways – ran between the three main chimney sections.

The pictures presented two big problems though. First, it was difficult to evaluate depth of field: what appeared to be a ledge might be a few feet wide or a few inches. Second, I had to get down – and back up – in the dark. Moonlight helped, but this was still something of a crapshoot.

The descent started well enough. First section wasn't much more difficult than going down an uneven stairway: plenty wide enough and no shortage of horizontal surfaces. It brought me to the highest of the two shelves. Squinting in the moonshine, I saw that it was broader than I expected, but much steeper – a forty, even fifty per cent grade. With my face to the sour-smelling rock, I moved crabwise, boots stubbing more often than I liked on the uneven rock. From somewhere below, two voices carried up from the mining complex. A couple of workers, I guessed, taking a break or moving between different parts of the mine. I was 120 feet above them so I couldn't make out what they were saying. Sounded casual enough, though, which was what I wanted.

I reached the middle chimney and immediately realized it was much tougher than I'd anticipated. As far as I could see, there were no rocky outcrops or crevices; just a smooth, almost sheer groove that dropped thirty feet or more. Good news was that it seemed narrow enough to negotiate by placing the soles of my boots against one vertical surface and my back against the one opposite. Also, I had to switch the backpack so it became a front-pack. Carrying the extra bulk on my chest was a complication I didn't need and the strain on my back made my ribs burn like hell where Regular Joe landed his blow. But I had no option.

The distant workers' chatter faded as I concentrated on getting into position. With my lower back braced against the rock face, I manoeuvred into the gloomy shaft using a step and slide technique I learned at the JFK Center for Special Warfare. The two surfaces I was wedged between widened and narrowed so I was constantly readjusting, refocusing, recalibrating.

I went deeper.

After some time I peered down, searching for a gleam of pale rock that would show the ledge below. But I saw nothing except fuzzy darkness.

A little farther down I started looking for a ridge to rest a corner of my butt on, or a fissure I could get the toes of my boots into. Anything to take the strain off my legs and especially the bruised area of my back. But there was no respite. The pack felt heavier on my chest with every downward movement. Sometimes it rode up and clouted me in the face. Not hard, but hard enough to break my concentration. Maybe I should have ditched the pack. But no camera meant no evidence. Without evidence I might as well have stayed home.

Times like this, a psychological disorder like mine becomes an asset. My brain gave up on anxiety a long time ago and this meant I could work out what to do next without getting distracted. If I fell, I'd be hamburger, that was a nail-on certainty. But I dug this in the way you know you'll likely die if you step off a sidewalk and get hit by a passing bus. So for me, descending that canyon wall was no more scary than walking along a busy street. Of course there's a downside: Fear comes in the same pack as joy.

Deeper still and the middle chimney entered a fully enclosed section where I was denied even moonlight. Only way was down, though. This was the toughest part so far: I couldn't see my feet, still less where I was placing them as I shuffled and slipped into the blindness. Deprived of sight and perspective, other senses began to deteriorate. I even started to wonder which way was up. Fingers felt numb on the cold, smooth stone. A fusty reek seemed to intensify.

Then my ankles hit solid rock and I realized I'd made it to the bottom. That, at least, explained the smell.

For a moment I thought I'd lowered myself into a dead-end. Then, looking over my shoulder, I made out a pale archway of light and beyond that, a broad platform gleaming in the moonshine.

The opportunity to take a short rest couldn't have come too soon. Moving out onto the ledge, I sat cross-legged with my back to the canyon wall and reached into the backpack for the bottle of water. My fingers had started opening the zipper when I felt his eyes on me.

Turning my head real slow I saw I was sitting next to a Mojave green rattlesnake. Getting up close with a rattler is never a good deal but getting up close halfway down a near-sheer canyon wall was the worst sort of bad luck. See, the habitat of the Mojave green, was grassy plains, dry washes, Joshua tree woodland. This dude just wasn't supposed to be here.

But then nor was I.

He was coiled on the flat rock three feet away, arrow-shaped head raised and pointed straight at me. No doubt as pissed off to see me as I was to see him. But there we were.

Way I saw it I had two choices. I could grab him by the neck and toss him over the cliff, or I could sit still and wait for him to move on. The head-grab would be high-risk but quick. Sitting it out was a less hazardous option, though clearly much more time-consuming. But, hey, I had all night.

So I waited.

As snakes went, I'd encountered far more dangerous ones than this fella. The bamboo pit viper for example. He was also known as the step-and-a-half snake because once he bit you that was as far as you got before you died. The Mojave green's bite was not as lethal, but his fangs could still deliver a powerful hit of neurotoxin. Depending on your circumstances it could be fatal. And since my circumstances were none too encouraging, I figured my decision to play safe was the right one. Fact that he hadn't shaken his rattle was a good sign. Having said that, Mojave greens sometimes bite without warning so I took nothing for granted.

Hard to tell how many minutes I sat there with that snake, but it was a lot of minutes. Twenty or twenty-five I guess. I didn't want to risk glancing at my watch because the movement might provoke him. Anyways, knowing how much time I was wasting wouldn't help. My companion just didn't appreciate that I had stuff to do.

Eventually, though, he began to move.

Lowered his head, he pushed himself forward. I hoped he'd move around me, but instead he came over my lap. He was a big mother, maybe four feet nose to tail. And heavy. A twelve-pound rattlesnake's belly pressing hard on your crotch is not a pleasant sensation. Once he'd gotten going, though, he picked up the pace and I relaxed a little. A few seconds later I watched him vanish into the dark base of the chimney and made a mental note to remember this on my way back up.

Finally I was able to move along the middle ledge. It soon became clear, though, that this was the inverse of the one higher up: The slope was gentle but the surface narrow. Worse still were vertical outcrops that blocked the way. Upshot was that I had to lean out to get by, the backpack hanging out over the precipice.

I was trying to get around one of these when I slipped.

TWENTY-SEVEN

I lurched backward, reached out. Fingers grasped a fracture in the rock with just enough of a ridge to cling onto. Fingernails split and tore. But I hung on.

First with one hand, then both, I hauled myself around the buttress and managed to get my feet back on the ledge.

Not before I kicked a little scatter of pebbles.

I froze as they went bouncing to the ground, maybe fifty feet below.

Two voices drifted up. Now I was close enough to hear what they were saying.

'Hey, Burt, what was that?'

'Dunno. Critter of some kind.'

'What sort of critter?'

'Fuck knows, Gene. Lizard. Rat, maybe.'

'I ain't never seen no lizards or rats up there.'

The guy called Burt was reassuringly dismissive. 'They don't go around in high-viz vests.'

But Gene was not going to give it up. I heard a click, saw the beam of a flashlight playing on the canyon wall just a few feet below me. The cone of light moved closer. Then it was dancing all over me.

I kept still, face turned to the rock. The light stayed on me for five or six seconds before moving away to my right. It hovered there for a few moments more, then the guy called Gene killed it.

'See, Gene? Nothing up there.' Burt sounded bored. 'Not tonight. Not any night.'

Was I relieved? Sure I was. Surprised? Not entirely. See, folk are often so busy looking for what they expect to see that they miss what they *do* see. And the very last thing Gene or Burt expected to see was some crazy guy climbing down the canyon wall in the wee small hours.

I reached the last section of chimney soon afterward. This was the longest and sheerest of the three, though there were lots of hand and foot holes. Just as well because the nearer to the ground I got, the more visible I became to the likes of Gene or Burt.

Finally on the deck, I moved quickly into some shadow between two of the Wild West replica buildings. My target, the processing plant, was two hundred yards along the main drag. Going the opposite way, I noted the prefabricated office block where Rex Hambly hung out. Beyond that was the wire fence and security checkpoint.

A glance at my watch told me it was gone 2.30am. I'd taken more than an hour and a half to get down here, and a third of that was spent rattlesnake-sitting. One day I might laugh at the ridiculousness of it. Right now it meant I had even less time to get what I needed. And it sure would have helped if I'd known what this was.

Seemed I'd left bad luck behind me, though, because the place was virtually deserted. I moved quickly between the fake silver-rush structures toward the processing building.

As I got closer, I saw one, two, three doors along the side, as well as the big sliding doors on the front.

Side entrances seemed the best bet. I made it to the processing plant and took the camera and lock pick set from my backpack. I was stooping by the keyhole when I heard footsteps approaching on the other side.

I retreated to the shadows, waited.

A key turned in the lock, the door swung open and a worker in navy blue coveralls came out. He walked thirty feet from the door and lit a cigarette. I guessed the chemicals stored inside the plant made it a no-smoking zone.

With the smoker's back to the open door, I got inside without a hitch.

I expected to see other workers moving about the place and took cover behind some oil drums. The whole building was lit up by fluorescent strips, but I heard nothing, saw nobody. This surprised me.

So did the smell. I'd done some research before I came out and gleaned a basic understanding of the leaching method used to extract silver from the ore that comes out of the ground. It involved complex chemical and mechanical operations that I imagined would create smells of industrial lubricant, engine oil, muck and speciality substances including cyanide. But the only smell was a chalky staleness. It was as if the operation had been set up and immediately mothballed.

This was underscored by the state of the equipment. The big hall was filled with steel hoppers, conveyor belts, jaw crushers, pumps and pipes. There were other pieces of plant I identified as ball mills, agitators, flotation machines and magnetic separators. All different sizes and shapes, but the one thing they had in common was their newness.

The only exception was a little hopper, compact crusher and short conveyor. They were set apart, right at the back of the building. Unlike the big machinery, these were mired in dust. Beside the hopper was one of the muck carts I'd seen running on rails from the mineshaft toward the processing plant. The cart was piled with freshly mined ore and I guessed this was ready for feeding into the compact crusher when work resumed in the morning.

Sound of footsteps told me the guy who had gone for a smoke was coming back. I glanced over my shoulder and watched him close the door, lock it, and hang the key on a nearby hook. Then he walked over to a little office with glass walls.

This was a particularly lax security practice but it suited me fine. The rebalancing of the bad luck I had on the way down seemed to be continuing. The guy sat behind a desk, took out a newspaper and started reading.

I made my way along the side of a ball mill that resembled a horizontal Saturn V rocket and wasn't much smaller. Paintwork was shiny blue, floor space around it unblemished. Like the other machines, it looked more like a trade fair exhibit than a piece of operational equipment.

As I approached the grimy sub-plant at the back I trod on a small object. It crumpled under my boot like the ring-pull on a soda can. Looking down, I realized I'd flattened a silver earring.

Surprise was quickly replaced by suspicion.

I moved closer to the conveyor. It had been switched off with a cargo of fine graded rock at the midpoint between the compact crusher and a yellow collection bin.

On an adjacent workbench, two plastic trays had been

left either side of an engineer's vice. The tray on the left contained a pile of silver jewellery similar to the earring I just stepped on. The other contained silver shavings. A six-inch rat-tail file completed the picture.

Lined up on the floor were five Perspex cylinders, each filled with pulverized ore, no doubt ready for shipping as samples to a testing laboratory.

You didn't need a PhD in minerology to dig that the silver filings were being mixed in with the ore samples in order to skew the lab results.

I started taking pictures. First of the workbench and ore samples, then some long shots of the vast, unused factory.

Like the miners with their movie star teeth, all this sophisticated technology had been put in place for one reason: to look like something it wasn't.

TWENTY-EIGHT

This time Finn Sheldon agreed to meet me in a more civilized location: his downtown hotel room – but only on condition that I followed elaborate instructions to make sure I didn't get tailed.

He showed me into his room, brushing potato chip crumbs off his chest. Nylon drapes were pulled across the window and a weak electric bulb did little to compensate. Air conditioning wasn't working and the stuffy atmosphere carried a cargo of tobacco smoke and deep fried food. He sat on a two-seater couch, almost filling it. I took a seat on a plastic chair opposite and he invited me to tell him what I knew.

When I was done he made a sour smile. 'You can take the man out of the Green Berets, but you can't take the Green Berets out of the man. That it?'

I smiled back. 'I'd have nailed the story one way or another.'

'You really shouldn't have gone in there like that.' He was condescending in the way of a schoolteacher berating a kid who'd done something dumb. 'Are you absolutely certain you weren't detected?'

I shook my head. 'Getting out was a damn sight easier than getting in. I was passing Rex Hambly's office when I heard him tell a colleague he was done for the night and was heading home. There were only three vehicles outside: a Dodge pickup, a minibus, and a big Kawasaki motorbike. I couldn't imagine Hambly on the Kawasaki any more than I could see him driving the minibus. So I concealed myself under a tarp sheet on the back of the pickup and waited.'

'Your insight into the human condition never ceases to astonish.' My buddy's tone dripped sarcasm.

I let it pass. I got that he was pissed. No point arguing. 'Fifteen minutes later Hambly drove the pickup to the security gate. My gamble that the guard wouldn't inspect the manager's vehicle paid off. Forty-five minutes after he pulled up at a set of traffic lights in downtown Hicks and I jumped off.'

Sheldon remained doggedly unimpressed. 'What you discovered is what we suspected. The technique is called salting. Fraudsters typically use a ratio of around three ounces of silver for every ton of rock so they don't attract too much attention. But I suspect they've been using a much greater proportion up at High Rock because attracting attention was the whole point. That's what made the value of the business go sky high overnight. They knew they could get away with it because the mob would have been squeezing selected individuals at the labs.'

He gave me a solicitous look. 'Got a cigarette?'

I handed him my pack of Camels. He took one, lit it and continued speaking through a wreath of smoke. 'You do understand that you can't run the story?'

'Tell me why not.'

'One, you'd wreck a three-year CIA investigation. And two, you don't have all the pieces.'

'I got pictures of the silver flakes and the ore samples. And that pristine processing plant that's been built at great cost but never used.'

'Compelling stuff, I agree. But on its own it wouldn't be enough. You might catch some small fry like Hambly. But the big fish would let him take the fall and swim away. And remember you can't use any of the deep background I gave you without blowing me as your source. You can't mention the CIA or the mob. Not without independent corroboration.'

I made a frustrated sigh. He was right.

'Hold your fire until we can establish the mob connection and you get an exclusive.' His demeanour switched from irascible to amenable. 'How does that sound?'

It sounded like something I already heard from Lee Caraway about Gary Gerwitz's secret meeting with Frank Hazeldene, but I couldn't say so without revealing my other half-baked exclusive. So I nodded and said sure, I could wait.

But that didn't mean doing nothing.

*

First thing I did was call Lee Caraway and arrange to meet her later.

Next I phoned a contact at the Immigration and Naturalization Service to ask a favour. Caraway had already confirmed my belief that Rex Hambly was the manager at High Rock who phoned Carmody at the diner immediately before he got shot. You come from another country to work in the USA, the INS would certainly open a file on you and

I was keen to know what was in Hambly's. Corporate fraud, that's serious shit. Cop a rap, you'll do a stretch. Aiding and abetting murder, though, that's different league.

My pal at the INS said he'd do what he could, strictly off the record, and I hung up with him.

Then I drove over to the scene of the triple murder. I parked outside the New Life Episcopal Church and walked over to where I figured the shooter would have been standing when he took aim at Hazeldene and Carmody.

Now I was thinking Carmody was the mark and Hazeldene the decoy. The congressman's movements had been purposely and widely publicized; Carmody's were private and unpredictable. When Carmody got out of bed each morning the guy himself didn't know where he was going to end up that day, or when. He simply went wherever he was needed. Some days he worked from his office in downtown Hicks; other days he stayed up at the mine. And then there were days when he started at one and moved to the other. Whichever way you looked at the happenstance of the two men's deaths, Hazeldene's was bound to appear premeditated and Carmody's accidental.

So if you could somehow get Carmody's path to cross Hazeldene's, you could shoot them both and leave no trace of your intention. The cops would focus their resources on the logical victim – the decoy victim – and your trail would never be looked for, still less followed.

Equally interesting was that I'd run this idea by Sheldon out at the Silurian Hills and he hadn't contradicted me. *Credible hypothesis* was the phrase he used. For a spook who never said much, that said a great deal.

Even more interesting was that now I had Carmody

pegged as a huckster caught up in a $20 million money laundering caper run by the mob. If that didn't make you a hot target, it was hard to imagine what would.

I looked again at the crime scene, trying to visualize events from the shooter's point of view. He'd have parked his bike by the kerb and waited for the two men to appear. Maybe he sat awhile on the low brick wall that separated the parking lot from the sidewalk. Until now, it seemed Hazeldene's arrival was the key. But maybe the real key was Rex Hambly.

Suppose he was the mob's placeman.

Suppose he somehow arranged Carmody's schedule that day so he ended up eating alone at the diner? More you thought about it, the more plausible it became. Hambly could have told Carmody that an investor or supplier wanted to meet with him there. He might even have said a mob boss demanded the meet. That would have guaranteed Carmody's presence.

And suppose the shooter contacted Hambly from the phone booth opposite, with instructions to call the diner and lure Carmody into the parking lot? Even more straightforward, the shooter could have called the diner direct, claiming to be Hambly. Later, when questioned Hambly, simply told the cops he made the call. According to Hazeldene's itinerary the congressman was available for a photo opportunity in front of the church from 2.00 to 2.15pm. That gave plenty time for Hambly or the shooter to bring Carmody into the kill zone where Hazeldene was hanging around for press photographers who never showed. For the shooter, the rest would have been easy.

'Hey, Wat! Buddy!'

Norm Dibbitts was striding toward me, spoon collar

shirt unbuttoned almost to his naval, flared pants flapping around high platform shoes. A few days ago I'd have made some excuse and split, but I was beginning to see Norm in a different light. There were good reasons why he was suffering from paranoid delusions. And despite these problems, he'd shown grit and loyalty out there on Harvard Road. Least I owed him was a little time.

Besides, standing in 100 degrees of desert heat had made me thirsty. So I accepted Norm's offer of a cold beer and followed him into the bar.

He plucked a Lucky off the cold shelf and asked me how I'd been after those goons attacked me. I said I'd been good. They hadn't showed since and although their disappearance was a mystery, I had no complaints.

'We vets, we gotta stick together.' Norm looked up at me as he finished pouring my beer. 'Ain't that so, Wat?'

I nodded yes and took several big swallows of beer.

'You read the Good Book, Wat?'

'Not so much these days, Norm.'

'I read it cover to cover, seven times.'

Setting down my beer glass, I took out a Camel and lit it. 'That must have taken a while.'

'More you read, faster you get. Last time I took a week's vacation and read it in six days and six nights – same time it took the Lord to create the world.' He hesitated and made a hangdog expression 'Gotta admit I skipped some bits.'

'Maybe God did too. Maybe that's why we live in the world we do.'

Norm shook his head vehemently. 'The Lord would never do such a thing, Wat. And you shouldn't entertain thoughts like that.'

'Just a throwaway comment, Norm.'

'Throwaway, that's the devil's shit.' He gave me a straight, hard stare. 'You and me, Wat, we was put on this planet to do the Lord's work.'

'How so, Norm?'

'We been chosen.'

Norm's assertion wasn't unusual. A lot of guys tried to get through the war by telling themselves God had chosen them for some higher purpose. They thought this meant they'd survive. But I saw a lot of chosen guys going into body bags, often in a lot of pieces. I said nothing, though, and waited for my buddy to continue.

'When I read the Good Book for the seventh time, it was kinda like the opening of the seventh seal. You know, in the book of Revelation? That was when I realized the US military was created by the Almighty. And I don't just mean created along with everything else, I mean created specific.'

I sipped my beer more slowly. 'There was me thinking it was Uncle Sam's work.'

'Sure it was Uncle Sam's work. But who do you think created Uncle Sam? It's all in the Good Book, Wat, if you know where to look.' Norm made a triumphant smile and reached over the bar to collect a couple of empty beer glasses. The action made his shirt sleeve ride up and I saw a tattoo on his upper forearm: the word *Bro* inscribed above an American eagle.

'That's an interesting tat on your arm, Norm.'

'You like it?'

'Sure do.'

'It's for your brother, right?'

He rolled up his sleeve so I could see the artwork more clearly. 'We both served. We was in the Nam together.'

'He get home okay?'

'Yeah he did.' My buddy's mood seemed to nosedive. 'But we got split up over there. I ain't seen him since we came back to the States.'

*

Lee Caraway was waiting in a booth in the Say When. She was wearing a pale blue chambray shirt with mother of pearl snaps and a suede skirt. She looked real cool and made me wish I'd showered and changed instead of coming straight here in my work stuff.

I told her what I discovered at High Rock Mine and explained my theory that Carmody, not Hazeldene had been the mark.

'You need to interview Hambly again,' I said. 'He's in real deep. Not just the silver strike fraud but putting Carmody in the shooter's sights. Arrest the guy if necessary.'

I could tell from her stony expression that this was not an option. 'The only person likely to get arrested is you, Wat. You can't go around breaking and entering like you're on some recon patrol. And you know perfectly well I can't use photos you obtained illegally.'

'I get that. But if you brace Hambly about Carmody, he'll cave.'

'Will he? We have nothing to prove he didn't have a genuine reason for calling Carmody on the day of the shooting and no evidence to link him, or the mine, to the mob. We'd achieve nothing and show our hand in the process.'

A bartender came over and I ordered a Lucky the same

as Caraway's. 'So you do at least agree that Carmody was the real target?'

'After what you just told me, the idea has legs.' She took out a menthol cigarette and accepted my offer of a light. 'Can't your CIA source give you any more on the mob's involvement?'

I shook my head no. 'This person is out on a limb already. Any further information I have to get on my own.'

When Grover Burdick entered the bar I assumed he was here for a routine after-work drink. I could tell from his expression, though, that some significant shit had gone down. Hard to tell whether he was looking for me or Caraway, but he came over and addressed us both.

'Bobby Peeples was just found unconscious. He's been badly beaten. Currently in a coma at the hospital.'

Caraway reacted first. 'You know what happened?'

The lines in his big face deepened. 'Do *you*?'

I leaned forward. 'C'mon, Grover, if you even suspected either of us did it, you wouldn't be here with the tip off.'

'Give your brain a chance, Wat.' He gave me a pissed look. 'What I suspect don't matter squat. Bobby was left for dead in a side street near where you live. Half the station thinks the pair of you had something to do with it. Bull Turner is furious and Pop Peeples is demanding he has you both arrested.'

I took out my notebook. This was a hot news story regardless of who was responsible. 'What do you know about the attack, Grover?'

Burdick took a Camel from my pack and lit it with my lighter. 'Severe bruising to the base of Bobby's skull shows he was hit from behind with a blunt weapon. Baseball bat or some such like.'

I made notes. 'Will he live?'

Burdick held out a flat hand, palm facing the floor, and wiggled it. 'Could go either way. Even if he does recover, there could be permanent brain damage.'

My buddy looked from me to Caraway, then back at me. 'You want my advice? Get a rock solid alibi for last night. Both of you.'

TWENTY-NINE

Saturday September 22, 1973

I drove my Bug up to Fort Irwin early the following morning.

In my pocket was a press pass from Stokes Honeysett for a demonstration of the M60A1 main battle tank fitted with Amalgamated Metal torsion bars.

This was my first visit to Irwin, forty miles north of Hicks in the Calico Mountains. During the Vietnam War a lot of artillery and engineer units trained and deployed from the base, but these days it was used mainly as a training area by the Army Reserve and the National Guard. With more than seven thousand square miles of desert to go at, there was no shortage of elbow room.

On the drive over I listened to Iggy and the Stooge's *Raw Power* album. First up was *Search and Destroy*, a high voltage rock song about the world's forgotten boy who walked the street with a heart full of napalm. After the Nasty there was a lot of anger on the streets for a lot of reasons and Iggy's new record was the angriest I heard in a long time. If there was a soundtrack for the national mood right then, this was it.

Whoever attacked Bobby Peeples sure wasn't short on

anger. There had been no change in his condition overnight. *Still critical* was the phrase used when I called the hospital. I phoned Caraway straight afterward. Pop Peeples was all over Bull Turner, demanding he sling us both in the tank. Bull wasn't going to roll over, at least for now, but the problem was that neither of us had an alibi. Caraway had been alone in her apartment that evening and I'd been alone in mine, preparing to break into High Rock.

A little over thirty minutes later Iggy was thrashing out the final track, *Death Trip*, as I approached Irwin's security post.

I was directed to a parking lot where an Army Reserve major was waiting with Suze Carter, who had come direct from another job.

The major introduced himself as Jim Caldarelli. He was a short, swarthy man of Italian descent and I liked him immediately, mainly because he never mentioned my Medal of Honor, the Green Berets or Vietnam.

He ushered Suze and me into a Jeep, but instead of heading toward the main cluster of buildings, he drove northeast, past the airfield, in the direction of the desert.

I gave our host a quizzical look. 'Mind me asking where we're headed?'

Caldarelli made an affable grin. 'Mr Honeysett wanted to give you an insight, sir, and the CO agreed.'

'What sort of insight?'

The major hung a right and the jeep swung around an islet of rock. 'That sort.'

Ahead of us was an M60A1. Eleven feet tall, twelve feet wide, and thirty-one feet long if you included the 105mm gun barrel. Weighing more than fifty tons, this was America's biggest, baddest battlefield beast.

Behind it was a squat cinderblock structure.

'I understand you never rode in a tank, Mr Tyler.' Caldarelli said. He guided us toward the cinderblock building. 'Mr Honeysett and the CO thought the experience would be helpful if you're going to write about the suspension system.'

Inside the building a briefing room was laid out with plastic chairs and a film projector. Caldarelli ran a short film about the layout and safety procedures of riding the M60 and explained what the exercise would involve. Then he handed me a fire resistant tank suit along with a Kevlar helmet and showed me to a locker room where I could change my clothes.

Caldarelli was right about my inexperience of tanks. Vietnam wasn't a war for tanks and the M60 was never deployed there. Instead we used the M48 medium tank, which was considered sufficient to handle any armoured threat Charlie could muster. And since most of my active duty was spent in enemy controlled territory, I saw very little of the M48.

This wasn't to say I didn't respect tank crews and I respected them a whole lot more as I hauled myself onto the M60's hull and followed its commander, Sergeant First Class Lafferty, into the turret. Getting down to the gunner's station was like crawling inside the drum of an industrial-sized washing machine that had been crammed with control gear and hydraulic systems. No doubt you'd get used to working in the confined space, but right then it was a tall order not to bump my head or skin my elbows on the sharp-edged metal objects that stuck out all over the place. Apart from the crew's seats, I couldn't see a single soft surface. Then I realized why: The type of plastics and fabrics you find in an automobile would burn instantly if the M60's armour got penetrated.

The interior was painted gloss white, which looked a little strange because in my experience the only colour the US Army ever painted anything was olive drab. Apparently the shiny whiteness was there to reflect light when the tank was buttoned up.

There were four crew members and I was there instead of the gunner. The driver sat up front on his own, the gunner on the right of the 105mm gun, the commander above and behind, and the loader to the left of the gun.

SFC Lafferty's voice crackled in my headphones, 'You okay there, Mr Tyler?'

I said yes and the driver hit the gas. The ride was surprisingly smooth: much more so than Caldarelli's jeep. There was a front-and-back rocking motion that I realized was due to the cushioning effect of the torsion bar suspension.

The driver took his foot off the gas and the tank rolled to a halt. Looking through the telescopic sight, I realized we were on the crest of a low rise. Dead ahead, at a range of one thousand metres, was our target: A Sherman tank of World War II vintage. Through the naked eye it looked like a matchbox placed at the opposite end of a basketball court. When I zoomed in, though, it looked close enough to spit at.

'Up!' The shout in my headphones came from the loader, indicating that a 105mm round was in the chamber.

There was a whirring noise as the hydraulics coaxed the heavy ordnance to the correct range and bearing.

'You wanna fire the gun, Mr Tyler?' This was Lafferty's voice.

'You'd trust a reporter with the 105mm, Sergeant?'

'Not really a matter of trust, sir.' Lafferty made a throaty chuckle. 'I already acquired the target. Gun's ready to shoot.

All you need do is take hold of the Cadillac and squeeze the top switch on the right handle.'

I knew from the briefing that the 'Cadillac' was the control mechanism right in front of me – so called because it carried the manufacturer's logo.

Taking both handles, I took a look through the main battle sight then squeezed the trigger switch. The M60 rocked back. I felt the torsion bars absorb the colossal force as the shell left the barrel at 1,800 feet per second. I was impressed, no argument there. The round landed but all I saw through the sight was a column of churning dust. When it drifted clear it seemed the Sherman's turret had skewed around to the left.

'Direct hit,' Lafferty announced. 'Great job, sir.'

Of course I hadn't done anything except press the fire switch when I was told to. But it was good of the guy all the same.

*

First I felt the earth vibrate, then the air was filled with a bass growl as the seventeen M60s of the demonstration company approached. Next I picked up the squeal and clank of steel tracks passing over cog wheels and return rollers, then the sizzle of tread plates crushing the rocky ground as if someone was frying eggs. The column appeared on the left of a small grandstand where Stokes Honeysett, Suze Carter and I were sitting with the Armor Branch generals this show was being laid on for. Despite the space age technology, there was something primordial about those steel monsters that fit right in with the Mojave's ancient anger.

Honeysett leaned close and shouted into my ear. 'Where would you rather be, Mr Tyler? Inside or out?'

I grinned. 'Where do you think? That was a much smoother ride than I'd been expecting.'

He smiled back. 'That's why we do what we do at Amalgamated.'

The tank company roared away into the desert, fanning out, hulls rising and dipping as they cruised over mounds and crashed through gullies.

Their targets, ten scrapped Sherman hulls, were arrayed along the top of a ridge 3,000 metres from the grandstand. The M60s stopped in line abreast and fired a ragged salvo at a range of around 1,500 metres. Through my binoculars I saw the tanks lurch back then spring forward as their torsion bars absorbed the recoil. Gotta say it was as mind-blowing from a mile away as it had from the gunner's seat.

Panning right, I watched the practice shells rain down on the Shermans, throwing up spouts of ochre dust that hung in the air long enough for Suze to capture the scene with her zoom lens and power-winder.

The officer in charge of the exercise picked up a radio handset, spoke to the guys on the target range, and announced on the PA system that all seventeen M60s had scored hits. This triggered applause from the generals and I joined in.

With the main event concluded we retired to a marquee for club sandwiches and coffee. This was where I had to sing for my supper as a former Special Forces officer, fielding questions about the Vietnam War from a bunch of generals and colonels who never served there. Many had fought in tank units in World War II and Korea, but since then their heavy armour commands kept them in the European theatre.

The conversation wasn't all one-way, though and I got some useful quotes about the operational performance of the M60A1 and how it stacked up against its intended adversary, the Soviet T62.

Later Honeysett took me to a private room in the Officers' Club where we did the main interview for my feature. For a man who was meant to be dying, the old boy seemed remarkably well. He was attentive, indulged my technical ignorance and couldn't do enough to help me get the detail and colour I needed.

Toward the end of the session I broached the subject of the torsion bar contract. Without mentioning the absence of Gary Gerwitz, I asked if Honeysett was confident of landing the order.

He patted his jacket pockets to locate his pipe and tobacco tin. 'Our torsion bars are the finest and most competitively priced in the world. And if that sounds boastful, I make no apology. Our research and development programme for speciality steel alloys is acclaimed by universities from Berkeley to Oxford. We understand better than anyone the consequences of a tank failing in the field, which is why we invest so heavily in our laboratory testing resources.'

I looked up from my notebook. 'When you say a tank failing in the field, am I correct in thinking you mean a torsion bar breaking?'

'You are, indeed, Mr Tyler.'

'So what happens in a situation like that?'

He removed the lid from his tobacco tin and started loading his pipe. 'Depends on the circumstances. If the tank is performing a dangerous manoeuvre when a bar fails, that could result in a catastrophic loss of control. At best it would reduce mobility, but there could be more serious consequences because the failure of one bar would inevitably load the others beyond their design limits. That could cause multiple failures and total loss of mobility.'

'So the tank would be a sitting duck?'

He struck a match and dipped the flame into his pipe bowl. 'Precisely.'

'And if one tank was affected, presumably a whole formation could be?'

'In the worst case, yes. But the chances of failure are remote.'

I looked up from my notepad. 'How remote?'

He paused to get his pipe going. 'With appropriate maintenance, the chances of an individual bar failing are negligible. Ninety-nine per cent of our bars have a life-span of 300 miles – appreciably greater than the Department of Defense specification of 99 per cent and 260 miles.'

'What happens when this mileage threshold is exceeded?'

He sucked on his pipe and released a veil of fumes. 'Well, at distances over six hundred miles, there's a fifty per cent probability that a bar will fail. But the Army operates a regular maintenance and replacement programme to make sure that never happens.'

With the interview done, I was preparing to leave when Honeysett went and bushwhacked me.

THIRTY

'I do love my daughters, Mr Tyler.'

This was as close to embarrassed as I ever got. 'I don't doubt it, sir.'

'Nonetheless, I think you may have reason to.'

'You don't need to explain anything – least of all to me.'

He went on, though, as if he hadn't heard me. 'I know you were with Lee at Florine's Nest when Bobby Peeples told everybody who cared to listen – and everybody who didn't – about my arrangement with the mayor and Chief Turner. Bobby is a malicious piece of work, much like his father.'

For a moment I wondered if Honeysett put Bobby in a coma. But not having anything good to say about a guy doesn't translate into attempted murder. Besides, it wasn't Honeysett's style. Honeysett would have hit him from the front.

'Perhaps one day, Mr Tyler, when you have children of your own, you'll understand the pain of having to watch them fail.' Old boy pinned me straight. 'That's what happened with Lee after she joined the LAPD. Every time she took that sergeant's exam the paper was marked 'fail' before she put a pen to it. I never wanted her to pursue a career in law enforcement, but I did respect her decision. What I found myself unable to do was stand back and watch her ambition being slowly suffocated. So I persuaded her to apply for the Hicks PD job, then I had a word with the mayor.'

'I don't blame you, sir.' I held his gaze. 'And I don't believe Lee will. She just needs a little time.'

'Which, of course, is the very thing I don't have.' He gave me a knowing look. 'Lee did tell you about my heart condition, didn't she?'

Not for the first time lately, finding the right words was tough. 'I'm sorry, sir.'

He made a sigh someplace between anger and sadness. 'When you reach my age you tend to avoid making long term plans. But this news could not have come at a less convenient juncture.'

I had to admire the old boy's scrappy contempt for the hand he got dealt.

There was a note of resignation, though, when he continued. 'I don't expect to see next summer. But I'll have long enough to secure the Chrysler contract. And, I hope, for Lee to forgive me.'

'If there's anything I can do, sir...'

'That's very kind, Mr Tyler, but I'm afraid there isn't.' He made a tight smile and held out his hand.

I left him in that room at the O Club and drove back into Hicks.

In my office I sifted through a stack of notes and memos.

When Sheila called from reception it was a relief.

Until I heard what she had to say: Bull Turner wanted to see me at the police station. Right that minute.

*

'This is an unusual step,' Bull Turner said.

He was sitting behind a desk that made the flight deck of a nuclear powered aircraft carrier seem cramped. In front of him, Caraway and I were sitting on visitor chairs. She was already there when I arrived so there was no opportunity to get our stories straight.

'The pair of you put me in the damndest situation with Chester Peeples.' Bull Turner was the opposite of happy. 'The very damndest.'

I never found out how he got his nickname. At five six and one hundred twenty pounds, he didn't look bullish. His uniform was no doubt the smallest available, but still too large. The starched collar orbited his neck without touching it and the gold eagles on his epaulettes dragged the garment forward from his shoulders. Features were delicate, even dainty. His hair was fine-spun grey and pebble lensed glasses magnified his eyes. If he hadn't been wearing a uniform I'd never have pegged him as a police chief. Maybe the Bull nickname was ironic.

When he spoke he looked alternately at Caraway and me, as if to make clear he was addressing us equally. 'Here's what I know: Bobby Peeples overstepped the mark giving out like he did at Florine's Nest and got what he deserved from you, Caraway. Two days after that, you, Tyler, were attacked out on Harvard Road by four thugs who then made themselves scarce pronto, even though you left two out cold and the others barely able to walk. Two days after that, Bobby got the back of his head caved in, probably with a baseball bat.'

He paused just long enough to light a fresh cigarette from the butt of the old one. 'Here's what I *don't* know: What the heck is going on.'

'Sir, I think – ' Caraway's sentence got sawed off.

'Here's what *I* think,' Turner said. 'I don't like women cops and I especially don't like you, Caraway. I heard from your lieutenant over in West Hollywood that you're a bra-burning trouble-maker. But I got you anyways and I don't – you hear me? – *don't* hang my own out to dry.'

Caraway started to speak again, but Turner held out a flat hand in the manner of a traffic cop making a stop signal. 'You can complain when I'm done.'

He turned to me. 'You, Tyler, I respect. Fellow pulls himself up by his bootstraps like you did, you gotta respect that; comes back from Vietnam with the Medal of Honor, you gotta respect that too. I even respect what you write. Well, some of it. Anyways, I don't hang folks I respect out to dry either.'

By now I'd figured out that the 'Bull' tag wasn't one bit ironic. It came from his attitude.

He leaned forward on his pointy elbows. 'So I got Chester Peeples on my back and he's convinced one or both of you put his boy in the hospital. I don't agree. And as long as that's the case, that's all that matters.'

He let the silence play a long five seconds. 'But if you give me any reason – any reason at all – to make me think you've been playing me, I'll throw both your asses in the tank faster than you can blink. You understand?'

'Yes, sir.' Caraway seemed to get that we were there to receive information, not give it.

We left Turner's office and said nothing until we were in the parking lot, headed toward my Bug.

'Turner's a sexist bastard.' Caraway was plainly disgusted and I got why she felt that way.

Even so, I thought she needed to put the scene with Bull Turner into some perspective. 'If the chief really didn't like you, he wouldn't have had you in there at all.'

She raised one eyebrow. 'I'm supposed to be grateful that he's an *honest* sexist bastard?'

'At least you know where you stand with him.'

'Yeah. Eyeball deep in shit.'

'Way I see it, it's gonna get deeper.'

'How *do* you see it?'

I stopped by the VW. 'If Bobby regains consciousness he'll say you or I did it, or we both did it.'

She frowned. 'But he was hit from behind. He couldn't know who attacked him.'

'He'll invent a story. He'll say he saw us sneaking around immediately before he got whacked. Or he saw one of us coming at him in his peripheral vision. And if Bobby doesn't invent a story, his dad will put one in his mouth.'

She nodded and completed my train of thought. 'And if Bobby dies, the rap is murder.'

'Which Chester will do his damndest to pin on us.'

'He has no evidence.'

I said nothing. We both knew how evidence could be acquired by a big man in a little town.

She checked her watch. 'I gotta go.'

I was going to mention my meeting with her dad up at Irwin, but she was preoccupied. And the more I thought about it, the more I realized that I'd probably make matters worse.

So I watched her drive off then turned to unlock my car.

'Hey, Tyler!'

Schwenk was homing in on me, shoulder-holstered ordnance bulking out the left side of his suit coat.

'Hi there. You got something for me?' I grinned, but the G-man's mouth stayed in a tight line.

'Sure I got something for you. Another warning. Butt out.'

Didn't give up my grin. 'Butt out of what? My First Amendment rights?'

'Don't give me that boy scout crap, Tyler.'

'Or what, Schwenk? You'll give me what you gave Bobby Peeples?'

'You really think the Bureau would pull something like that?'

'Quite honestly, I don't know what to think.'

He came close, the loophole eyes and boxy face filling my vision. 'What happened to Bobby Peeples, that was on you, Tyler. So was the incident with Caraway at Florine's Nest. And the assault out on Harvard Road.'

I met his gaze. 'So you're now accepting the Harvard Road attack actually happened?'

'The sheriff and the chief are giving you the benefit of the doubt, so I guess I will too.'

'That's mighty generous of you, but how is that, and those other two incidents, on me?'

'I can't tell you any more. But if you want to do Caraway and Peeples – *and yourself* – a favour, you'll back off right now.'

Schwenk stepped back, straightened his coat and started toward the police station doors.

I called after him. 'Hey, Schwenk. Can't tell me, or won't?'

'Can't.' He didn't look back.

*

I drove straight to Gary Gerwitz's place and used one of my lock picks to open the side door.

In my experience the best stories came from breaking the rules one way or another, and I sensed this was no different. If Supervisory Special Agent Schwenk cared to explain why he reckoned I was responsible for events outside my control, then I might consider taking his advice. Until then, he could go fuck himself.

Even so, this latest encounter with the Fed was concerning and puzzling in equal amounts. The logical inference was that the scene at Florine's Nest, the bushwhacking on Harvard Road and the assault on Bobby Peeples were intended to throw me off the scent. But which sent? The Ray Carmody scent or the Frank Hazeldene scent? Or was there some other scent Schwenk thought I was following, that I simply hadn't picked up?

I figured Gerwitz's house was a good place to start looking because last time I was there I got interrupted by Caraway. That meant the search we carried out was superficial so as not to disturb potential evidence and render it inadmissible in court. As a reporter I wasn't concerned with rules of admissibility. I was after a story.

I found nothing in the kitchen and the plate of leftover spaghetti Bolognese had started to smell real bad, so I moved quickly to the living room. When Caraway and I had been here she searched the living room while I focused on the study. Her determination to leave the place as we found it even extended to switching the TV back on. Now it was showing an episode of *Kung Fu*. Sounded real loud.

Behind the TV set was a burr walnut writing bureau with a hinged lid that folded outward to form a writing surface.

The lid was locked but I had no problem opening it with my lock picks. Inside the bureau were untidy piles of bills and unopened mail – stuff a gambling addict with money problems would want to ignore. Half buried under a pile of unpaid parking tickets I noticed a binder with the logo of a bank on the spine. It contained checking account statements in Gerwitz's name. I scanned the money-in and money-out columns. My eyes snagged on a name I recognized: Stacey Honeysett. It appeared next to a $2,000 payment into Gerwitz's account. Then another, also for $2,000, and another, and on they went.

This was not what I expected. According to Caraway, Gerwitz had been behaving weird for some time. What did she say? *Forgetful. Short-tempered. Distracted. Prone to moodswings – and freaking out for no apparent reason.* Apparently the ex-wife got so concerned she stopped the kids coming over. I got the impression Gerwitz was being shaken down. But this substantial income stream from Stacey suggested *he* was doing the shaking. I'd never have picked out Stacey as a dupe though.

Then I realized *I* was a dupe.

Someone was in the room behind me. I heard the ratcheted click of a revolver being cocked.

I thought of Schwenk, but this wasn't the G-man. He couldn't have known where I was headed when I left the cop shop. And whoever had the gun on me was already here when I arrived. No doubt he turned up the volume on the TV to drown out any noises he made.

In that instant a lot of things went through my mind. Fortunately a bullet wasn't one of them. At least for now.

THIRTY-ONE

You got a gun on someone, you're the Man.

Leastways you think you are. See, a lot of folks believe whoever they're pointing a firearm at will do exactly what they're told. Few people expect resistance and getting hold of that revolver before it put a hole in me was gonna hinge on my ability to spring a surprise.

What the guy said next, though, was the biggest surprise I heard in a good long while. 'Turn around real slow, Gerwitz.'

I said, 'I'm not Gerwitz.'

The other guy chuckled. 'Sure you ain't.'

Even so it was in my interest to follow his instructions. I needed to see who I was dealing with.

The news was good and not so good. On the plus side he was half-way handsome with a trendy haircut and profuse dark brown sideburns, decked out in a bottle green suit with tulip lapels. The collar of the red silk shirt was turned over his coat collar and the top four buttons were open to display a gold St Christopher medallion. It nestled in a nest of thick chest hair. The niff of Brut 33 was so overpowering I was surprised I didn't smell it earlier. My overall assessment? This guy was not a professional killer. If anything, I'd say he was a socialite, a party animal.

On the negative side, he was young – mid-twenties. And young men with guns tend to be cocky, nervous and jacked on adrenalin. That's a volatile mix.

'Really, I'm not Gerwitz.' I spoke in a light, familiar tone, as if this party cat and I would be buddies if only we could get past this small misunderstanding. 'Not your fault. This is Gerwitz's house. But you got the wrong man.'

'Into the study. Put your hands in the fucking air.' The party guy jerked the revolver – a Colt .38 snub nose – in the direction of the hallway. 'Move!'

I moved, he followed.

My hands were raised either side of my head with the pistol pointed at the base of my skull. I walked toward the doorway, weighing up what this entailed. In some ways I'd have preferred him to have gun on my torso. On balance, though, my head suited me better.

'Listen, man,' I said, making sure I had this amateur's full attention, 'I'm sure we can sort this out if you just let me – '

'Keep your mouth shut, Gerwitz, or I'll shut it for you.'

'But I just want to explain – '

I was still talking as I started to spin. Only stopped when my already-raised left arm knocked his gun-arm to one side. He squeezed the trigger. This close, any gunshot will hurt your ears. But I was used to it and he wasn't. Shock and pain registered in his expression. In the same motion, I wrapped my arm around his and locked it tight, giving me control of the weapon. I could have hit him in the head at that point, but I needed information he couldn't give if he was unconscious. So I kicked his right foot off the floor and drove the heel of my free hand into his shoulder, levering him off balance. Party guy hit the floor hard. I pinned him with a knee-drop just below his ribs and kept his gun arm locked. But the fight had gone out of him. He released the revolver without further struggle.

I kept my grip tight though.

'Where you from?'

'Vegas.'

Should have guessed. The entertainment capital of the world and a natural habitat for a good-time-guy like him.

I released the arm lock and stood over him with the revolver. He was scared shitless and with good reason. Seconds ago he was the motherfucker; now he was plain fucked.

'You co-operate, I won't hurt you. Understand?'

He nodded yes and I stepped back, allowing him to get up off the floor.

He came to his feet, nursing his right arm where I'd wrenched it.

'Where in Vegas?'

'The Maharaja.'

I hadn't heard of it, although casinos came and went in Vegas. 'On the Strip?'

'Across from The Sands.'

'What's your name?'

'Marty. Marty Millard.'

'Well, I gotta tell you, Marty, that I still ain't Gary Gerwitz.'

'You ain't?'

I knew genuine puzzlement when I saw it.

'I'm a journalist. Looking for Gerwitz just like you, though for different reasons. I assume he owes your boss money?'

He nodded yes.

'How much?'

'I don't know exactly, but it's a lot. Twenty grand, maybe more.'

That tallied: I'd counted a dozen payments of $2,000 from Stacey's checking account to Gerwitz's. Didn't take a genius to figure out that Gerwitz owed the Maharaja $24,000 and Stacey gave him the cash to pay it off. But the debt never got settled and I had no doubt Gerwitz simply blew those $2,000 payments at other casinos.

'Lot of money,' I said. 'Double, even triple what most folks earn in a year. Debt that big could get you killed.'

I didn't think it was possible, but Marty Millard's face got a shade paler. He held up his hands defensively. 'You got it wrong, Mister. I didn't come here to off Gerwitz. Just to put the squeeze on him. I mean, killing him would make no sense. If Gerwitz ended up dead, my boss would never get his money.'

This stacked up. I knew from the outset that Millard wasn't a hitman. He arrived at Gerwitz's house without even knowing what the dude looked like. I figured his boss just gave him the address and sent him over.

'Relax, Marty.'

I gave him a Camel and a light.

'What's your boss' name?'

He sucked on the cigarette and gave me an anxious look.

'Hey, remember I'm a reporter. I just want to ask some questions about Gerwitz. I'll even call ahead and book an appointment. My name's Wat Tyler, editor of the *High Desert Herald*, the local paper here in Hicks.'

I showed him my press card and that seemed to convince him.

'My boss's name's Randy Pasqual.'

'Okay, tell Randy I'll be in touch.' I nodded toward the side door. 'Now beat it.'

*

Stacey Honeysett peered over the top of the *New Yorker* and regarded me with an easy smile. 'My dad's over at the factory.'

She was reclined on a chaise longue by the pool at the Honeysett mansion. A black bikini covered very little of her thoroughly desirable body.

'I'm here to see you.' I prized my eyes off the display of taut flesh. 'I called the house an hour ago and spoke to your maid, Constanza. Didn't she tell you I was coming?'

'She must have gotten sidetracked.' Stacey put her teeth on show. 'But it's no big deal – you're here now. Take a seat. Can I get you a drink?'

'No thanks.' I sat on a beach chair. 'I won't take up much of your time.'

'That's a shame.' She made a disappointed pout. 'Such a long drive if it's just for a short visit.'

'I'm here about Gary Gerwitz.'

She walked slowly into the shade of a eucalyptus tree where a bottle of white wine lay in an ice bucket. 'Sure I can't tempt you?'

'Sure I'm sure.'

She poured herself a large glass and came back to the chaise longue.

'So, what's this about Gary?'

I said, 'Why did you give him twenty-four grand?'

She was clearly shocked. She asked what I meant and I told her what I knew. Then I repeated my question.

'I gave him the cash because he was an old friend with serious money problems.' She picked up a pack of Gitanes and lit one. 'What was I supposed to do?'

'He's a gambling addict. Giving money to a guy like that is like giving booze to an alcoholic.'

'Pardon me for caring.' Her voice trembled and I pegged that she wasn't as hard as she liked to appear.

'I'm sorry,' I said. 'I'm not trying to be mean. But he didn't repay the casino. He just went to other casinos and pissed it all away.'

Her eyes were moist. 'I'm worried about him, Wat. What if other people he owes money to send more guys to get him? Gary's not tough like you. He couldn't handle it. And if my dad finds out it'll finish him.'

I put my hand on hers and squeezed it. 'I'm sure Gary is out there somewhere. We just gotta make sure we find him first.'

She placed her other hand on mine and held on. The militant socialist I met in the greasy spoon had been replaced by a freaked out girl.

'If I lose Dad *and* Gary, I don't know what will happen – to me, the company, everything.'

'Listen,' I said. 'You're going to be all right. One way or another, we'll get this mess cleaned up.'

'And you're not angry with me?'

'I'm not angry. You've been a good friend to a guy who doesn't deserve you. But I do have stuff to do. Stuff that won't wait.'

I stood up.

She stood up.

We were close. I felt her breath on my face.

She said, 'Let's go to bed.'

Her tits brushed my chest; my cock mobilized.

I took a step back. 'It wouldn't be right.'

'Dad won't be back for hours. Constanza is very discreet.'

Offer like that, it's tough to say no. But I knew this much: if I didn't say no I was headed straight into a Force 12 shitstorm.

'It's not that I don't want to – '

'But you'd rather fuck Lee.'

'That's not true.'

'It's fine. I'm used to it.'

'I haven't laid a finger on Lee. We're working together is all.'

'Fuck off, Wat.' She turned her back to me. 'Please, just fuck off.'

She was humiliated and angry and I understood why.

So I left.

I took a short cut home along a dirt road between the Honeysett place and Interstate 15. I'd driven maybe five miles when I noticed another car coming toward me. The road was too narrow for both vehicles to pass so I pulled over.

The profile of the Rolls Royce Silver Shadow was unmistakable. When I pinned the cardinal red coachwork, so was the owner. The limo cruised by, the chauffeur waved his thanks, and I pinned Stokes Honeysett reading a newspaper in the back.

He'd arrive home several hours before Stacey expected him.

I tried not to think what might have happened if I hadn't said no to the hottest offer of sex that came my way since I left New York.

THIRTY-TWO

Last time I saw Stuart Van Loon was in a foxhole in the central highlands of Vietnam in the fall of '69. He was the executive officer of one of the other A-teams in my company and his people had taken heavy casualties completing a tough operation. Van Loon came from privilege, but that was okay because he never shoved it in my face like so many so-called brother officers.

Back then I called him Loony – the most ironic nickname I ever heard – and he called me sir, leastways in front of the brass. But that military stuff seemed ridiculous in our current location: his family's investment bank in the business district of Los Angeles. He didn't look old enough to be a vice president, but then he never looked old enough to lead a Special Forces detachment. A shiny-smooth complexion and short brown hair gave him the somewhat plastic look of a GI Joe soldier doll. It would play well in the corporate arena, though.

We'd talked on the phone the previous evening so I went straight in. 'You got the information I asked for?'

He looked at me with a faint smile. 'Do I get the deal I asked for?'

I nodded yes. 'Absolutely you get the deal. Most of the time sources don't want their names in the paper. Guy of your stature goes on the record, that's gold dust.'

My buddy offered me a cup of coffee from the pot by his desk, but I declined. It was difficult to take notes and drink coffee.

'This story will go around the world, Wat. I want my firm's name in it. Money couldn't buy the publicity.'

'Okay, Stuart, tell me what you got.'

He poured himself some coffee and stirred it with a dainty spoon. 'In a nutshell, High Rock Mine could be the biggest fraud in American corporate history.'

I started writing: a dozen words that would make the lead for my second national exclusive in two weeks. I still needed Finn Sheldon's cooperation but I was confident of getting it when I returned from LA.

'High Rock originally listed as a penny stock on the Western Nevada Exchange in March 1970. Back then it was classified as a visitor attraction but when silver was discovered six months later, the stock rocketed from two cents a share to $3 in less than a year. This continued until last month when it peaked at nearly $10 a share, yielding market capitalization of more than $20 million.'

'That's the value of the company, right?'

'Right.' He lifted the cup from the saucer and took a sip of coffee. 'During this period Ray Carmody remained the majority shareholder. When he died he still owned 51 per cent of the equity. And this was despite him selling shares worth one million dollars last November.'

'Was that the first cash taken out of the company?'

Van Loon shook his head no. 'Two other investors –

a venture capital firm here in LA and a private individual named Anthony Dexter Martin – also took a million bucks apiece a month earlier.'

'Any idea who Anthony Dexter Martin is?'

'Not a member of the LA corporate finance community is all I can tell you. Whoever he is, though, I'm pretty certain he and the venture capital outfit are cash conduits for the mob.'

I scribbled some notes. 'Two million is an impressive number.'

'Sure is – but in relative terms it's chump change.'

I stopped writing. 'Relative to what?'

Van Loon sipped more coffee. 'A proposed new listing on the Pacific Coast Stock Exchange valued the company at fifty million. That's according to an official filing with the Securities and Exchange Commission in DC. Flotation on the Pacific Coast market would have made the stock much more liquid – far easier to sell to the general public, as opposed to large institutional investors. Just as crucially, the amount of cash available would have doubled overnight.'

'Would have? What went wrong?'

My buddy placed his cup back in the saucer real slow, as if it was the Apollo lunar module touching down. Then gave me the sort of hard look that belonged in Charlie country. 'Twelve days ago Ray Carmody instructed his lawyers to pull the plug on the Pacific Coast share issue. He was murdered the next day.'

My mind had gotten blown a lot of times lately and I was sort of used to it. This, though, was a whole new experience.

I looked up from my notes. 'You come between the mob and fifty million bucks, you better run. So why didn't Carmody run?'

'Must have had his reasons. Can't imagine what they were.'

I drew a line under that section of notes. Caraway was in LA with me. Maybe her enquiries would shed some light on this latest revelation.

In the meantime I had more questions for Van Loon.

'What I really don't get is how it was possible to pull a scam like this. Carmody must have dodged stock market regulators all the way from Western Nevada to DC. How come they swallowed his jive? It's not every day some backwoods businessman shows up claiming to have found America's biggest silver deposit since the Comstock.'

Van Loon took another sip of coffee then made a sardonic smile over the rim of the cup. 'This was the real smart play. In the early days High Rock placed its stock with private investors. This meant the public disclosure requirements were substantially less rigorous than if the company had sold direct to the public. It may sound inconceivable, but the only prospectus the company ever filed was in 1970 when Carmody listed it on the Western Nevada Exchange as a visitor attraction. To this day there's never been any mention of silver mining operations. Not to the Securities and Exchange Commission or any other regulator.'

Van Loon was right: it *was* difficult to believe. Shavings from silver jewellery scattered in worthless chunks of Mojave rock had apparently suckered experts who were supposed to protect investors.

'What about the big brokerages and corporate finance firms? Surely they do intensive due diligence before signing off millions of investment dollars?'

He hesitated and I sensed there was more to this than loyalty to his own kind.

I gave him a nudge. 'How would *you* have approached the situation, Stuart?'

Van Loon winced. 'That's the thing, Wat. We *did* approach it. We were on the verge of joining the syndicate underwriting the Pacific Coast share issue. We didn't go ahead because another opportunity came along and we couldn't do both. At the time, we were kicking ourselves... That's not for publication.'

He gave me an angry look. 'You can put this in your piece though: If somebody like Ray Carmody tells a massive lie and people are determined to believe it, all the disclosure rules under the sun won't stop the ordinary investor, or the world's biggest investment bank from getting ripped off.'

THIRTY-THREE

It said something about Hollywood Boulevard that two of the stars embedded in the Walk of Fame had gotten chiselled out and stolen. It said something else that another star had no inscription – presumably waiting for some kid to get famous enough to cop a chunk of immortality. And it said even more that a double amputee was sitting by the next star down, begging nickels and dimes. As I drew nearer I saw a cardboard placard hanging from his neck saying *Vietnam Vet – Please Help*. Only when I dropped two quarters in his wool hat that I realized he was sitting crossed-legged with his feet tucked tight under his thighs and a blanket arranged to hide them.

That said it all.

Some handbill distributor in a nylon Spiderman costume went by, big belly and king-sized ass stretching the fabric in all the wrong directions. Sweat patches spread from the armpits and red gumboots squeaked as he walked. Spidey spotted the scam too and wheeled around, telling the phoney amputee that he was a disgrace to the country and insisting that he refund my donation.

I didn't have the time or inclination to get involved so I moved on.

Caraway was waiting outside a little café at Hollywood and Vine called the Grub Club. She was wearing her hair up under a floppy straw hat and shades with blue hexagonal frames, a low-cut tank-top and miniskirt with platform-soled boots up to her knees.

'This is my old beat and people know me,' she said. 'The guy we're seeing after lunch can't be seen talking to a cop.'

'So you figured to attract one type of attention in order to deflect another?'

'Does it work?'

'If you're asking me if you look like a hooker, I gotta say yes you do.'

'Good.' She made a faint smile. 'You can be my pimp.'

She nodded toward the Grub Club and we went inside to grab a sandwich and exchange information. The place was almost empty, which suited us.

Caraway had come to LA after finally agreeing that Ray Carmody's links to the mob via a big money fraud were worth investigating. She got even more interested when I told her what I just learned from Stuart Van Loon. Her own enquiries among former LAPD contacts had led her to a crime family capo called Rocco Bonfiglio who knew a lot about the mob's financial dealings.

I was hungry and began to eat my sandwich. Between bites I asked if she'd told the guy I was a reporter.

'That's the only reason he agreed to speak to us.'

'So he wants something. Any idea what?'

'None. We should be grateful he's willing to talk at all.'

'Any news on Bobby Peeples?'

'Condition still critical.' She took a bite of her sandwich, swallowed some and pushed the rest into the side of her mouth.

She hesitated and I could tell there was something else. Finally she said, 'Rex Hambly has gone missing.'

I frowned. 'Missing how?'

'Schwenk put a tail on him. He shook the tail and didn't show at the mine this morning.'

'You told Schwenk about this?' Couldn't help but sound pissed off. Little wonder she held off telling me this until last.

'You wanted me to come to LA.' She shot me a stinging look. 'And since I can't be in two places at once I had no choice but to ask Schwenk to help.'

She had a point. I let it ride.

Back on Hollywood she steered me across the street in the direction of a strip joint with a huge sign over the entrance announcing "Hollywood's Hottest Showgirls".

Big speakers pumped out Kool and the Gang's *Hollywood Swinging*. Falsetto vocal and funky guitar hung right in the hot fuggy bar room. Caraway led me toward the far side, past a stripper in mid-routine. As we went by she took off her glitzy top and whisked it around her head. On the third time around the wire fastener got caught up in her hair. She tried to tug it free. It wouldn't budge. She tried over and over, but it was no use. The dudes in there were so busy watching her tits bouncing around that they only realized what was going on when she stopped dancing to disentangle the wire. Then they began laughing and shouting. Some threw coins and beermats onto the stage. Poor girl stood there, tits out, fiddling with the hook and that scene said as much about Hollywood as the fake amputee begging bits on the Walk of Fame.

Caraway led me through a door at the back of the bar.

We were confronted by a pair of homeboys with droopy moustaches and neckties with fist-sized knots.

One took us up a narrow flight of stairs that smelled of booze and cheap perfume, then into an office that was every bit as chic as Stuart Van Loon's suite in downtown. Except for the two Rottweilers salivating on the leather couch and a bar in one corner that carried significantly better quality liquor than the much bigger one downstairs.

Rocco Bonfiglio was standing by a window and turned to greet us. He was short, maybe five-seven or eight. Well quilted, just short of podgy. His nearly bald scalp was spattered with pale freckles and his round features were dominated by heavy, black-framed glasses. In a double breasted suit with polished wing-tip shoes, he looked more like Phil Silvers in the role of a banker than a senior mobster.

Placing a fat cigar in an ashtray as he extended a hand and guided Caraway and me to a couple of chairs in front of his desk. He offered us a drink and poured himself a modest Bourbon when we declined.

He relit his cigar. 'Not every day I do this sort of thing.'

I took out my note pad. 'We can all of us agree on that, Mr Bonfiglio.'

He made a belly laugh that was too loud to be genuine. 'Okay, Mr Tyler, let's be honest with one another. I got something you want and you got something I want.'

I suspected he hadn't been honest with anyone since he was old enough to talk. I said, 'What *do* you want?'

'I want you to kill a guy.'

'I'm a reporter not a hitman.'

Bonfiglio seemed to find this amusing. 'Where this guy is

right now, bullets can't touch him. Words are a whole other deal. You can't hide from words.'

'You can't hide from libel laws either.'

'Someone told me the truth is a complete defence.'

'Only if you can prove your story is true.'

He laughed again, this time more gently and, I suspected, more genuinely. No one would call Bonfiglio an intimidating guy; devious, you'd hear that plenty.

He laid his cigar in the ashtray. 'First of all, tell me what you got on High Rock Mine.'

I glanced at Caraway. She nodded to go ahead. So I told the mobster the truth. More or less and up to a point.

Bonfiglio smiled appreciatively. 'Okay, Mr Tyler, I can tell you that your facts are essentially correct.'

I was about to start writing but he wagged his index finger at me.

'The information I give you, it's strictly Deep Throat stuff, right?'

'Right.'

'And you reporters, you protect your sources at all costs, am I correct?'

'Entirely correct, Mr Bonfiglio. I'll do jail time rather than give up a source.'

'If this goes bad it won't be a judge asking you to give me up.' He looked at me hard but seemed satisfied with my response and reclined in his studded leather chair.

'Okay, first off, here's some background for you.

'Right now the LA families are not happy families. There's a power vacuum around the corner and people are antsy. The boss, Nick Licata, and his number two Joe Dippolito, are in very poor health. Neither is expected to see another summer.

The coming man is Jimmy Brooklier, but there are other contenders and nobody is really sure which horse to back.'

I wrote this in shorthand and looked up when he stopped speaking.

'Okay, that's the background.' He leaned forward and picked up his cigar. 'Here's the specifics.

'The High Rock Mine deal was, like you said, part of a money laundering caper involving venture capital investment. Some guys, including me, had doubts from the start, but we needed to bring cash back into the country so it got the go-ahead. Management was delegated to an ambitious douchebag named Vito Occhipinti, also known as Anthony Martin.'

I looked across at Caraway. That was the name of the guy Van Loon said had sold High Rock shares worth a million dollars last fall.

Bonfiglio noted the interaction and continued. 'Occhipinti happened to be shaking down a corporate financier named Harold Burbridge, whose liking for young boys had come to Occhipinti's attention. So Occhipinti made a deal with Burbridge: The money man devised the scheme and in return he got his life back.'

The mobster paused, grinning to himself. 'The plan Burbridge came up with was meant to be slow but safe. He set up two venture capital funds to buy equity in fast-growing businesses, the idea being to sell the shares in two or three years and bank the cash. It got called slow-motion laundering, but it was more like no-motion. Patience was required, but Occhipinti was not a patient man. He liked the High Rock scheme in particular because silver is sexy and the company was already publicly traded. And so – without the say-so of the high-ups – Occhipinti told Burbridge to list the mine on the Pacific Coast Exchange. Like you said, Mr Tyler, the plan was to hike the share price and raise fifty million bucks in relatively liquid assets. Occhipinti was ecstatic. The asshole could smell the money.'

Bonfiglio made another pause for dramatic effect. I was done with dramatic effects though. I looked up from my notes. 'But?'

He shrugged. 'But Ray Carmody panicked. He told his suits to pull the plug on the new share issue.'

Again I looked at Caraway. Her question was the same as mine: Why would Carmody trash a deal that would have propelled him from filthy rich to obscene rich?

'You want me to tell you why?' Bonfiglio was lapping this up – a cop and a reporter unable to see what he considered to be obvious. 'All the extra shares created by the new share deal would have cost Carmody his majority stake. He'd gotten used to being the top dog. If he couldn't be in the driving seat, he was gonna run the car off the road. Can you believe it?'

'I can believe it.' Caraway lit one of her menthol cigarettes. 'Little guy from a little town becomes a national celebrity, he'll get off on the fame a lot more than the fortune. And after a lifetime feeding off scraps he'll do anything to keep that sense of control.'

Bonfiglio sucked on his cigar. 'He was still a dumb fuck.'

I was more interested in what happened next. 'Where did this leave Occhipinti and Burbridge?'

The gangster chuckled. 'It left Burbridge in the Los Angeles River with most of his head taken off by a sawed off shotgun. And it left Occhipinti on the lam. Word is, though, that the cocksucker's negotiating a sit-down with Joe Dippolito. Occhipinti is an oily tongued bastard who could talk his way out of the most shit you can imagine. I wanna make fucking certain that never happens. You print the story I just gave you, Mr Tyler, and Occhipinti becomes the kind of liability the LA families absolutely do not want. With this out in the open, there's no way Dippolito's gonna give him a pass. You understand what I'm saying?'

'I understand what you're saying Mr Bonfiglio.' I gave him a curious look. 'Might I ask why you're saying it?'

'Sure you might ask.'

He killed his cigar, stabbing it in the ashtray over and over, then crushed the butt until it was flat. 'Ten years ago Occhipinti put a blade between my ribs. I was lucky to survive.'

'So you want revenge?'

'Sure I do. But I've been waiting a long time. It has to be done right – so there's no coming back.'

Caraway exhaled menthol tobacco smoke. 'So it was Occhipinti who ordered the hit on Carmody?'

Our host gave her a dismissive look. The deal was that I asked the questions and Caraway was here as an observer. That way, Bonfiglio could truthfully say he hadn't been quizzed by a cop.

So I repeated the question.

Bonfiglio shrugged. 'Carmody did not get stiffed on the orders of Occhipinti or anybody else in LA.'

I stopped writing. This was a big surprise. Bonfiglio could be shitting us, but I couldn't figure out why.

'How can you be so sure?'

'Carmody would have been dealt with at some point,

sure. But this hit went down way too fast, even for a shit-for-brains ditz like Vito Occhipinti. Look at the sequence of events: Carmody pulls the stock market flotation and gets iced in less than twenty-four hours. We don't waste time when something's gotta be done. But this was too rushed, too obvious and too sloppy.'

I said, 'Sloppy in what way?'

The mobster gave me a give-me-a-break-look. 'If the contract was for Carmody, he and nobody else would have gotten hit. Not Carmody plus a congressman plus a fucking barmaid. The moment Hazeldene was killed, the FBI was all over this. Like I said, these are not happy days for the LA families. A lot of important people got real pissed off having to field questions from the Feds about a huckster politico they had nothing to do with.'

There weren't many times when I took the word of a mobster at face value, but this one.

I looked over to Caraway and had no doubt she was thinking the same: So who *did* kill Carmody? And why?

THIRTY-FOUR

We ate ribeye steaks with mashed potatoes and sautéed broccoli at the Pacific Dining Car at West 6th and Witmer. Then we walked back to the Majestic Hotel on Wilshere Boulevard. Hicks PD was picking up Caraway's tab and the *Herald* mine, which left us with not much choice. So we registered at the Majestic, which was anything but. The six storey hotel was built in the twenties but its once-elegant façade was neglected and the art deco interior, shabby.

The owners had taken good care of the bar, though, and Caraway agreed to a nightcap.

I ordered some drinks while she used the pay phone to get an update on Bobby Peeples and Rex Hambly.

She agreed that Bonfiglio had levelled with us about using me to get even with Vito Occhipinti. By putting the already busted scam in the public domain, Bonfiglio would make damn sure Occhipinti got thoroughly investigated. That would make him one hundred per cent toxic to the crime family bosses. No doubt they'd want him silenced before he could turn state's evidence and implicate the higher-ups. In that sense my story would be Occhipinti's death warrant. Did I give a fuck? What do you think?

Caraway also accepted Bonfiglio's claim that the mob wasn't behind the killing of Ray Carmody. Sure, Carmody was a dead man walking after he pulled the plug on the new share issue. But his only direct link to the mob was Harold Burbridge. And he was eliminated already. So rushing to Hicks to kill Carmody, who was apparently awaiting his fate, made no sense.

The question of why Carmody didn't run still dogged me, but I was sure the answer wasn't in LA.

When Caraway returned I could tell from her expression that she had no more news on Peeples or Hambly.

We took a seat at a table near the window. The room was full enough to be lively but empty enough for privacy. Juke box was playing *Touch Me In the Morning* by Diana Ross.

I didn't want to ask her what was on my mind but felt I owed it to Stokes Honeysett.

So I jumped right in. 'How are things with your dad?'

She sipped her drink. 'You mean have I decided to forgive him?'

'I didn't say that.'

'You didn't need to.' She fidgeted with her pack of Belair menthols but didn't take one. 'I get that he was trying to help. I'm just so angry that he presumed he had a right to interfere.'

I waited for her to continue.

'What really pisses me off is that everyone in Hicks knows how I got the job. They think I don't deserve it. And they're right.'

'You're already proving them wrong. The thing is though...'

I paused. How to phrase this?

'Go on.' She looked right at me.

'Okay, the standard advice here is that you shouldn't leave important stuff up in the air because none of us knows what's round the corner. But the argument is even stronger in your case because your dad *does* know.'

She drank some more. 'That's decent advice. I'll sleep on it.'

Then she threw me a curve ball. 'Tell me about *your* parents.'

'I don't know if they're still alive.'

She seemed to find this surprising. 'That must be tough.'

'Actually it's not. Parents like mine, not having them around is a bonus. I haven't seen my dad since 1957 when I was fourteen and my mom brought me to New York City. I don't blame her for running. If she hadn't he'd have beaten her to death. But I haven't seen her since 1965 when I went to Vietnam.'

'You said she had a booze problem.'

'She had a lot of problems although booze was far and away the biggest. I tried all sorts of tactics to get her to quit, but you gotta want to and my mom just didn't. When I went back to Brooklyn three years ago, she was gone. Nobody knew where and after a time I stopped looking.'

I was glad when we switched to small talk.

After another drink we rode the old cage elevator to our rooms on the fourth floor.

Caraway's and mine were at opposite ends of a frowzy hall, separated by five rooms and a shared bathroom. I walked to her to her door and waited while she opened it.

The door swung open and she turned to face me.

I said, 'I guess this is goodnight.'

She smiled. 'I guess.'

I hesitated.

Lee was looking real gone sexy. But she already made clear that she wasn't ready for anything more than friendship and professional partnership.

I could see why.

Or could I?

What to do?

In the end, though, it wasn't even a tough call. I kissed her cheek, told her to sleep tight, and backed off.

Maybe this was what happened as you grew older. You quit thinking with your dick. You got responsible. You got boring. Yesterday I passed up the opportunity of sex with Stacey. Now I'd done the same with Lee.

I went to my room, cleaned my teeth, climbed into bed.

City noise seemed amplified in the musty room: a car horn honking; a bus grumbling by; booze-fuelled babble from folks on the street rising up then falling back like waves on a harbour wall. Somewhere distant a police siren wailed.

I thought about Lee.

I tuned into hotel noises: the ancient elevator doors rattling open and shut. Groans and clanks from the Calvin Coolidge-era pipework.

I tried to sleep but the act of trying only made me more awake. And the more awake I got, the more I thought about Lee.

Sodium streetlights penetrated the thin nylon drapes and a flashing neon sign winked pink against the peeling wallpaper.

I counted sheep. I don't know how many sheep I counted but it was a lot of sheep.

More gurgles and clanks from the ancient plumbing tore it.

I pulled on my jeans and T-shirt and stepped into the hallway.

Lee was approaching from the far end. She seemed as shocked to see me as I was to see her.

We met in the middle. She was wearing a short bathrobe.

I said, 'I was going to the bathroom.'

She said, 'So was I.'

We glanced at the bathroom door, then back at each other. Hard to say who started talking first.

She said, 'I was coming to see you.'

I was already saying, 'I was headed for your room.'

She took my hand. We went to her room and she led me to the bed, kissing me hard on the mouth like she did that night at Florine's Nest.

She smelled of smoky vanilla. She was every bit of desirable.

We got it on fast but not furious. And we kept it on, varying the pace, staying in tune. Caraway was agile and responsive. I liked the way she let control pass back and forth between us, making it last until we were both ready.

At last we fell sideways and lay looking at each other with small smiles.

Later we shared one of her Belair cigarettes – I'd left my Camels in my room – and she propped her head against my chest.

After some time I kissed her hair. 'You miss LA?'

'Not the sexist cop shit. I don't miss that.'

'Big city life, then. Your friends.'

'The big city buzz, sure. A few friends, maybe. But most

of the folks I socialized with were friends of my ex. He's a cop too. So when we split it made things kind of difficult. In a way, Hicks was the answer.'

'What sort of ex? Husband? Fiancé?'

'We were living together and thinking about getting engaged, but it didn't happen. I caught him cheating and that was the end.'

She took a pull on the Belair and passed it back to me. 'You?'

'Long term relationships aren't my thing.'

'I find that hard to believe.'

'I can't make them work.' Gotta say I was bushwhacked by my own candour. 'Harder I tried, the worse it got, so I quit trying.'

'Don't you get lonesome?'

'It's what I'm used to.'

She interwove her fingers with mine. 'Why is that?'

'You don't wanna know. It's boring psychological stuff.'

'I do wanna know.' She banged her fist on my ribcage. 'C'mon, spill.'

'Okay, if you insist.' I sucked hard on the cigarette. I really didn't like the menthol deal but wanted the nicotine fix. 'It's called an attachment problem. It starts in violent or chaotic homes where very small kids fail to bond with their moms.'

'That must have been horrible.'

I shrugged. 'The damage was done before I can remember. Obviously I have memories of my dad beating my mom, but these came as I grew older.'

'So how does that really early stuff affect you now?'

'My kiddie brain went into survival mode and stayed that way. So I process negative feelings differently – especially anxiety. But it also distorts positive feelings.'

'How so?' She took the cigarette from me.

That was a tough question. I took a few seconds to think about it. 'It's as if the volume control on my emotions has been dialled right down. There are ways I can pump it up – rock music, poetry, sometimes my work – but they're just snapshots of what it might be like to be normal. There is no permanent fix.'

'You don't strike me as a guy with problems.' She gave me a puzzled look. 'Just the opposite. You're good with people.'

'All part of the coping strategy. Truth is I'm not so good with any sort of domestic scene and I struggle with stuff like affection and empathy. I never get particularly angry, and I rarely get excited.'

She made a puzzled frown. 'But you've got insight. Surely that helps?'

'Sure it helps. It also helps that I had therapy after Maggie took me off the street. But childhood shit is especially tough to deal with. Adult trauma – combat fatigue, for example – that's like a car crash. You know where it happened and you can see what the damage is. Childhood trauma is like a car getting damaged on the assembly line. It rolls through the factory doors looking fine, but all sorts of stuff doesn't work like it should. And you have no idea what until it starts going wrong.'

'There's not much wrong from where I'm looking.'

'You don't know me, Lee. I sometimes wonder if I do.'

She kissed me on the lips again, slow and tender.

After a while she drew back a couple of inches, her big eyes flooding my vision. 'I can get to know you – if that's what you want?'

'Sure it's what I want.'

I meant it. What I was less sure about was whether wanting would ever be enough.

THIRTY-FIVE

I parked my dusty old Bug next to Stokes Honeysett's gleaming Rolls Royce and found myself looking at the sublime and the ridiculous. Having said that, my sound system was as good as any and that was what really counted. Leastways in the world I lived in.

I glanced at the copy of the *Herald* I'd placed on the passenger seat. Under another exclusive byline, the lead paragraph read:

Businessman Ray Carmody was slain the day after he aborted a $50 million stock market shares fraud backed by the Los Angeles mafia.

This was my second national story in two weeks. I sure wasn't complaining, though it was the most irony ever that my résumé had significantly benefited by my quitting a big city paper for a small town rag. Sheldon had been happy to contribute as an anonymous CIA source. Combined with the naming of Vito Occhipinti and the pictures I got of the fake silver operation up at High Rock, this gave me a story that ran like a rat. Spooks, mobsters, a multi-million dollar scam, a triple murder, this yarn had it all.

I headed toward the mansion just as Stacey appeared from a gate in the walled garden. She gave me a frosty look and turned away. She couldn't have known I spent the night with Lee but was clearly still angry with me.

I wanted to make it right with her, but now was not the time. Now I was calling on Stokes Honeysett. He phoned my office and invited me over, insisting he'd explain why when I got here.

The maid, Constanza, showed me into his office.

Honeysett came toward me, swinging his prosthetic legs, hand extended.

He looked exceptionally healthy, but this didn't strike me as uplifting. Just the opposite. I thought it was a cruel illusion.

He poured two tumblers of bourbon and handed one to me.

'Another scoop in today's *Herald*, I see. Congratulations, my boy.'

'Thank you, sir.' I felt the bite of the sour mash whiskey on the back of my throat. 'If it wasn't for Lee's help, though, I'd never have nailed it.'

'Oh, I think you would. You may have taken a little longer, but you'd have gotten there.'

He lowered himself into one of two armchairs by the french windows. 'No doubt you're wondering why I asked you to come over?'

I took a seat opposite. 'It had crossed my mind, sir.'

He unlocked the mechanism that allowed his prosthetics to bend at the knee and looked up, grinning. 'Lee came to see me this morning. We had our most civilized talk in a very long while. At the end of it she told me she's willing to forgive me – or at least to try.'

'That's marvellous news, sir.'

'Isn't it just? Of course I realize that I hurt her deeply. The healing process may take a while. But we made a start and that's the important thing.'

He sipped his bourbon. 'I want to thank you, Mr Tyler. Your name was never mentioned, but your influence was very clear.'

'Sir, I—'

'I can see I've embarrassed you, for which I apologize.' He made a faint smile. 'I am, nonetheless, deeply grateful.'

He seemed to realize there was no place for this conversation to go and changed direction.

'When a man reaches the point in life that I'm at, he thinks a lot about what he's leaving behind; about his family; about achievements and regrets.'

'I'm sure your accomplishments are comfortably in the majority, sir.'

The topic was deep serious for sure, though his tone stayed light. 'I took some tough decisions during the Great War, but the sterner test came when I set up Amalgamated Metals. Certainly I've enjoyed commercial success, but I never lost sight of the fact that one bad decision could sink the whole enterprise – and twelve hundred families would lose all they had. I know you agree with Stacey that I should have let the unions in—'

'Sir, that's not for me to say.'

Honeysett raised an eyebrow. 'But it is what you *think*, isn't it?'

'As a reporter, I have no view.'

'And as a friend?'

That was the second time in two days a member of this family knocked me off balance. Not often I ever get to say this, but I was moved. Got my shit together quick though. 'As your friend, I'd have to say I think organized labour can benefit a business as well as its workers.'

'You could be right. And if I had the time available I might even have put it to the test.'

'You *have* got time, sir. Some time anyways.'

'You're being kind. But we both know I don't have *enough* time.'

He drained his whiskey glass. 'Rightly or wrongly, you should always believe in yourself, put faith in your judgment – even when other people doubt it. Especially when other people doubt it.'

The old boy's gaze moved to the french windows and the lawn outside. It was freshly mowed and perfectly smooth. Eucalyptus trees ran along one side and cerise bougainvillea the other. A stone birdbath stood at the centre of the grass.

'Will you look at that?'

A brown bird with a white eye-stripe was perched on the rim of the birdbath. It drank from the still water, then hopped in and started flapping its wings to douse itself.

'It's a cactus wren.' Honeysett craned forward, squinting. 'They get their water from the berries they eat so they very rarely drink, still less bathe. I've been watching birds in that bath for more than a half century and I've never seen a cactus wren go anywhere near it.'

'A memorable day, then,' I said.

'Lovely creature, isn't he?'

I just saw a bird splashing around in a dish of water. But I pretended to be fascinated for the old boy's sake.

I waited until he turned back toward me. 'What will you do, sir? With the business, I mean.'

He grimaced and adjusted his posture. 'Stay here to secure the new contract, then move to a place I have in the San Bernardino Mountains. It's much smaller than this, but everything I need is there. That's where I plan to die.'

This surprised me. Live most of your life in one place, you'll likely want to spend your last days there. Leastways that was how I saw it.

'Gary Gerwitz owns one third of the business and my sixty-six per cent will be divided equally between Stacey and Lee.' He made an ironic chuckle. 'Finally Stacey will be able to let the unions in – and maybe that will be a good thing. As for Lee, she can do what she likes with her shares, though I doubt she'll give up her police work.'

He lifted his empty glass from the little table at his side and asked me to fix him another drink.

I went to the sideboard and poured a finger of bourbon for each of us. I had mine straight but couldn't recall if he took ice. I asked him. There was no reply. So I skipped the ice and took the drinks back. Easy enough to get ice if he wanted it.

In the garden, the cactus wren was still flapping in the water. It stopped and cocked its head. I got the absurd impression it was looking right at me. Then it took off, quickly vanishing among the eucalyptus leaves.

I went over to Honeysett and offered him the glass.

'Did you want ice, sir?'

He didn't reply and he didn't take the glass. His head was

tilted to one side and I thought he was studying something else in the garden. Then I saw the unblinking eyes, the slack face muscles.

He had died.

THIRTY-SIX

I called 911. Then I found Stacey and told her what had happened. She stood in front of her father, refusing to speak or look at me. I guessed it was the shock. Next I phoned Lee at the police station. She arrived ahead of the doctor. When Lee came into the room, Stacey left. Lee kept it together, told me she'd handle things from there and promised she'd see me soon. I told her what I had to do and she was cool with that.

The story I wrote about her dad wasn't the story I planned. That was an upbeat feature about a World War I veteran who used his combat experience to build better tanks for US soldiers and create jobs for folks in Hicks. Instead I wrote a page-one lead about those jobs hanging by a thread due to Honeysett's death, Gary Gerwitz's unexplained absence and the impending torsion bar contract.

With the paper put to bed I left the office and went for a drive. Soundtrack was Mike Oldfield's instrumental *Tubular Bells*. The absence of lyrics fit my mood. I wanted to think and vocals sometimes got in the way. I thought about Stokes Honeysett and how I wished I could have known him better and longer. I thought about the randomness and brevity of life.

In the end, though, my thoughts went from Honeysett to Gerwitz to Hazeldene and then back to the murder scene. That was where my drive took me.

Standing in the spot where the shooter would have stood, I ran the sequence of likely events in my head. I'd done this time and again. No reason to suppose this latest attempt would prove any more fruitful, but my reporter's brain wouldn't give it up.

Something was wrong with the whole triangular homicide deal. It didn't really have three angles. There were only two: Ray Carmody and Frank Hazeldene. Marsha Houtrelle wasn't an angle. Marsha wasn't relevant. This wasn't a geometric equation. There was no symmetry or logic. Just a mind-fuck of action and incident. Some of it related, some not.

I went over to the Million Dollar Nugget. The prospect of hearing more of Norm's paranoid notions didn't exactly gas me, but I could use a cold beer.

The place was quiet. Two barflies on tall stools; no music on the jukebox; nobody shooting pool; nobody playing pinball.

The barmaid was Lucinda, the scraggy girl I'd met at the burger joint after those guys came at me on Harvard Road. I recalled Norm had a thing for Lucinda and that she juggled jobs at the Million Dollar Nugget and the burger place.

'Well hello there, Mr Reporter. What can I get you?' Her smile showed discoloured overbite teeth.

I asked for a Lucky and if Norm was around.

She shook her head no. Norm had gone to see a sick cousin down in Hesperia and would be gone till late. I went over to a table to drink my beer.

Lucinda appeared at my shoulder. 'Mind if I join you?'

What could I say?

She sat opposite.

'I read your story in the *Herald*. Bad deal over at Amalgamated. Poor Mr Honeysett. And some time for Gary to go AWOL, huh?'

She spoke about Gerwitz as if she knew him. I asked if this was so.

She nodded yes. 'He comes in quite often.'

This surprised me. You wouldn't expect to see the senior vice president of a substantial business to visit a dive like this. Without being rude about the place, I said as much.

Lucinda lit a Kent cigarette and made an amused smile. 'Gary don't come here for the ambience.'

'Why does he come?'

'He likes – *liked* – Marsha.'

I gave her a sharp looked. This was a surprise.

'I didn't know they had a thing.'

Lucinda leaned forwards to tap her cigarette in the ashtray. 'Not sure if I'd call it a thing. Gary was one of Marsha's waifs and strays. She listened to his blues and gave him a shoulder to cry on; he took her to nice places, even Vegas a couple of times.'

'Was there anything more between them?'

She pulled a puzzled face. 'You mean did they fuck? Guess they did. Be surprised if they didn't.'

'Marsha fuck a lot of guys?'

She flashed me an angry glance. 'She weren't no whore if that's what you're saying.'

I held up my hands in a gesture of surrender. 'I'm not saying that.'

Lucinda gave me a long look and seemed satisfied with what she saw. 'Like I said, she had her waifs and strays – men with problems. Gary was one of them. But I got the impression it was more about taking a little comfort. For Marsha too.'

'Marsha was a nice lady, wasn't she? Kind I mean.'

'She was my friend. She was a lot of folks' friend.'

I pictured the woman sprawled on the ground just outside, part of her head missing, big entry wound under her sternum. I knew why Carmody got hit. I could imagine why people wanted Hazeldene dead. But I couldn't put any sort of 'why' next to Marsha's death.

'I want to tell Marsha's story,' I said. 'But I can't get the information I need.'

Lucinda tilted her head and peered at me through the fog of tobacco fumes. 'What sort of information?'

'Where she was from. Where her family lives. What happened to her before she came to Hicks. Why she came.'

Lucinda smoked her Kent right down to the filter and examined it to see if there might be one last pull. 'She never talked much about what she did before here. Bar work in the San Fran Bay area was all she ever said. But she came from Coeur d'Alene, Idaho. That's her home town. Dunno if her family's still there, though.'

I'd be lying if I said this information didn't give me a jolt. It was the break I'd been looking for. After all this time, I couldn't believe how easily it came.

Lucinda killed her cigarette. 'I'm from Spokane, see. Just over the Washington state line. But we grew up close enough to have stuff in common. Sometimes we teased one another. She said I was from Spoklahoma and I said she was from

Coeur de Lame. We'd mimic one another's accent. It was like a joke between the two of us.'

It was easy to see why Marsha and Lucinda traded banter. Oftentimes local rivalry brought people together when they were a long way from home.

What was less clear was why Norm didn't tell me Marsha and Gerwitz were seeing one another. Something else: Stacey was friends with Marsha and Gerwitz and she never mentioned them getting together either. Maybe Marsha and Gerwitz wanted to keep things between themselves. It wasn't as if they were going out in the conventional sense.

'That's really helpful, Lucinda.' I took out a five dollar bill and pushed it toward her. 'Get yourself a drink.'

She gave me a leery look. 'I'm not after your money.'

'I'm sure you're not. I'm grateful is all.'

She took the five-spot like she was doing me a favour. 'Have one with me?'

'Love to. But I got things to do.' I stood up and headed for the door.

'Where you going in such a hurry?'

I said, 'Coeur d'Alene.'

*

Next morning I drove the Beetle to Los Angeles and flew to Spokane in a little under three hours. Then I rented a car and followed Interstate 90 along the Spokane River to where it empties into Coeur d'Alene Lake.

Fifteen minutes later I was in the town of Coeur d'Alene. It was home to 16,000 people – similar size to Hicks – which made it small enough to justify my gamble that somebody would remember Marsha Houtrelle. Coeur d'Alene was also like Hicks in that it was surrounded by mountains, although these peaks were much loftier and shawled in pine forest. Located on the lake's northern shore, it was a picturesque resort town. Water sport and leisure was a major part of the local economy. Plenty of excursion craft and sail boats out on the lake; sunbathers and swimmers on long sandy beaches with bathhouses and diving towers. Not the sort of place I would have associated with Marsha Houtrelle's apparently tough and impoverished life.

I began my enquiries at the county recorder's office. I went through the public records relating to anyone called Houtrelle but came up with zip. This was puzzling because the records went back to 1891. Next I tried the city clerk's office. Still nothing. Then I visited the police department. I produced my press credentials and laid all my cards on the table, including the photo from Marsha's apartment of her with the woman I assumed was her mom. The desk sergeant was cooperative but couldn't help. Same story at the county's sheriff's office, the high school, and the junior college.

Finally I went to the local newspaper office. The city editor was an old-timer named Arnie Duden. He walked to the front counter with a stoop. His features were scooped out, fingers nicotine yellow, breath booze-laden. I guessed he'd given himself unreservedly to an unforgiving profession and reminded myself not to go the same route. Easier said, though.

Duden listened attentively – especially when I told him his paper could land a major news story if Marsha was from these parts. When I was done, though, he shook his head.

'That's an unusual name – the sort you tend to remember,'

he said. 'But I've been on the editorial staff here since 1946 and I never heard it before today. Wish I could tell you otherwise.'

He went to check the clips library but I could tell from his expression when he came back that he'd drawn a blank.

I was mighty frustrated after so many dead ends and Duden sensed it. 'Sorry, son, but there's nothing more I can do.'

'I've been on some ass-busting wild goose chases,' I said. 'But a twenty-six hundred mile round trip makes this the longest by some distance.'

He made a sympathetic expression.

The picture of Marsha with her mom had to be worth one last shot so I slid it across the counter.

The old timer glanced at it. He'd started to push it back when he hesitated and looked again.

'When was this taken?'

'Not sure. Fifteen, maybe twenty years ago.'

He scratched his chin. 'That would be sometime between '53 and '58?'

'Give or take.'

'Hang on. We may have something.'

He vanished into the newsroom again. I lit a Camel. I'd smoked less than a third when he came back with a manila file. He opened it and pushed it toward me.

'I don't know where you got the name of Marsha Houtrelle from,' he said. 'But the name of the girl in this photo is Marsha McMeekin. She's pictured with her mom, Barbara.'

The story was there in the clips. Marsha McMeekin's family came to Coeur d'Alene in 1945 when she was six. She attended grade school and high school in Coeur d'Alene, enrolling at Portland State College in 1960 and enlisting in the Washington State Police after she graduated. There were short pieces with pictures about the graduation and appointment as a woman police officer.

It was in September 1972, though, that Marsha made a splash in the local newspaper. This was when she became one of the first women to complete the FBI's special agent training programme. Woman joins the Bureau these days, it's no big deal. Not in the seventies though. Back then the new female recruiting programme was a pioneering, even controversial development. And that made it front page news.

THIRTY-SEVEN

Lee Caraway poured a little cream into her coffee and stirred it in a series of agitated whisks.

'Even as a federal agent, Marsha McMeekin as the mark makes zero sense. That would mean Hazeldene and Carmody were the collateral. Any halfway competent shooter would have closed the range and made absolutely certain of taking her out.'

'Maybe that's what he intended. Then the two guys arrived on the scene. They took him by surprise and the shooter panicked.'

She shook her head no. 'Hazeldene *or* Carmody stepping out at the wrong moment, that's credible. But both? What are the odds?'

'Could be Marsha was investigating Carmody. Trying to stop the hit. The shooter could have taken a couple of shots to warn her off as he bugged out.'

'That's more plausible.' She sipped her coffee. 'Do we know of any contact between Marsha and Ray Carmody?'

I'd already run through these permutations. I was sure Caraway had too. It often helped, though, to talk stuff through.

'None. But then we didn't know about Marsha's relationship with Gary Gerwitz. I'm sure there's a lot we don't know.'

'Schwenk must have known about Marsha.' She sounded angry. 'He should have shared that information.'

I fixed myself some coffee but skipped the cream. 'To be fair on the guy – and I really don't wanna be – he'll have his reasons. There could be other people mixed up in this. People who'd be vulnerable if Marsha's cover got blown.'

We were sitting in the kitchen of Caraway's apartment at Whipple and Third. I'd just gotten back from Coeur d'Alene and needed to sleep, but first we needed this conversation.

'I'll talk to Schwenk,' she said. 'He'll be massively pissed that you got hold of this stuff.'

That was no overstatement. Schwenk had gone to extravagant lengths to conceal the undercover operation. Why else would he have tried to warn me off with two visits to the *Herald*, and the pep talk in the parking lot at Hicks PD?

'You can tell him the secret's safe with me. I won't print anything until I have the whole picture.'

She raised an eyebrow. 'What about the paper up in Coeur d'Alene?'

'Arnie Duden is an old pro. The type with integrity.'

'You don't know that, Wat. You only met him once.'

I couldn't resist a smile. 'I met him every time I walked into a newsroom since I was a cub reporter. And anyways, it's in his interest to cooperate. Duden plays ball, he gets a joint exclusive with a righteous Coeur d'Alene angle.'

'What's to stop him doing his own digging?'

'Nothing to find, not in Idaho. Marsha has no family

left there. Her dad died in '63 and her mom left town the following year. There may be some old high school friends of Marsha's, but teen memories don't make a news story and Duden knows that.'

'Yeah, I guess.' Her voice quavered a little.

'You okay?'

I kissed her forehead and smoothed her hair. We'd talked on the phone before I left Coeur d'Alene. She said she was holding up, keeping busy with the funeral arrangements. But folks often said they were fine when they weren't, especially grieving folks.

'I'm glad he knew I was ready to forgive him.' She gripped my hand. 'That was thanks to you.'

'Your dad was an old school gentleman. With some folks you don't need to know them long to know them well. Your dad was one of those.'

'It was a good piece you wrote, Wat. Balanced and measured.'

'Those are my middle names.' I paused. 'How's Stacey taking it?'

'Not well. When I talk to her all I get is one-syllable answers. I understand that bereavement affects people in different ways, but she's totally imploded. She's leaving everything to me, although that at least isn't out of the ordinary.'

'It's not just your dad.' I tried to sound as balanced and measured as she said my piece on her dad had been. 'I'm sure she's also worried about the future of the company with him gone and Gary still missing.'

'She should have thought about that before she handed Gary twenty-four thousand dollars to blow on the blackjack tables.' There was deep rooted bitterness in Lee's voice. I thought it went beyond sibling animosity. Perhaps it was part of her grief; perhaps there was something else. I'd find out soon enough.

'I gotta go see this guy Randy Pasqual, owner of the Maharaja Casino.' I pushed back some hair that spilled over her face. 'I'd like it if you came to Vegas with me, Lee, but I dig why you probably can't.'

'I'd like it too, Wat.' She looked at me through her smoky eyes and I sensed forlorn longing. 'But you're right – it's out of the question.'

THIRTY-EIGHT

Drive a 1965 Bug with 80,000 miles on the clock, you won't go very far very fast. You get a straight choice: bust a gasket or sit back and enjoy the ride. So I calculated my journey times by albums played rather than hours taken. Hicks to Las Vegas, that was a clear three-album trip. I played *Me and the Captain* by the Doobie Brothers and Led Zeppelin's *Houses of the Holy*. Then I listened to Bob Dylan's *Bringing it All Back Home*. Difficult to believe it was released in 1965 – the year the Beetle rolled off the production line, the year I went to Vietnam. The three albums sounded solid on the eight track as I followed I-15 to Vegas. I took the off-ramp for Flamingo Road, then a left onto the Strip.

Vegas is different every time you visit. Some folks think this makes the city fake and cosmetic. For me, though, the constant changes are part of the show. The Greco-Roman deal of Caesar's Palace was the same as last time, but at the Flamingo a 130 foot sign in the shape of a feathered plume had replaced the neon bubble. Johnny Carson topped the bill at Caesar's, Connie Stevens at the Flamingo.

The Maharaja was located next to Castaways, across the street from The Sands.

The place was a low-rise stucco complex, except for a purple onion-shaped dome. I guessed this was meant to resemble a psychedelic Taj Mahal, but it looked more like a dick. Inside, there were *Karma Sutra*-style pictures of Indian folks getting it on, along with sculptures of bare-breasted oriental women with elaborate headgear. Maybe the psychedelic phallus was cleverer than I first thought.

At the check-in I told a pasty-faced clerk in a rhinestone turban that I wanted to talk to Randy Pasquale. I said I was a reporter and mentioned my encounter with Marty Millard, the guy Pasquale sent over to Gary Gerwitz's place with a .38 snub-nose Colt and very little idea of how to use it.

I took a look around the tables while I waited. The male croupiers wore scarlet fez hats with golden vests and baggy sleeved shirts; females wore belly dancer costumes studded with plastic gems. Both get-ups had more to do with Hollywood notions of *Arabian Nights* than the Indian subcontinent, but you gotta remember this was Vegas and it was also the seventies. The Maharaja was not the sort of place you expected to see high rollers, especially at 10.30 on a Saturday morning. The few gamblers that were here were balls-to-the-wall casino junkies. A guy with two days' stubble on his jaw pushed a burger into his mouth with one hand and dimes into a slot with the other. A middle-aged woman with messed-up make up sunk whiskey while shooting craps.

'Mr Tyler?'

The slim guy approaching me wore a maroon velvet suit with delta-wing lapels and bellbottom pants that covered his shoes. His features were small and delicate, as if they stopped developing when he was a seventh grader. Feather-cut hair fell onto his shoulders, but there was almost nothing up top – just a patch of loose matted strands.

I looked round. 'Mr Pasquale?'

'Randy, please.' He extended his hand, revealing a chain-link ID bracelet that seemed too heavy for his bony wrist. 'Can I get you something to drink?'

I asked for a cold beer. I didn't usually drink this early, but the drive had been long and hot. Pasquale snapped his fingers and a waitress took my order.

'Marty told me what went down at Gary Gerwitz's place.' He gave me a stern, though not unfriendly look. He had a Midwest accent and talked as if he had some education. 'Clearly a misunderstanding. But tell me, what brings you to Vegas?'

'I thought we might be able to help each other out tracking down Gary Gerwitz.' I handed him a copy of the previous day's *Herald*. 'As you can see from my story, he's the boss of a big company that could go under unless he turns up soon.'

The waitress arrived with a glass of Brown Derby. I took a long swallow and felt the cold beer slide into my belly.

Pasquale made a wish-I-could-help shrug. 'What can I tell you? He still owes me a lot of money and my shareholders are getting more and more impatient. That was why I sent Marty over.'

I took a long swallow of beer and took out my spiral notebook. 'How much does he owe?'

He made a dubious expression.

'Is it around twenty-four grand?'

'I really can't say.'

'If I was to print that number, though, would it be inaccurate?'

'No it wouldn't. But you didn't get it from me.'

'Has he made any attempt to clear the debt?'

This brought a bitter chuckle. 'All I got is that big shiny Cadillac taking up a space in my parking lot. I guess it does look the part – but the guy from the auto dealer is picking it up Monday morning.'

I looked up from my shorthand. Hadn't clocked Gerwitz's Cadillac when I arrived, but then I wasn't looking. 'Would that be a '71 Coupe de Ville, electric blue, with a dented front bumper?'

'Sure would.' He gave me a puzzled look. 'How'd you know about the bumper?'

'He rear-ended me over in Hicks. This was a couple of weeks back – Thursday the thirteenth. I'm guessing he turned up here later that day.'

'Yes he did. Slippery bastard offered the Caddy in part-payment and promised to give me the rest by the end of that week. Late model Coupe De Ville, gotta be worth six large, so I took the deal.'

'What happened?'

'He took off in an old Power Wagon I gave him as part of the agreement. The end of that week arrived but his money didn't. Another week went by, still nothing. My shareholders got on my back again, demanding some sort of action. So I sent Marty to Hicks in hopes of squeezing something – anything – out of Gary.'

I could tell from Pasquale's expression that the situation had gotten worse since my encounter with Marty.

'When Marty drew a blank I went to the Cadillac dealer here in Vegas and asked how much I could get for the Coupe De Ville. The guy there said a two-year jail term for grand theft auto. Seems Gary bought the car on credit but skipped payments. The dealer was taking repossession action when I took delivery of it. Net result: I copped the liability for the Coupe De Ville repayments *and* lost another two hundred bucks, which is what I'd have gotten for the '59 Power Wagon he drove off in.'

It was easy to see why Pasquale and his shareholders were pissed off big time.

Also easy to see why Gerwitz was keen to swap the two-year-old Cadillac for a 14-year-old Power Wagon. Apart from evading his creditors, he needed a change of vehicle to throw whoever was chasing him off his trail.

'Did Gary say where he was going?'

'Yeah – Hicks.'

'Okay if I take a look at the Caddy?'

My host made a longsuffering smile. 'Be my guest. You won't find anything, though. I already turned it inside and out.'

The car was parked in an unshaded area of the lot. The heat trapped inside stung my face when I opened the driver's door. I stepped back to let it cool a little. The scene in the car was not dissimilar to his study back in Hicks. Styrofoam burger boxes and candy wrappers were piled up in the passenger footwells, front and back. A crumpled suit coat and pants had been thrown onto the rear seat, suggesting he'd changed clothes in a hurry before he cut out of Vegas.

I leaned inside. The air reeked of gone-off junk food.

Lowering myself into the driver's seat I searched the interior but found nothing. Pasquale was standing by the hood, arms folded over his chest, wearing a told-you-so expression.

I was climbing out when I pinned an empty Alexander the Grape candy pack behind the gas pedal. The thin card had been folded over so the blank inner surface faced outward. I picked it up and smoothed it out. All I saw, though, was blank white card.

'You got something?' Pasquale sounded more hopeful than expectant.

'Just more trash.'

I was about to throw the pack back into the car when I saw faint handwriting indentations on the printed surface – right across the cartoon figure of Alexander the Grape. Numbers, though, not words.

Seemed Gerwitz turned the pack inside out and folded it over so he could use the unprinted side to write on, then tore it in two and kept the half he'd inscribed. As a reporter I often scribbled hasty notes on all kinds of products – napkins, cigarette packs, anything to hand. But it was always in an emergency and everything I knew about Gerwitz said emergency in 72-point upper case bold.

I turned to Pasquale. 'Is there someplace I can get a better look at this?'

We went into his office and I sat at his desk. I used his desk lamp to examine the pack more closely. Taking out my notebook, I started to transcribe what I could see. It wasn't easy because the impression was faint, the handwriting erratic and Alexander the Grape's grinning face made the surface confusing. Eventually, though, I produced two sequences: 352221 and 1155387.

I showed them to Pasquale. He squinted. 'Phone numbers?'

I couldn't think what else.

'Okay to use your phone?'

'Go ahead.' He leaned over my notebook and examined the numbers. 'That first number you got, though, it's only six digits. All the local numbers in Vegas have seven.'

I dialled the seven digit sequence but it didn't produce a ring tone. I tried the six digit number on the off-chance Pasquale was mistaken, but got the same result.

'Could be another city,' he said. 'Try dialling the LA area prefix – 213.'

I did, but no phone line in LA corresponded to that number. Same went for San Francisco, Phoenix and Chicago. We could have been there all day.

'Maybe Gerwitz wrote the numbers down wrong,' I said. 'Or a couple of digits didn't make a legible impression. Maybe they just aren't phone numbers.'

'What then?'

I made a puzzled expression. 'Combinations for a safe. Bank account numbers. Some sort of encrypted shit. Maybe they're nothing to do with anything.'

I spent the rest of the day making enquiries at a dozen other casinos but nobody knew Gerwitz – or was prepared to admit it. Back at the Maharaja I told Pasquale I was driving back to Hicks but would keep him informed. Then I asked to use his office phone again and called the *Herald* newsroom.

Jacinta was at the city desk. Only message she had for me was from my source at the Immigration and Naturalization Service regarding Rex Hambly. He came to the USA six years ago and worked at a number of silver mines in Alaska. In '71, though, he was involved in a bad accident that left six men dead. Hambly wasn't to blame but the owners scapegoated him and he never worked in another American mine. The

INS was about to revoke his green card when he landed the job at High Rock. Made a lot of sense from the mob's point of view. Guy on the verge of becoming an illegal immigrant, he'd do exactly what he was told and no questions.

Next I called Lee Caraway and she told me the question of Rex Hambly's whereabouts had already been answered. He'd been found dead last night in a motel room near San Diego. Cause of death: Gunshot to the back of the head.

THIRTY-NINE

I got home a little after dusk.

A slender figure stirred in the shadows behind the stoop.

I made a silent groan. The drive back from Vegas had been hard and hot. Last thing I needed was another bunch of dudes coming at me with violent intent. Or worse, Norm Dibbitts with more theories from Planet Paranoia.

So I was gratified when I saw Lee Caraway walking toward me. We'd arranged to meet at her place after I'd showered and eaten. This made her presence at mine somewhat unexpected.

'You seem disappointed to see me.' She made a puzzled expression.

'Surprised is all.' I opened the front door and followed her inside. 'Anything wrong?'

'No more wrong than when we talked on the phone.'

'What then?' I grinned. 'You came round here early to get your hands on me as soon as you possibly could?'

'Not entirely.'

Even so, she leaned forward and kissed my mouth. It wasn't a making out kiss, more of an affectionate one. Like, this was what we did; what normal folks did. It made me feel warm rather than sexy and this was unusual for me. Horny, that was familiar; warm was an unexplored continent.

She pulled back and went to business. She asked about my meeting with Randy Pasquale and I told her.

'Pretty much a wasted journey, then?' she said.

'Pretty much. Anything more on Hambly?'

'A little. He was found dead on the doorstep of his room at a cheap motel in East San Diego. Other guests were alerted by a single gunshot. There was no suggestion of a struggle, nothing stolen, so we're working the theory that it was a straightforward professional hit. Killer approached Hambly from behind as he opened his door and shot him point blank in the back of the head. The local cops are cooperating.'

'Presumably linked to the triple homicide?'

'Figures.'

I went into the kitchen and opened the refrigerator. 'Sandwich? Beer?'

Caraway said no to the sandwich, yes to the beer. 'Getting rid of Hambly has to be part an orchestrated plan. And coming so soon after your story appeared in the *Herald*, it must be linked to Carmody. We know from your source at the INS that he was desperate for work when he was taken on at High Rock. That would have made him easy to manipulate. Hambly called the Desert Diner seconds before Carmody walked out to his death. I'm sure Hambly was coerced into making that call and I'm equally sure there was no emergency at the mine.'

The butter was hard and chewed up the bread when I tried to spread it. 'My piece on the High Rock shares fraud put the whole thing in the public arena. It would have made Hambly even more vulnerable.'

She nodded. 'He was killed because of what he knew. Poor bastard went on the run but he couldn't run far enough or fast enough.'

'Surely that points to a mob hit.'

'You'd think so. Vito Occhipinti probably had more reasons than anyone to want both Carmody and Hambly dead.'

I watched the evening heat soften the pat of butter on the tip of my knife. 'But?'

She swallowed some beer. 'Occhipinti entered a witness protection scheme the day before Carmody and the others were shot. Seems he cut a deal with the Feds.'

'Did you ask Schwenk about that?'

'Says he doesn't know anything about it.'

'You believe him?'

'He could be telling the truth. You know what the FBI is like. Wheels within wheels. And I still believe what Rocco Bonfiglio told us. Sure, the mob would sooner or later have eliminated Carmody. But the triple homicide deal doesn't feel like their sort of thing. A mob hit is workmanlike and, more than anything, precise. This was too hurried and at the same time too complicated. As far as the mob is concerned the whole thing was too...I dunno...tricksy.'

That was an interesting word-choice and I got what she meant. Whoever was behind the Desert Diner shooting had thought about it from many angles and on many levels in a very short space of time – 24 hours tops. And we didn't even know the whole deal.

The thought of Occhipinti getting his neck saved by the Feds was perversely amusing. Bonfiglio's long-cherished scheme to avenge himself had come to nothing. In fact it wasn't too much of a stretch to imagine Occhipinti getting the last laugh. He could easily finger Bonfiglio for some other rap and the Feds would be knocking on *his* door.

I laid some pastrami on the buttered bread and added cheese and a sliced tomato. 'You think Hambly's death ties in with the Marsha angle?'

'It ties in all right. We just don't know how.'

I bit into my sandwich and chewed the food on one side of my mouth. 'What did Schwenk say about Marsha?'

She sipped her beer. 'He confirmed she was working a deep cover operation when she got hit. But he refused to tell me anything more. The operation is still live. National interest still at stake. Lives still at risk. And Hicks PD should back off.'

'That's the Feds for you.' I picked up my sandwich and beer then followed her into the living room.

She sat next to me on the couch but craned forward, clearly agitated by the way Schwenk had treated her. 'I asked if the murders of Hazeldene and Carmody were related to Marsha's and he said yeah, they were. But we'd figured that already so it's hardly illuminating. It's the question of *how* that's the problem.'

I ate my sandwich, swallowed some beer. 'How about we go back to the murder scene tomorrow? Take another look at the angles and lines of sight. But from the perspective of Marsha as the mark.'

'We both know every square inch of that grubby little patch.'

'Maybe we know it *too* well. Maybe that's part of the problem. We need to ditch all our preconceptions and start over. Besides, where's the harm?'

She finished her beer. 'Worth a shot I guess.'

'Wanna stay tonight?'

She said yes she did. She was weary. Her dad's death was hard to handle and she needed a shoulder to rest on.

We went upstairs and she borrowed my toothbrush, then we got naked and into bed. But we didn't screw, just lay together. It was the first time I spent the night with a woman without having sex and that was something – a whole other aspect of closeness. Made me wonder if I was more capable of commitment than I thought. Made me wonder about a lot of stuff I thought was beyond me.

We woke early, though, and sex was the first thing we did – and that was one thousand degrees hot.

FORTY

Later I made some coffee and Caraway called the cop shop.

There was good news. Bobby Peeples was off the critical list, though there was still a lot the doctors didn't know. They didn't know when – or if – he'd regain consciousness, or if he'd have neurological damage. But he *was* expected to live.

We ate waffles and eggs for breakfast and drove over to the Desert Diner.

It was 8.30 on a Sunday morning and the place was quiet, although a service at the New Life Episcopal Church was scheduled for 9.30. The air was still cool and damp. Soft sunlight glistered on particles of moisture. Like the quiet, though, it wouldn't last. By mid-morning the temperature would ratchet up to ninety degrees and we'd be breathing dusty heat.

We tried to reimagine the shooting, with Marsha as the intended victim. We traced the steps of all three victims, looked again at the lay of the land from the shooter's point of view. But being here on the ground made the sequence of events seem even more of a puzzle. We couldn't get past the implausible proposition of an assassin shooting Hazeldene and Carmody point blank, then firing at Marsha at long range. He'd have been in entirely the wrong position. If Marsha was the mark, the whole thing could – *should* – have failed. In fact, it would never have been attempted.

The only credible scenario was that Marsha was not the intended victim. That, for some reason we could only guess at, she was trying to stop the assassination and got hit by two random shots.

Even this seemed unlikely.

There was something crucial missing from our interpretation of what went down. Something that was staring right at us. Something real basic.

I turned to Caraway, re-spooled yet again.

Realization came in fits and starts.

Facts that seemed at odds began to link up. Focus sharpened, blurred, sharpened again.

I started to see a different picture – clearer and clearer and clearer until I couldn't figure out how I never nailed the whole deal at the outset.

I turned to Caraway. 'You fire a .45 automatic at seventy-five yards, how many times out of ten would you expect to hit your target?'

She gave me an odd look.

'Why do you ask?'

'Just play along.'

She wrinkled her nose as she gazed across the scene. 'In a situation like this, with a moving target, seven out of ten, maybe eight if the gods were smiling.'

'How confident would you be of making a kill with one shot?'

Her brow wrinkled. 'Hard to say. Too many variables. Rough guess: less than twenty per cent.'

'How about the odds of firing twice and making a kill shot with both bullets?'

She took a beat to think it through. 'Slim to zero.'

'Yet that's what our guy did.'

'Where's this leading, Wat?'

I didn't answer directly. I was still working this out. 'What was Marsha doing while the shooter was taking out Hazeldene and Carmody? I mean, he must have done that first, right?'

'Well, yeah.'

'How long does it take to get off six rounds from a .45 automatic? As many seconds?'

'I guess.'

'But that's easily enough time to find cover – especially if you're an FBI agent. So why did Marsha go against all her training, all her instincts, and stand still?'

Caraway thought about that. 'Maybe she was moving toward the shooter, trying to stop him.'

'Unarmed? On open ground?'

'Okay, it's unlikely.' She stood beside me and looked across the splintered concrete lot toward the Million Dollar Nugget. 'Tell me what you're thinking.'

'What if someone else fired the shots that killed Marsha? What if there was a second shooter, much closer in? Somebody nobody noticed because everybody was looking at the guy making his getaway on the motorbike?'

I watched her face. I could almost hear her mind accelerating, running the facts we knew and the assumptions we'd made.

She lit a Belair and blew the menthol-tanged smoke into the still air. The absence of any contradiction told me she saw exactly what I'd seen.

She began walking toward Norm's place and I followed.

She said, 'Remember Mrs Sanchez? The elderly blind woman who lives across the street? The one who complained about your Talking Newspaper reporting eight shots when she said she heard ten?'

I remembered. Caraway was referring to the old bat who nursed a grudge since the *Herald* got her husband's name wrong not long after Johannes Gutenberg invented the printing press. 'You reckon she was right all along?'

Caraway nodded yes. 'That would account for eight shots from the biker's gun, plus two fired by the second shooter – the two that hit Marsha.'

Caraway quickened her pace. I hurried after.

'Where are you going?'

She was looking straight ahead. 'We need to locate where this second shooter was positioned. The whole deal went down real fast. The second guy must have left in a hurry to avoid being seen. He might have left something.'

Two dark stains in the concrete marked where Marsha had fallen. We stood there and looked around for places where her killer could have hidden.

She indicated a small patch of dirt between the street and the lot. Its rectangular shape suggested some sort of heavy equipment once occupied the space, maybe the base for some gas pumps. A couple of creosote bushes had taken root and reached a height of three or four feet. They were scrawny weeds and wouldn't offer much concealment. But perhaps it had been enough – especially if everybody was looking the other way.

Caraway stopped by the creosotes and turned to look back at the spot where Marsha got hit. The distance was around twenty feet. 'This would be about right,' she said. 'Close enough to be sure of two kill shots.'

I took out my pocket knife and kneeled by the bushes in the spot where I'd have placed myself if I'd been taking those shots.

'What are you doing?' Caraway crouched beside me. 'This is a crime scene, or had you forgotten?'

I gave her a dubious look. 'You really want to play this by the book, Lee? Alert Schwenk and let the whole town know what we're doing?'

She thought about the options. 'Okay. Go ahead.'

I used the pocketknife to plough rows of small furrows in the dirt. It was so thin and dry it spilled right back into the grooves almost immediately. This, though, was what I was counting on. Any hard object falling onto it would be covered over almost immediately.

I scraped two furrows, then three, and four. The sun beat on the back of my neck. Spiky creosote branches scratched my face. The whole patch was no more than six feet by four, but my tiny excavations were getting no place slowly.

The blade bucked as it struck something hard and metallic.

I used my fingers to brush the dirt away.

It was a nickel, 1930s vintage.

I handed it to Caraway. 'Not the sort of pay-dirt I was hoping for.'

I went back to ploughing.

Another half dozen furrows; and another. Still nothing.

Caraway sensed my frustration. 'Maybe we ought to bring in a metal detector.'

'Maybe you're right. One more shot.'

I moved to the opposite end and began working back toward the middle.

Somewhere behind me tyres crunched on grit. Car doors opened and shut as the churchgoers began arriving. Last thing we needed was a bunch of curious Episcopalians crowding around.

I heard someone approaching. A little boy's voice, 'Hey, Mister, what you doing?'

I didn't look up. 'Searching for treasure.'

'You won't find much with a pocket knife. You're not digging deep enough.'

'Sometimes you don't need to, kid.'

I started to feel a little pissed off that Caraway hadn't told the boy to scoot.

Then the blade scraped against another piece of metal. This time, though, it rolled around the object, as if it was tube-shaped.

I pinned the brass casing lying in the centre of the trench.

Taking out my pen, I inserted the tip in the open end of the brass cartridge and picked it up.

I tilted it toward me and examined the head stamp. Then I looked at Caraway. 'Federal .45 Auto.'

'Gotcha!' She sounded excited.

But I stayed focused, carried on ploughing the same trench, sensing the other casing was nearby.

After nine inches the blade hit metal again. The second cartridge rolled slowly into the furrow and lay winking in the sunlight.

Jubilation wasn't my thing. Satisfaction was, though. Right then I felt supremely satisfied.

I stood up, grinning.

Caraway looked at me the same way.

The kid must have thought we were crazy people. This was fine, though, because it freaked him out and he ran back toward the church.

I used the back of my forearm to wipe sweat from my brow. 'What do you think?'

She shaded her eyes from the strengthening sunlight. 'Second shooter used the bushes for cover, waited for his compadre to open fire on Hazeldene and Carmody, then hit Marsha at close range. She couldn't take cover because she didn't have time. The first shooter must have fired two rounds into the air because he left eight casings behind and only hit the two men with six. We wrongly assumed the two bullets that hit Marsha came from those two extra casings. That was smart. Really, really smart.'

'Maybe too smart.' I pointed to the ground. 'This dirt is so fine and dry that it would have covered over the second guy's casings the second they hit the ground. Clearly he didn't have time to hang around and dig them out. Look how long it took me.'

She watched the Episcopalians file into church. 'I gotta call the lab. We need verification.'

I waited by the dirt patch while Caraway went to the phone booth opposite to call the cop shop. She wanted the area closed off and the forensic folks back on the scene.

I got why she had to go through the motions. But we already knew what the lab was going to tell us: Marsha was gunned down at short range by a second shooter whose presence went completely unnoticed – except by an elderly blind woman.

FORTY-ONE

It was late afternoon the next day before Caraway got the confirmation she needed from the lab: The bullets that killed Marsha came from a different gun to the one used to hit Hazeldene and Carmody.

We met at her place after work and she filled me in on what went down at the cop shop when she told Chief Turner and Agent Schwenk about the second shooter. Schwenk had seemed shocked. But he still knew a lot of stuff about Marsha that we didn't, so maybe he wasn't as mind-blown as he wanted us to think. Turner acknowledged Caraway's detective smarts, but his praise had been meagre and reluctant.

'He said it was good work, but too bad we didn't figure it out two weeks ago. And there are still a lot of unanswered questions.' Caraway sounded pissed off and I understood why. 'If I'd been a guy it would have a whole other story. Slaps on the back, beers on the chief.'

'Turner's a bigoty bastard,' I said. 'But he's right about one thing: We still don't know why they went to such lengths to make Marsha's death look like an accident.'

She took two cans of soda from the refrigerator and

handed me one. 'I'd say she got made and the people she was investigating didn't want to alert her handler. Staging an accidental death meant they could carry on with business as usual.'

I opened my soda can. 'Stacks up. They'd have shaken off Marsha and put the federal investigation back to a square one. We don't know how much she communicated with her handler. Deep cover op like this, though, you keep a hell of lot of stuff in your head. All that would have died with her.'

Caraway glugged some soda. 'We need to find out who they are. Also, what Marsha was investigating.'

'Schwenk must know. I wouldn't be surprised if he's playing both ends against the middle.'

'Can you get any more on him from your CIA source?'

'I can try. But the bottom line is that Schwenk is devious, ruthless and resourceful. And those are precisely the qualities you'd need to pull this second shooter stunt.'

She sounded doubtful. 'That would mean the Feds taking out one of their own.'

'Marsha could have gotten turned.' I made a quizzical expression. 'She could have been a double agent. Or a triple or a quadruple. These are paranoid times. Maybe we're all Manchurian Candidates now.'

I stopped, smiled at my own words. 'And maybe I sound way too much like Norm Dibbitts.'

She finished her drink and crushed the can. 'I did get some clarity on Ray Carmody and his apparent death wish.'

I pricked my ears.

'His wife came in to see me. Seems you and I were both wrong about the guy.'

'How so?'

'Carmody suffered from chronic depression. Not just the blues. Real bad shit that was diagnosed by a shrink. According to his wife the High Rock venture was an escape. The money and the celebrity status were part of it, but the main thing was the purpose and sense of belonging it gave him.'

'C'mon, Lee.' I couldn't keep the cynicism from my voice. 'He must have known it was a scam from the very beginning.'

'Sure he did. But that didn't matter. He'd been given a role to play and that was enough to keep his depression at bay. Leastways that's what his wife told me.'

'How did you get her to talk?'

'We did a deal. She agreed to give me the truth and I agreed not to go after her with an aid and abet rap.'

'Smart move.'

She tossed the empty soda can in the trash. 'Not so much where Ray Carmody was concerned. He knew the Pacific Coast share issue would be the end of his head honcho job. And he knew pulling the plug on the flotation was a death sentence. But he wouldn't give up control of the mine.'

She paused and made a wistful expression. 'In the end Carmody accepted there was nowhere to run and no point trying. Life without being the King of High Rock wouldn't be worth living. So he flipped the finger to the mob and waited for the inevitable.'

I smiled. 'You kind of admire that, don't you?'

'Guess I do. He went out on his own terms, with some integrity.'

She opened a kitchen cupboard and produced a pack of spaghetti. 'Hungry?'

I said yes and she tossed me the spaghetti.

'You fix that, I'll handle the Bolognese.'

With the spaghetti simmering, I asked how the funeral arrangements were coming along.

'I'm still having to do everything. Same with the probate arrangements.' She started chopping an onion with more force than was necessary. 'Stacey's worried about what's going to happen to this Chrysler tender without Dad or Gary. But she doesn't seem to understand that we have to get through the probate process before she and I can take control of the company. And until that happens everything is at risk – including the torsion bar contract.'

Clearly the death of Honeysett had hit Stacey hard. Not for the first time I thought Lee was being a little unfair. 'Surely there are other people in the company who can take up the reins? At least in the short term?'

She started frying the ground beef. 'There are other members of the management team. If push comes to shove they can handle the tender. But confidence is a big part of it. Chrysler is our number one customer and we have to show we have an effective succession plan. If Gary comes back, well and good. If not, we have to move on.'

'You think he won't come back?'

'I really don't know.'

'You think he might be dead, don't you?'

She took the pan off the stove, gave me a hard look. 'He's been missing for nearly three weeks. We know he owes a lot of money to the wrong kind of people. We know he had some sort of relationship with Marsha, probably related to her undercover work. And we know he was due to meet Frank Hazeldene on the afternoon Hazeldene – and Marsha – got killed. Gary is in this way over his head, in ways we can't even guess at. I hope he's alive. But I'm not optimistic.'

FORTY-TWO

One problem I didn't have the next morning was finding stories for the front page.

The lead was Stokes Honeysett's funeral. It took place in a white timber frame church on the edge of town and was attended by civic dignitaries, politicians and business leaders from Hicks and miles around. A lot of ordinary folks were there too, and that said a lot about the man's commitment to his local community. Lee held up well, Stacey did not. At the graveside her sobbing almost drowned out the pastor's words. She was consumed by grief in a way I couldn't begin to understand.

Second main piece on the front page was a public appeal by Turner and Schwenk for information that might reveal more about the second shooter. As things stood, there was next to nothing: the two shell casings Caraway and I found; and the blind lady's statement that she heard ten shots, not eight. This was another *Herald* exclusive. Just as importantly I was given priority access to Turner and Schwenk. If the chief and the G-man wanted local folks to come forward with fresh information, the *Herald* was their best shot – way ahead of the big hitters. For this reason Turner let me have everything I wanted. Even Schwenk gave me a solid quote and confirmed that Marsha had been murdered because she was an undercover FBI agent. He wouldn't be drawn, though, on the investigation she was working on. All the same, I kept my word to Arnie Duden up in Coeur d'Alene and made sure he got all the information I did.

When I finished working on the next day's news budget I drove over the Million Dollar Nugget. Norm Dibbitts had called at the front desk that morning but I was too busy to see him. A message came back, though: Norm said he'd catch up with me later. Rather than waiting for another ambush, I bit the bullet and went to him.

He saw me come in and reached for a cold bottle of Lucky.

'On the house, Wat.'

'Sorry I couldn't see you earlier, pal.'

'No problem at all. I dig you're a busy guy.'

'So what can I do for you, Norm?'

Norm levered the cap off the Lucky bottle and found a glass. Then he made a bashful grin. 'You know, I clean forgot.'

'That's cool.' It wasn't cool though. I suspected he'd wanted to offload another paranoid notion but couldn't remember which one.

He started pouring the beer. 'We can talk about other stuff, right?'

'Sure we can.' I recalled Norm had been visiting a sick relative last time I called. 'How's your cousin?'

He didn't reply at first, as if pouring the beer took up all his available brain capacity. Then he handed me the filled glass like it was a work of great craftsmanship.

'My cousin? He's fine. Lives down in Hesperia.'

'Yeah, Lucinda told me. She also said something about him being sick.'

My buddy seemed puzzled. 'I ain't sick.'

It was like talking to someone hard of hearing. 'No, I meant your cousin. Lucinda said your cousin was sick.'

Norm took an overflowing tin ashtray from the counter and emptied it in a trash can. 'My cousin? He's fine now, but he ain't been too good lately. Diabetes.'

On the far side of the room Lucinda started clearing empty glasses. Norm's eyes went out on stalks tracking her butt as she worked her way from table to table.

'Ain't she the livin' end?'

'Why don't you ask her for a date?'

'Guy like me?'

'You shouldn't put yourself down, Norm.' I felt something akin to comradeship. Norm was crazy as a loon, no argument there. He was also full-on exasperating. But he dug loyalty. He'd been there for me out on Harvard Road and I had no doubt he'd be there again if I ever needed him.

'Just ask her out for something to eat. Take her someplace nice and see how – '

'You see 'em?' Norm was looking through a window into the parking lot. His eyes were wide and jittery, his right arm outstretched, finger pointing. 'It's them people again. You see 'em, Wat?'

He was indicating a sky blue station wagon with faux wooden panelling. It left the lot and turned right, moving slowly along Main Street. I nailed it as a Mercury Colony Park.

'Them fuckers been following me everywhere I go.'

'There's an awful lot of those old Mercury station wagons around, Norm. Sure it's the same one?'

'It's Nixon's people. They got my name on the super enemies list – the secret one. I gotta stop 'em.'

He moved crabwise to the end of the bar, ran out through the front door. Moments later his Chevy Nova accelerated along Main Street in the direction the station wagon had taken.

'He'll come back soon enough.' Lucinda appeared beside me and placed a tray-load of beer glasses on the counter.

'Does he do that often?'

'It's how he is. He gets confused and panics. But you shouldn't worry.'

She started to shift the beer glasses from the tray to the sink, then hesitated. 'It's good that you watch out for him, though. He thinks you're the most.'

I drank some beer, looked her in the eye. 'He thinks you're the most too.'

'Nah.' She looked away, flustered, and started washing glasses. 'Anyways, not in *that* way.'

'Sure he does.' Here was a problem I never faced before: trying to get two people together who were convinced they weren't good enough for one another. 'He says you're the girl for him.'

'So why ain't he asked me out?'

'He thinks you'd say no.'

'Well I wouldn't.' She made a quirky smile and headed off to clear more glasses.

I sat there awhile, musing how I could get these two knuckleheads together.

Next minute, Lucinda was back behind the bar. 'I just read the story you wrote in today's *Herald*. About Marsha being a federal agent and all. Blew my mind. You think you know someone, then you realize you didn't know them one bit.'

'That's what working undercover is all about. Marsha was a true professional.'

'Did you discover that stuff after I told you about Marsha coming from Coeur d'Alene?'

'Sure did. And I owe you one.' I felt for my wallet. 'What can I get you?'

She shot me an angry stare. 'I wasn't trying to get no drink out of you.'

This wasn't the first time Lucinda flared up when she thought I doubted her integrity. Yet again I held up my hands and made my best appeasing smile. 'Hey, I didn't mean to offend.'

'I was trying to help catch Marsha's killer is all.' Her temper subsided, melting into a canny grin. 'But if you're offering...'

I pushed a one spot across the bar.

She fixed herself a vodka coke and walked around the bar to perch on the stool next to mine. 'I got *more* information if you're interested.'

'I'm interested.'

She helped herself to a Camel from my pack and I offered her a light. 'See the guy by the juke box?'

I saw a tall sinewy fellow, with dark wiry hair that merged with dense sideburns. Plaid shirt and oil-smeared jeans. He fed the juke box and the room filled with Deep Purple's *Smoke on the Water*.

Lucinda lowered her voice. 'He just told me he saw Marsha take a call on the pay phone here in the bar just a few seconds before she went outside and got shot.'

I gave her a curious look. 'Who is he?'

'Teamster, name of Billy. Don't know his second name.

Passes through Hicks every few weeks, sometimes stays over. I can introduce you if you want.'

Billy was still checking out juke tunes as we approached. Lucinda told him I was the reporter who broke the story on Marsha being an undercover fed and said I wanted to talk to him about the phone call she took.

Billy looked at me with a leery scowl. His eyes were dark, close set in a sun-baked face that had seen a lot of wear. I guessed he'd been on the road since he was old enough to drive a rig. 'What if I don't like reporters?'

'Then you don't have to talk to me.' I made a so-what shrug. 'But that undercover fed was a nice lady with a lot of salt. Anything you got might help catch the people who killed her.'

Billy pushed more change into the juke, tapped in some codes, and nodded okay.

We took a seat and he explained that he was shooting the shit with Marsha when the pay phone started ringing. Marsha picked it up, listened but didn't talk, and said she had to go outside. Seconds later Billy heard the gunshots.

I looked up from my notebook. 'Did you mention this to the police?'

Billy made a world-weary expression. 'Fuck knows I tried. Pasty-faced young cop at the police line told me someone would come over and talk to me. No one did, though. I took off next morning and haven't been back in Hicks since.'

I recalled Shane Phillips, the rookie officer, fishing barricade tape from the trunk of his cruiser with shaky fingers and a lardy complexion. His first homicide, a messy one at that, with back up slow to arrive. It was easy to imagine how a brief conversation with the teamster might have slipped his mind.

Billy carried on talking. 'I only mentioned it to Lucinda just now 'cause we was talking about how scary life is. One minute you're minding your business. Next, you're fucking dead.'

I thanked him for the information and said so long to Lucinda.

Then I headed for the door, contemplating tomorrow's front page lead and the humble pay phone as an instrument of murder.

*

I drove to Caraway's place and told her what I'd learned from Billy. There were no other developments so we distracted ourselves with an early night and that was highly agreeable. Sex with Lee Caraway was the best. Not so much for technique – though she sure hit my on switch – but for commitment and intensity. It was doing stuff *with* somebody, not *to* them. Caraway was real gone and in those hot moments and I loved her for it.

Afterward she said, 'You good?'

I touched her face with the back of my hand. 'Sure I'm good. You?'

She nodded yes. 'How about us? Are we good?'

I thought about my reply, to be certain I meant it. 'Yeah,' I said. 'We're good.'

Early the next morning we were back outside the Desert Diner. The most obvious place to start was the phone booth across the street. This was the one I used to file my copy on the day of the killings so I knew before we arrived that the location gave direct line of sight to all three locations: the diner; the church; the bar.

I explained this to Caraway on the way over, though I appreciated why she wanted to see for herself. She stood awhile by the pay phone, running the probable sequence of events in her head.

When she was done she joined me in the shade of a raggedy cottonwood tree. 'You're right. Whoever pulled the strings did it from that booth. The moment Hazeldene left the church, they called the diner, claiming to be Hambly, and asked to talk to Carmody. Next they called the bar and said something to Marsha that they knew would bring her into the open. Both calls could have been made in sixty seconds, maybe less.'

I looked from the diner to the church to the bar – a total distance of seventy or eighty yards. 'And all the while, the first shooter was waiting on his motorbike and the second in those creosote bushes. Each shooter could have used hand signals to communicate with whoever was pulling the strings. As soon as all three marks were in position, bang.'

She followed my gaze. 'Odd, though, how nobody noticed the guy using the pay phone or the shooter in the bushes.'

I glanced at the spot where most of the shots had been fired: right in front of the diner and the church. 'Not so much if the biker deliberately sucked in all the attention. He'd have made damn sure everybody was looking at him and no place else.'

Caraway frowned. 'That's part of it, but I think there's more. You wanna pull off something like this, you need tradecraft. Sure, the biker would have provided misdirection, but it's equally telling that the string-puller and the second shooter were capable of going about their business unseen.'

'Telling in what way?'

'This wasn't a hit, it was an operation. Conceived, planned, executed in a very short time-frame. Maybe the clock started ticking when Carmody trashed the High Rock share issue; maybe when Gerwitz called Hazeldene to set up the meeting that never happened. At most, seventy-two hours; quite possibly just twenty-four.'

Caraway looked east along Main Street, shielding her eyes from the strengthening sunlight. 'Who would have the skills and resources to do that?'

I looked the opposite way, along the tar-seamed street toward the Million Dollar Nugget. 'Feds, CIA, KGB. And now I really am turning into Norm Dibbitts.'

She touched my arm. 'It's natural to feel paranoid. This is a paranoid situation.'

She dropped me at the *Herald* office and went on to the cop shop.

When she called me just forty minutes later I knew something deep serious had gone down.

'It's not good, Wat. Hang on...' She broke off to talk to somebody.

I heard her say, 'Yes. Get onto it right away.'

She went quiet. In the background I heard crackly voices on a police radio.

Then Caraway was back, her voice low. I sensed she didn't want to be overheard. 'It's your friend Lucida Hannity. She's dead. Body was found under the bridge at Third and Congress. Her throat was cut.'

FORTY-THREE

I drove to the latticed steel truss bridge that carried Third Avenue over the railroad yards to its junction with Congress Street.

A small posse of black-and-whites and an ambulance marked the spot. It was near one of the bridge's big concrete piers, maybe one hundred yards from Third Avenue. I parked on the street and set off across the half dozen derelict acres toward the squad cars. Sometime past the land had been part of the railroad yards, though the tracks and crossties had been ripped up long ago. All that remained was hard ochre dirt and thin scrawls of sage bush. Candy wrappers and plastic shopping bags had snagged in the branches. They twitched occasionally in the lazy breeze.

I stood at the police line and waited for Caraway. She was talking to Bull Turner, Schwenk and some other feds in a tight knot at the back of the ambulance. The first edition had gone to press with a lead story desperately light on detail. I had couple of hours to get something more substantial for the second edition.

Suze Carter arrived with her camera bag and I asked her

to get some crime-scene shots. Investigators looking busy, that sort of stuff.

Schwenk detached himself from the group and headed toward me. His cuboid face was glossed in sweat but he hadn't loosened his shirt collar. Stick him in hell, he'd keep his coat buttoned and his tie knot tight.

The G-man was clearly pissed.

He came so close I smelled garlic on his breath, a hint of whiskey too.

'That woman's death is on you, newspaperman.' His stubby finger jabbed my chest. 'I warned you, but you wouldn't give it up. This is still a live operation and you're still putting lives at risk. And don't give me no BS about your First Amendment rights.'

I kept my tone even. 'I don't need to. Fact is you still need my paper to make your public appeals. So one way or the other you'll continue to cooperate.'

He ducked under the barricade tape and headed toward the clapboard houses on Third Avenue.

Caraway came soon after, but she didn't break stride as she passed me. 'Meet me at the station at 11.30. I'll have something for you by then.'

The show of formality was no doubt for the chief's benefit so I played along.

Besides, I needed a picture of Lucinda and Norm Dibbitts was the most likely source. As her employer, he'd also be good for a quote.

Except Norm wasn't good for much.

The bar was closed and I found him in the back yard. He was sitting on an empty beer crate in a fug of whiskey fumes. There was a reek of vomit too.

He heard me coming and looked over his shoulder, eyes agitated yet spaced out. I guessed he'd been on substances as well as booze.

'Can't believe she's dead.'

I rested a hand on his shoulder.

'What did the cops tell you?'

He shook his head. 'They ain't told me nothing. She was found by some kids. One of their dads is a pal of mine. He told me everything.'

I made a sour grimace. Town like this, who needed a newspaper?

'It's Nixon's fault. He put Lucinda on that fucking enemies list – the secret one. Them goons of his, they got her blood on their hands.'

This time I agreed his paranoia was justified, if his assignment of blame was not.

'Guys who did this, they don't deserve to live.' Norm shook his head, gazed at his shabby platform shoes.

I gave him a questioning look. 'Why do you say "guys", Norm? Did someone tell you it was more than one?'

He ignored my question and I didn't push it.

'I should have protected her better. Should've seen this coming.'

I up-ended a beer crate and sat opposite my buddy. 'Nobody could have seen this coming, Norm. This isn't your fault. If anything, it's mine.'

'How so?'

'Remember that story I printed about Marsha being an undercover fed? And the one yesterday about her taking that call just before she died? I'd never have gotten those stories without Lucinda's help. Looking back, I put Lucinda in danger more than anything you ever did.'

Norm continued to stare at his shoes, but his voice was softer. 'You was just doing your job, pal. Your duty. Can't blame a guy for that.'

Not for the first time, I was surprised by his offbeat decency. Lotta people in his situation would have lashed out. Grief turns to anger. Not with Norm Dibbitts. He'd sooner heap all that pain on his own shoulders than let me take any of it.

'Lee Caraway's a smart cookie, Norm. She'll get the bastards.'

He nodded vigorously. 'Them sick fucks gonna burn in hell.'

'They'll get what's coming.'

'Sure they will.' He looked up, but his gaze was unfocused. I hadn't seen the thousand yard stare since I quit the Nasty but I was seeing it now. It was a look guys got when they were left in deep serious shit long after they stopped being able to cope with it.

I lit a cigarette and offered it to my pal.

He took it, sucked in some smoke and returned for a moment from wherever it was he'd been. 'Lee Caraway, she's a real gone chick ain't she, Wat? Lucinda was too. Lucinda was my gal. Anyways, she might have been.'

'You meant a lot to her, Norm. She told me she'd have said yes if you asked her on a date.'

'Never happen now, though, will it? Not. Fucking. Now.'

The thousand yard stare was back.

FORTY-FOUR

Caraway glanced up from her desk as I went into her office. She looked worn-out and I got why. This was the fifth homicide in Hicks, or involving a local resident, since she took up her job less than four weeks back. And she was nowhere close to making an arrest.

She made a little smile. 'Sorry I couldn't talk at the scene. Turner's been riding me and the mayor's been riding him.'

I told her I understood the situation and was happy to print the appeal for witnesses she wanted in the second edition.

'You get much from the crime scene?'

She gave me a stern look. 'It's gotta be off the record.'

'Sure thing. But I can't imagine much of it would be fit to print anyways.'

'You're not wrong. I'm still waiting on the autopsy report, but I got some initial observations from the coroner.' She looked at some notes on her desk and read them out in a clipped monotone. 'Approximate time of death: 11.00pm to 3.00am. Cause of death: Cut throat – everything severed except the spine. Very sharp blade drawn across the neck, left to right, from behind, by a right-handed assailant. Hands tied behind her back with nylon cord and traces of cotton fibre in her mouth tell us she was abducted and gagged. Volume of blood at the scene and spatter pattern suggest she was killed right there.'

She pushed the notes to one side, looked up with an any-questions? expression.

I asked the obvious one. 'Any clue how she ended up in that place?'

'None whatsoever. Lucinda was last seen at 10.00pm when she finished her shift at the Million Dollar Nugget. But she lived alone – small apartment on Yardstick Road – so she may have gone home and come out again. Or she may not have gotten home at all. Neighbours didn't see or hear anything.'

'So she could have been taken to where she was killed from her place, or the Million Dollar Nugget? Or anyplace in between?'

She nodded yes.

There was a dragged-out silence. I figured that she, like me, was running what-if? scenarios.

At last I said, 'You think this is linked to the triple homicide and the murder of Rex Hambly?'

'I'd be astonished if it wasn't.' She pushed back from her desk and walked over to look out the office widow. 'But why Lucinda? And why last night?'

I went to stand by her. In the lot below black and white squad cars were lined up in perfectly symmetry. Only things spoiling the orderliness was Schwenk's gleaming Buick at one end and Caraway's dust-coated Plymouth at the other. Only vehicle that could have looked any worse than the Plymouth was my Bug.

I started thinking out loud. 'I figure Lucinda is dead because of what she told me. Without Lucinda we'd never have found out about Marsha's relationship with Gerwitz. We'd never have known that her home town was Coeur d'Alene, and without that we'd still be in the dark about her being a federal agent. Next, Lucinda told me about the teamster and the phone call that lured Marsha outside.'

I glanced sideways. I could tell from her expression that she thought the same.

I continued anyway. I wanted to get the words out. I was partly to blame for what happened to Lucinda. Normally I welcomed any hint of emotion. Not this kind, though. 'Whoever killed Lucinda wanted to make sure she didn't tell me anything else. She probably didn't know anything else, otherwise she'd have told me already. But the killer couldn't know that.'

I watched a fly buzzing round the window, thumping against the glass over and over, no idea why it couldn't get to where it needed to go.

Caraway said what I expected her to say: She agreed with my analysis and insisted that Lucinda's death wasn't my fault. 'No disrespect, Wat, but Lucinda was a talker. If she hadn't told you that stuff, she probably would have told somebody else. She may well have gotten killed regardless.'

I hadn't looked at it that way and it did make sense. So how come I still felt responsible?

I asked if she had any suspects. She said no. She asked me if I had any ideas.

'I still figure Schwenk's involved.'

'You always figure Schwenk's involved. And maybe he is. But not in the way you think.'

I chewed on that and had to admit the G-man was an unlikely suspect. When he confronted me at the police line he was either real angry about Lucinda's death, or a real good actor. For a guy like him, acting required way too much imagination.

I tried another line of thought. 'Chester Peeples?'

She took a few beats before responding. 'I can see why he'd want Hazeldene and his unionisation campaign out of the way. He's resourceful enough, and maybe malicious enough to get it done. But why would he want Marsha dead?'

'She could have been investigating Peeples. He's gotta be deeply corrupt.'

'I don't doubt it. But it's unlikely she was investigating him and Ray Carmody at the same time.'

'Unless Peeples had done a deal with Carmody. And if Rex Hambly knew about it, that might also explain why he got hit.'

She made a doubtful expression. 'I still think Peeples is too much of a small town businessman to pull off something as ambitious as this. But I'll grant you it's a crazy situation.'

I took my line of thinking a stage farther. 'Do you know if Peeples owned any High Rock stock? Or if he invested in the aborted shares issue?'

'No I don't.' She looked at me less dubiously. 'But it's time I did.'

'Peeples would have been majorly pissed if he lost money when Carmody pulled the plug on the flotation. And he was in the right place at the right time to get to Carmody before the mob did.'

She scribbled more notes. 'I'll look into it.'

Bull Turner walked into the parking lot below and

climbed into a squad car waiting to drive him someplace. I hadn't talked to the chief since the attack on Bobby Peeples. I sensed he was avoiding me.

'Any developments on Peeples Junior?' I watched Bull Turner's car move off along Whipple Street and turn left at Third Avenue.

'Still off the critical list; still in a coma.'

'If he wakes up and identifies his attacker, that would be a big help.'

'And if he wakes up and says it was you and me, that could mean jail time for the both of us.'

*

'Got a minute?'

Tom Ferris, the *Herald's* copy chief, came into my office without waiting for a reply. Tom was well north of sixty but never gave the impression of taking his foot off the pedal. If anything the approach of retirement seemed to make him keener.

It was late – gone 7.30pm – and I made a throw-away comment along the lines of didn't he have a home to go to? Then I recalled his wife died in the spring and that he hung around in the newsroom because he hated going back to the empty house.

He gave me a filthy look. It was what I deserved so I said nothing and waited for him to talk.

'It's those numbers on the candy pack.' He brandished the fragment of the Alexander the Grape candy box I found in Gerwitz's Cadillac. The one with two number sequences indented on the printed surface. I'd asked him to take a look because if anybody could spot anything, it was Tom Ferris. There were two reasons for this. First, he was the sharpest copy editor I worked with – he nailed tiny or obscure errors that nobody else noticed. Second, he was a whizz at cryptic crossword puzzles – his brain could make sense out of the most far-out shit imaginable.

'They aren't phone numbers.' He tossed the piece of cardboard on my desk. 'They aren't safe codes. And they aren't zip codes.'

I wanted to say, *So what the fuck* are *they?* but if he'd teased some meaning out of those numbers, a moment of triumph was the least I owed him.

'Hell of a puzzle, must admit.' He stuck his thumbs in the pockets of his knitted vest and looked down at the torn cardboard as if it was an alligator he'd just wrestled to submission. 'That's why it took me so long.'

Walking around to my side of the desk, he placed his index finger just below the first set of indentations. 'Can you see those small gaps between the second and third digits and the fourth and fifth? And there's something else written after the last number, the sixth? Not another number – possibly a scribble, possibly a letter.'

I squinted. I could just about make out what he was referring to.

His finger moved to the second sequence. 'Similar pattern emerges here. This time, the gaps are between the third and fourth numbers and the fifth and sixth. Ditto with the squiggle or letter after the final number – though this time it's a seven digit sequence.'

Again I peered at the indentations; again I struggled to see what he was getting at.

'There are faint superscript characters in those gaps. So faint I bet you can't even see 'em.'

'It's a bet you'd win, Tom.'

I looked up and saw the corners of his mouth nudge into a slight smile. He was loving this. Like I said, though, if he had a solution, he could be as smug as he liked.

'The superscript characters are the key to the whole thing. They're symbols for degrees, minutes and seconds. Also, there's a letter at the end of each sequence.'

I looked again at the number sequences. I still couldn't see these little symbols, but I *could* see the gaps where they went.

'What you're looking at is map coordinates.' He produced a sheet of copy paper and laid it flat on the desk, right beside the printed cardboard.

I leaned forward and saw what he'd written down:

$$35\ 22\ 21 = 35°22'21''N$$
$$115\ 53\ 87 = 115°53'87''W$$

A map reference had never occurred to me, but made a lot of sense. The place had to be related to Gerwitz's disappearance. Maybe where he was hiding.

'You're a genius, Tom.'

'Do I get a raise?'

'Maybe.'

'What if I tell you the location of the coordinates?'

'All right, probably a raise.'

He made a do-me-a-favour expression.

'Okay, definitely a raise.'

That seemed to satisfy him. 'The place is eight miles

north of I-15 at Halloran Springs. But I looked on the map. There's nothing there.'

I grabbed the paper with the co-ordinates written on it. 'That's exactly why there *is* something there.'

Then I called Caraway at home.

I said, 'I think I know where we can find Gary Gerwitz.'

FORTY-FIVE

We took I-15 to the Halloran Springs exit and drove eight miles north along a dirt road before leaving Caraway's car at the start of an old burro trail. This took us around the side of a rust coloured outcrop known locally as the glass mountain. In the distance a power line bisected the dry playa of Silver Lake. A little to the north, the Soda Mountains and Avawatz peaks gnawed the pale sky. Even farther north the white workings of a talc quarry glistened like snow.

A couple of miles along the trail we found the abandoned silver mine we were looking for. There was no headframe, just a parapet of rocks with a makeshift roof of old timber slats and tree branches. It was well hidden behind a stand of juniper trees and blackbush scrub.

The first sign that we were in the right location was a battered Dodge Power Wagon. Randy Pasquale said he traded a similar vehicle for Gerwitz's Cadillac. Dollars to dimes this was it.

We found the next pointer a few moments later: empty Spam and soda cans half buried in the dust.

Finally there was the stink of human body filth. It lingered on the air around the mineshaft, getting stronger as we got closer.

Caraway glanced around and gave me the thumbs up.

Cupping her hands to her mouth, she called out to him. 'Gary, it's Lee Caraway. You're safe now. You're not in any trouble we can't fix. But we need to talk with you right now.'

The silence played tense. Gerwitz would be paranoid. Holed up in this place for three weeks, who wouldn't be?

Caraway tried again. 'You gotta trust me, Gary. You can't stay out here for ever.'

Another strained hiatus.

Then he moved from behind the parapet wall, real slow, arms half-raised like a soldier in the act of surrender. Sunburn had turned the pasty face vivid pink and one of the lenses in his John Lennon glasses was cracked. The frizzy red hair was now accompanied by a mangy beard. He was wearing a grimy T-shirt and jeans. They were ripped at the knees, showing scraped skin where he must have fallen.

He stopped six feet from us and squinted in the intense sunlight. 'That really you, Lee?'

'Sure is.'

He took a step closer. 'Stay out here long enough, your mind plays tricks.'

'No tricks, Gary, it's me.' She turned to me. 'And this is Wat Tyler. He's the editor of the *Herald*. He's been helping me with the investigation.'

The ginger dude gave me a quick glance, then looked back at Caraway. 'How did you find me?'

She explained what happened after he left town.

He scratched his head and looked at her as if she was talking in a foreign language. 'Marsha can't be dead. She had it figured. We were gonna meet up here. We were gonna go away together.'

'She was a righteous operator, Gary, but she got unlucky.' Caraway spoke softly and I sensed she had some sympathy for this scared and confused guy. 'Whoever these people are, they made her as a federal agent before she could get out of town. We need to work out how that happened.'

'And your dad?' Gerwitz looked around at the empty landscape as if it might give him answers. 'That can't be true...'

'We need to talk, Gary.' Caraway's voice stayed gentle but acquired an insistent edge. 'You have information that's crucial to our investigation.'

'I'm not sure if I'm ready to go back.' He seemed freaked out. 'Marsha said to wait here.'

'We can talk here if you prefer.'

He jabbed his thumb over his shoulder. 'You wanna come into my camp?'

He indicated a patch of shade under the junipers and Caraway nodded okay.

We sat on some rocks under the leaves and I unslung the backpack.

'We figured you'd need some fresh supplies.' I pulled out a six-pack of Lucky and some candy bars.

Gerwitz's expression brightened as I tossed him a beer and a couple of Zagnut bars.

He popped the can, sucked it dry. Then he started on the candy. It was gone in thirty seconds.

Caraway said, 'Tell us what happened on the Thursday you quit town, Gary. How did you come to be here?'

He frowned, as if remembering was difficult. 'I got a call from Marsha. Shortly after midday. She told me she was a federal agent working under cover and just learned that my life was in danger. That was unreal. Like something out of a movie. See, Marsha and I, we had a thing.' He pushed his fingers through his hair and made a despairing expression. 'I thought I knew her. Fuck, I thought I loved her. Maybe I do. Or did. I dunno.'

Caraway's voice was consoling. 'She did all she could to protect you, Gary. That's gotta count for something.'

'I guess. She said her being a fed didn't change anything between us. She said we could be together once all this shit was over. But now she's dead and all this shit isn't over, is it?'

'It will be soon.' Caraway asked her next question slowly. 'Did Marsha say who was trying to kill you, or why?'

He shook his head no. 'She just gave me those co-ordinates and told me to get here right away and stay until she came. She said it might take a few days. But, Jeez, I never counted on three weeks.'

Caraway studied him. 'You didn't come here directly, though, did you, Gary?'

He shook his head. 'I panicked. My brain got fried. Barely knew what I was doing.'

'That's understandable.' I gave him a reassuring smile. 'Not every day you get a phone call like that. So what did you do when you left town?'

'Just drove east, fast. But by the time I reached Vegas I realized I needed to trust Marsha. So I went to Randy Pasquale at the Maharajah and traded the Cadillac for the Power Wagon. I figured the four wheel drive would give me a good off-road option. Then I bought a map and some provisions and headed out here.'

I kept my tone amicable. 'Randy says you owe him a lot of money. That true?'

Gerwitz made a what-can-I-say? shrug. 'You got another Zagnut?'

I gave him what he asked for.

Caraway's tone hardened. 'You got help with that debt, though, didn't you, Gary? Big help. From Stacey.'

He unwrapped one end of the Zagnut, said nothing.

I filled the silence. 'Why did you schedule a meeting with Frank Hazeldene for the afternoon he got shot?'

He looked at me, startled. Then his words came in a panicky rush. 'I had nothing to do with his getting shot. Or Ray Carmody, or Marsha. If I'd hung around in Hicks they'd have killed me too.'

'We believe you, Gary,' Caraway said. 'But that's not what you were asked. On the day he died, Congressman Hazeldene told Mr Tyler he was close to acquiring information that could shift the balance of power in the Cold War. And we know you called the congressman's office the previous day, asking for an urgent, confidential meeting. That meeting should have taken place at the Rich Vein café. But it never happened because Hazeldene was dead and you were on the run.'

Gerwitz stared at the ground.

Caraway leaned close. 'Why did you request that meeting, Gary? What was the information you were going to give Hazeldene?'

His shoulders rose and dipped in a barely discernible shrug. 'We've been sending faulty M60 torsion bars to Chrysler for over a year. I was under pressure to keep schtum. But it got so that I couldn't live with myself. I had to tell someone. Hazeldene was coming to town. I figured he was a guy who might be able to help.'

Caraway made a worried expression. 'When you say "we", who do you mean?'

'Amalgamated Metals. Your dad. Me. They're one and the same. Or they were.'

Caraway gave me a quick glance, then turned back to Gerwitz. 'Are you saying my dad knowingly, deliberately defrauded the Pentagon?'

Gerwitz nodded yes.

'I don't believe you.' Caraway was angry, incredulous. 'Dad devoted his life to the US Army. This is some bullshit story to get you off the hook, isn't it, Gary?'

Gerwitz said nothing. His silence said more than words. This was the truth. Deep down Caraway knew it.

I picked up the questioning. 'Tell us what happened, Gary.'

Gerwitz's eyes didn't leave the ground. 'In 1970 we started to develop a new high performance torsion bar. The product would be lighter and more resilient than anything yet seen. We named it Ultralite and the early results were encouraging. The following year Stokes committed most of the company's reserves to expanding the development programme. But we hit cash flow problems and ran out of funds before we could prove the product. We should have shelved it, but Stokes wouldn't hear of it and went ahead with full-scale production. He said we needed to have faith in ourselves, that he'd be vindicated as soon as we got the testing programme back on track.'

Honeysett's words, minutes before he died, came back to me: *Rightly or wrongly, you should always believe in yourself, put faith in your judgment – even when other people doubt it. Especially when other people doubt it...*Back then that declaration sounded inspiring and self-affirming. Now it sounded hollow and self-serving.

Gerwitz discarded the untouched Zagnut bar and turned to me. 'Got another beer?'

I passed him a Lucky. He snapped the ringpull and took a long swallow.

Now he sounded more weary than anxious. 'I tried to talk him out of it, I really did. But he wouldn't listen – even when it became clear that we'd spent so much on the Ultralite programme that we didn't have enough money to complete the order we were part way through. That was when Stokes took the decision to finish the current contract using the unproven Ultralite bar.'

He paused to burp, resumed in the same flat tone. 'When the testing started again, the results were my worst nightmare. The product fell well short of the Department of Defense specification. Ninety-nine per cent of the Ultralite bars would fail after just 175 miles. That compared to the DoD specification of 265 miles.'

I recalled what Honeysett told me at the M60 demonstration up at Fort Irwin. He said Amalgamated Metals bars had a life-span of 295 miles. Was the old guy lying or deluded? I wanted to believe the latter, but even that didn't reflect too well on him.

I asked, 'How many faulty bars did you supply?'

He finished his beer and squeezed the can. 'Three thousand five hundred. With another seven thousand to follow – enough for three armoured divisions of M60s.'

FORTY-SIX

Caraway said what I was thinking. 'So we're looking at nine hundred main battle tanks likely to break down or crash on manoeuvres. Or worse, in action.'

Gerwitz continued as if he hadn't heard her. 'Of course sooner or later we'd have gotten found out, but by then the damage would have been done. And the consequences would go way beyond US military capability.'

Caraway's voice had gotten a new note of concern. 'What exactly do you mean?'

He gave her a gloomy look. 'It's as much about prestige and confidence. If entire armoured divisions were subject to catastrophic failure, our NATO allies would lose a great deal of confidence. The US Army's main battle tank would become a byword for unreliability and failure. The Soviets would score a major propaganda victory. Just as crucially, we sell a hell of a lot of M60s to countries like Israel. Our export sales would take a nosedive and maybe never recover. I mean, who would want to buy a tank with a reputation for totally fucking up at the hour of need?'

Now Caraway sounded angry. 'If you knew all this, why didn't you come forward sooner?'

He went back to avoiding eye contact. 'Stacey persuaded me not to.'

Caraway wouldn't let up. 'Persuaded? Or bribed?'

'Does it matter?' Gerwitz was clearly beat so bad that one more blow made no difference. 'She found out about the flawed torsion bars last November after she overheard a fight between Stokes and me up at the house. I was threatening to talk to the authorities. Stacey came over to my place later that week. Said she was worried that the company could go to the wall and jobs would be lost if I went through with my threat. She knew about my gambling problem and proposed a deal: I'd keep quiet about the torsion bars; she'd pay off my debts.'

I asked, 'How did she find out about your gambling?'

'Dunno. Hicks is a small town but Vegas isn't. And that's where I racked up all my big debts. Stacey had me by the short hairs, though. She had the low-down on how much I owed and who I owed it to.'

I asked, 'Could your ex-wife have told her?'

He shook his head no. 'Barbara knew I owed money, but she didn't know any details.'

Caraway took over with the questions. 'So what happened to make you change your mind and go to Frank Hazeldene?'

Gerwitz let his empty beer can fall to the ground and used the side of his shoe to bury it in dirt. 'Two things, I guess. One, it slowly dawned on me that Stacey's money wasn't a solution. It actually made things worse. More to spend, less to stop me hitting even more casinos. And two, I couldn't live with the deception. Keeping schtum out of loyalty to Stokes made me a dupe; taking money to keep schtum made me a criminal.' He turned to Caraway with a faint smile. 'Call it conscience, or patriotic duty, or fear of getting caught. But

I decided to call it quits. I told Marsha everything. She was wonderful. Level-headed, didn't judge. She suggested talking to Hazeldene. She said he'd be in Hicks that next day. So I called his office and arranged to see him.'

I asked, 'Who did you tell about the meeting?'

'Stacey and Marsha – the only two people who stood by me.'

He threw back his head and raised his arms heavenward, like he was beseeching the Almighty. 'Of course, now I know why Marsha was so interested in me, why she was so understanding. She didn't have feelings for me at all. She was investigating me.'

'She must have thought something about you.' Caraway's voice mellowed. 'She could easily have cut out and let you hang. But she didn't and likely lost her life as a result. You should think about that.'

I added, 'Stacey must think something about you too. Why else do you think she ponied up all that money?'

He made a doubtful expression. 'Stacey's great. But she acted mainly to protect her dad and the workers.'

I tried again. 'C'mon, Gary, Stacey's been a true friend to you – loyal to the point of self-sacrifice.'

He thought about it and nodded. 'Yeah, that's true enough. But it's not been all one way. I bent over backward to get her a management position at the factory but Stokes wouldn't countenance it.'

'Why was that?'

I was a little surprised when Caraway replied. 'Partly Dad's sexist attitudes and partly Stacey's left-of-Lenin politics. But mainly because Dad had a rule of never mixing family and business. He lived two strictly separate lives. Never worried me because I had no desire to work at the factory. My sister did though. And for once I can sympathize.'

'Stacey did everything she could to get Stokes to change his mind.' This was the first time Gerwitz had volunteered information. 'She learned all there is to know about M60 suspension systems. She completed correspondence courses in business management and accounting. She even got a secretary's diploma to show Stokes she was willing to take letters and handle filing. Still no dice.'

'That sure was tough on Stacey,' I said. 'With Stokes' passing, maybe all that can change.'

Gerwitz looked hopeful. 'You think?'

Caraway gave him a non-committal look. 'Depends on how this plays out, Gary. First, though, you need to come into the station and make a formal statement.'

He threw an anxious glance in the direction of the old mine where he'd made his camp. It had been his refuge for three weeks, but now he seemed to get that staying out here was no longer an option. 'Okay,' he said. 'Let's go.'

*

Back in Hicks I went to the *Herald* office and wrote the next day's front page lead. It was solid.

A business executive fled for his life before he could expose a tank components scandal to a congressman who was murdered later the same day.

Next I drove to see Caraway at the police station. I expected her to confirm that Gerwitz had made a written statement.

What I didn't expect was the sight of Chester Peeples being hauled from the back of a black-and-white and bundled into the cop shop.

His hateful look gave me a jolt. It also gave me a great second-lead for tomorrow's paper. And a reason to use his picture again.

Caraway met me at the front desk.

She said, 'You were right to suggest running checks on High Rock stockholders. Pop Peeples' name came up over and over. He invested more than a half million dollars two years ago when the mine's value started to go through the roof. Then he subscribed a cool million to the Pacific Coast flotation. Lost the lot when the fraud was exposed. He's certainly going to go bust as a result. That's motive enough for murdering Ray Carmody.'

I frowned. 'We both know he didn't do it, though, right?'

She made a wry smile. 'Sure we do. But I want that bastard to sweat a while. He'll go down anyways for corporate fraud so it isn't as if he's wasting his time getting familiar with the inside of a jail cell.'

'What does Schwenk have to say?'

'Schwenk doesn't know – he was called to LA by his bureau chief this morning. Won't be back until tomorrow.'

This suited me fine. I wanted the G-man out of the way – at least for now. Was he involved in the torsion bar conspiracy? Possibly. Would he sabotage what I had in mind? Absolutely. Not if he was in LA though.

We went into Caraway's office. She told me about the interview with Gerwitz. It had gone well. He even added some illuminating detail to the account he gave us up at Halloran Springs.

I'd been quiet for a while when she realized I had something on my mind. She asked what it was.

I needed to explain the conclusions I'd reached since we arrived back in town. I struggled to get my shit together though. Finding out about her dad defrauding the Pentagon hit her hard. This would hit her harder.

But I had to tell her so I just started talking. 'This cover-up at Amalgamated Metals, despite what Gary said, it wasn't really about loyalty to your dad or keeping those folks in work.'

She gave me a hard stare. 'What are you getting at?'

I didn't – *couldn't* – go straight to it. So I took the scenic route. 'Let's look at what we know and what we don't. We know Schwenk came to town on a matter of national security. But what does he mean by that?'

'You better ask Schwenk.'

'I intend to. We also know three divisions of main battle tanks would have likely crashed on the front line if the deal described by Gerwitz went down. That's not to mention American prestige taking a major hit and the loss of substantial export sales. Who benefits?'

She made a you-tell-me shrug.

'Okay, let's take this one stage farther. We got a triple homicide in a little desert town – including the murder of a deep cover federal agent. Then a corrupt manager at High Rock Mine goes on the run and is found with a bullet in his head. Next, a talkative barmaid gets her throat cut after revealing the undercover agent's relationship with the senior vice president of the firm supplying faulty components to the Pentagon. Who has the motive and resources to make all that happen?'

She was plainly getting irritated. 'Quit the questions, Wat. Spit it out.'

I said, 'Your sister is working for the KGB.'

FORTY-SEVEN

First thing next morning Caraway drove us to the big house.

We said very little on the way over. This was going to be tough for both of us.

She parked the Plymouth beside her dad's Rolls Royce. The chauffeur came out of the garage with a wash leather and began polishing the hood. The sight of his grey uniform next to the cardinal red coachwork triggered an awareness, then another and another. This deductive process should have been a shock. In a way it was. But I'd been shocked a lot lately and once more made no difference.

I filed the thought, though.

We found Stacey in Stokes' office, standing by the french windows. She was wearing a floral pattern dress in navy blue and white. With her hair pinned up and her face made up she was every bit of businesslike. This was a remarkable transformation from the desolate figure at her dad's graveside two days earlier.

'If it isn't the lovers.' Stacey lit a Gitanes. 'What's with the joint deputation? A formal announcement, perhaps? You two getting hitched or something?'

Caraway's voice was brittle. 'Why did you do it, Stacey?'

Stacey made a puzzled expression. 'If you told me what you were talking about I might be able to give you a sensible answer.'

Caraway gave her half-sister a piercing look. 'Why have you been spying for the Russians?'

'Do you know how ludicrous that sounds?'

'Do you know how much I wish it *was* ludicrous?'

I intervened before this escalated. 'Humour us, Stacey, just for a few minutes.'

I joined her by the tall windows. 'Let me explain what we think has gone down. If it still sounds ridiculous when I'm done, you can put us straight and we'll apologize. If we *are* wrong, no one would be happier than your sister and me.'

Stacey sucked on her French cigarette. 'Okay, if it's so important I'll play along. Go ahead – regale me with your fantasy.'

I made a grateful smile. 'Back in April Marsha Houtrelle – aka FBI Special Agent McMeekin – came to Hicks. She was sent here after the Bureau got intelligence about a KGB handler running an asset inside Amalgamated Metals. Marsha's mission was to trace the handler and the asset – and thereby discover what was going on at Amalgamated. Now Marsha was smart. She soon developed a relationship with two key players: Gary Gerwitz, the company's troubled senior vice president; and you, a vocal left wing activist.'

'Seriously?' Stacey made a do-me-a-favour frown. 'If I *was* a spy – and I can't believe I'm even saying this – would I publicly associate myself with all that Marxist and Maoist stuff? Would I be so stupid?'

Caraway walked around the desk and sat in Stokes' chair. 'Not stupid, Stacey, clever. Those communist sympathies were a very effective double bluff.'

Stacey seemed to find this amusing. 'So I'm either unbelievably stupid or astonishingly smart. Truth is I'm neither of those things.'

Caraway wouldn't be deflected. 'Yet you gave substantial sums of money to Gary.'

Stacey sounded bored. 'I already went through this with your lover boy.'

Caraway made a tight smile. 'Gary says you used the cash to stop him going to the authorities about the faulty torsion bars. That's criminal bribery.'

'Gary's a gambling addict. He's also mentally ill. You spend three weeks in the desert feeding yourself Spam, you gotta be crazy.'

'Or scared shitless,' Caraway said. She paused a beat then pressed on. 'When did Marsha find out about your cash donations to Gary?'

'Marsha never knew anything.'

Caraway's voice got frostier. 'Gary made a formal statement just a couple of hours ago. He says he told you around 2.30pm on Wednesday September 12 that Marsha had persuaded him to talk to Hazeldene about the torsion bars the very next day. You got anything to say about that?'

'Gary's talking through his asshole. And so are you – both of you.' Stacey's expression changed from irritated to suspicious. 'What's this really about? You trying to get your hands on the company, Lee?'

I ignored the red herring attempt. 'Here's the thing, Stacey: You knew about the face-to-face between Gerwitz and Hazeldene when you met with me in that greasy spoon over at Third and Congress. You told me you thought Gary pulled out at the last minute because he lost his nerve.'

I let it hang. Stacey said nothing. I sensed cogs and ratchets spinning and clicking inside her head.

I went on, 'But that meeting was arranged in secret. So how *could* you have known? And here's another thing: The meeting wasn't arranged until 2.00pm the day before Hazeldene died. Yet you told me you last talked to Gary on Saturday September 8. You said this was after you both watched *M*A*S*H**, which ended at 9.00pm. That was five days before Gary called Hazeldene's office and asked to meet with the congressman.'

Stacey stubbed out her cigarette.

I tried to catch her gaze but she refused eye contact. 'You could only have known about that meeting if Gary's allegation is true: that he told you about it twenty-four hours before the hit went down.'

Stacey said nothing, returned to the french windows.

Caraway picked up the questioning. 'Is that right, Stacey? See, if it is, your next logical step would be to pass this information to your handler. He – or maybe she – then used the KGB's considerable resources to organize the triple homicide. And that would make you complicit in first degree murder, not to mention treason.'

For the first time, Stacey seemed shaken. It was like watching a boxer take the first heavy punch after several rounds of circling and ducking. 'I got confused,' she said. 'I can't remember who I talked to and what I told them all that time ago. But it doesn't make me a goddamn spy.'

I switched the line of attack. 'You also ran a pretty effective disruption strategy, didn't you?'

'I have no idea what that means.'

My smile became less friendly. 'Apart from me and my

city editor, you were the only person on the planet who knew where I was going to be when I got attacked on Harvard Road.'

Stacey laughed. But it was forced and nervy.

I pushed a little harder. 'When we talked to Gary over at Halloran Springs yesterday he spoke very highly of you. Explained how you tried to get your dad to let you work for the company by doing those correspondence courses in business management and accounting. And secretarial skills.'

I let that sink in. 'You learned Pitman shorthand, didn't you?'

Now she put on an exasperated expression. 'What the hell has that got to do with anything?'

'C'mon, Stacey.' I made a gimme-a-break expression. 'Back in the greasy spoon, you weren't looking in uncomprehending wonder at my shorthand notes. You said they looked like Sanskrit or Arabic. But that was bullshit. You were reading those outlines, weren't you? I'd written down the time and location of my meeting with Tab Thornley. With that information you could easily work out when I'd leave the office and what route I'd take. The moment I turned onto Harvard Road I was trapped.'

'That's plain silly.' This time Stacey made no pretence at laughter. 'Why would I do such a thing?'

I let the silence run, looked at the framed photos of Stokes Honeysett shaking hands with all those US presidents.

Without turning around I said, 'Because you – or more likely your handler – wanted to put me in the hospital to interrupt my stories about your dad's torsion bar tender running into difficulties.'

I turned back to look across the room. 'Whose interest

would be served by suppressing that story? Who would have most to gain from Amalgamated Metals continuing to supply substandard tank components to Uncle Sam? Here's a wild guess: The Soviet Union.'

Stacey stuck to mockery as her main line of defence. 'Have you been on those substances with Norm Dibbitts?'

My mind went back to the Rolls Royce's cardinal red coachwork, the grey-uniformed chauffeur. Last time I saw him he was at the wheel wearing his peaked cap, driving Stokes Honeysett back home – thirty minutes after my poolside encounter with Stacey.

'The interference you were running didn't stop at Harvard Road, did it?'

'What was it? Mushrooms? Acid? Must be some real heavy hallucinogenic shit.'

I crossed the room and stood close to Stacey. 'That show of vulnerability by the pool was a sham. The maid *had* told you I was on my way out. As soon as you heard that, you put on your skimpy black bikini and played the helpless little girl. You wanted to get me into bed, didn't you?'

She tried to slap my face. I caught her wrist and held it tight. Caraway knew nothing about this. Neither did I – leastways not completely – until I saw the chauffeur polishing the Rolls Royce when we arrived twenty minutes ago.

'You knew your dad would be back in thirty minutes, not several hours like you told me. You *wanted* him to catch us.'

'That's outrageous.' Stacey tried to yank her wrist free.

I tightened my grip, felt her pulse against the heel of my hand. 'It would have been outrageous if you'd gotten away with it. You'd have put a wedge between your dad and me *and* your sister and me. That way you'd have driven me farther from Amalgamated Metals and farther from finding out about Marsha.'

I knew Stacey was desperate when she turned to Caraway for help. 'Your boyfriend's flipped, Lee. Can you believe this crap?'

Caraway stood up from her dad's desk chair. 'Tragically, yes.'

I let go of Stacey's wrist.

Caraway came around to the front of the desk. 'It's time to cut the crap, Stacey. We got you over so many barrels I lose count – and you know it.'

Stacey said nothing.

Strange quietness filled the room. I imagined Stokes Honeysett's ghost trying to explain this mire of deceit to the ghosts of the presidents in the framed photos. The only one still alive was Nixon. And he'd soon enough wish he wasn't.

Caraway spoke first. 'Right now, Stacey, you're facing a charge of treason, five counts of conspiracy to murder, and a felony bribery rap. I'm sure we'll find more, but unless you start cooperating you're looking at spending the rest of your days in a jail cell.'

Still nothing from Stacey.

She turned to look out through the french windows. I wondered if the cactus wren was still out there.

Thirty seconds went by, and another thirty.

Caraway was about to turn the screw again when Stacey made her decision.

'Okay, I wanna make a deal.'

'Tell us everything.' Caraway's voice was harsh.

'How do I know I can trust you?'

'Because we're not complete assholes like you!' Never saw

Caraway lose her cool like that. 'For Chrissakes, Stacey, what would Dad think of this...*this*...'

I moved a little closer to Stacey, kept my tone even. 'Why did you do it?'

I expected a volley of revolutionary zeal, a denunciation of capitalism and its evils.

Her voice, though, was surprisingly mellow. 'I thought I was doing the right thing. I thought I was helping ordinary folk. At first I thought it was exciting. Then I got scared. Then there was no turning back.'

FORTY-EIGHT

I picked up one of Stacey's Gitanes, lit it and handed it to her. 'Tell us what happened.'

She took a pull the cigarette and looked at Caraway. 'They persuaded me to work for them three years ago. I met these people at an anti-war demonstration at UCLA. I didn't hear anything from them, though, until the back end of last year. They came to Hicks and told me about Gary's gambling debts. They wanted me to blackmail him into revealing confidential stuff about the M60 programme.'

She smoked more of the cigarette. 'You can imagine how impressed they were when I told them I had a better idea – that I heard Dad and Gary fighting over the faulty torsion bars.'

Caraway's voice was less the angry sister, more the professional cop. 'So why the switch from shakedown to bribery?'

'They wanted to keep the supply of substandard product going as long as possible. They thought Gary would be more compliant if he was presented with an incentive rather than a threat. They gave me the money, I gave it to Gary. For a time it worked. But Gary started to get cold feet. They told me to watch him even more closely, but there was only so much I could do, especially with Dad not allowing me into the factory.'

Stacey bit her lip as if she was thinking about what to say next. For a beat I thought she was going to stop talking, but she continued in an almost relaxed tone. 'Then Marsha arrived. She was the most. Someone to talk to, someone who really listened, who understood how complicated life gets. How you think you're in control when you're absolutely not. We never talked specifics, but it was as if she knew what I was doing. And, of course, she *did* know. Maybe I should have cottoned on when she started her thing with Gary. But at the time I thought she was good for him – and that was good for me because she was helping him to keep his shit together.'

'She was one cool operator,' I said. 'The complete professional.'

'Then they came back to town.' Stacey spoke these words much more solemnly. 'I was called to a meeting toward the end of August. They knew the feds were onto them, but they hadn't made Marsha. They didn't do that until I betrayed her. I didn't mean to. But that's what happens when you lose control.'

Caraway said, 'So you *did* contact them after Gary told you Marsha had persuaded him to talk to Hazeldene?'

Stacey nodded. 'But I had no idea what was about to go down. That was when the whole thing went spinning away from me. If I'd known what they were planning, I'd have...' She made a helpless shrug. 'I'd like to say I'd have tried to stop them. But I don't know. I was in so deep I didn't know which side was up.'

'What happened after the hit?' Caraway said.

'They thought Marsha tipped off Gary because he'd gone on the run. They were really angry about that.'

'Did they plan to kill Gary too?'

'I dunno. Probably. He'd become a liability. They must have realized I couldn't handle him any longer. But Marsha was the main threat to the operation and she'd been eliminated in a way that seemed like an accident. They'd have needed to do the same with Gary.'

Stacey turned to me. 'Next, you came on the scene with your questions about the torsion bar tender and Gary going missing. You got close to Dad. He really liked you. They even thought Dad might spill the beans to you in a fit of remorse. They certainly thought you'd find Gary before they could. That was when I got the instructions to disrupt your investigation in any way I could.'

Stacey looked away. When she spoke again there was something like embarrassment in her voice. 'Like at Harvard Road. And yes, like at the pool.'

'What about throwing Lee and Schwenk off the trail?' I said. 'Surely they were a much bigger problem than me?'

She made the faintest smile. 'You shouldn't underestimate the KGB. They sure didn't underestimate you. The feeling was that law enforcement – federal and local – could be managed. You, on the other hand, were the Peasants' Revolt. You were the wild card.'

'Thanks for the vote of confidence.' Caraway gave her sister a gloomy look. 'So what did they say about the killing of Rex Hambly and Lucinda Hannity? And the attack on Bobby Peeples?'

'They didn't say anything. They only told me what I needed to know so I could do what they needed me to do.'

I said, 'Sooner or later you gotta name names. Now is probably the time.'

Another long silence. This was the moment of betrayal. After all Stacey went through it was going to be tough. It would be like saying: *I used to be a revolutionary. But I gave up that shit. Couldn't hack it.*

Time went by.

And more time.

I started to wonder if Stacey had lost her nerve. I glanced at Caraway. She made a dubious expression.

Stacey said a name.

My mind got real blown.

Never saw that coming.

Except I did.

I'd seen it coming for fucking ever.

FORTY-NINE

Finn Sheldon bit off a chunk of cheeseburger and swallowed it in one. He also had a side of french fries and a pack of Oreos on the go. A half-smoked cigarette rested in an ashtray next to a tumbler of whiskey. How he could ingest all that shit at the same time was beyond me.

I took a seat opposite him on one of the couches in his hotel room.

He said, 'You got a name for this KGB handler?'

'You know I do.'

I ran Stacey's information by my CIA buddy. He was almost certainly the only person this side of the iron curtain in a position to validate the name she'd given us.

For all sorts of reasons I needed to do this alone. Caraway wasn't happy but she accepted that Sheldon simply wouldn't talk if she was there.

He pushed a half dozen french fries into his mouth. 'I always helped you when I could, Wat.'

'I know that, Finn.'

He took a mouthful of whiskey, a pull on the cigarette, another mouthful of burger. 'If I help you on this, I won't be able to help you again. Not ever.'

I made a rueful smile. 'I realize that.'

'And you're still asking?'

'I got no choice.'

More of the burger-fries-cigarette-whiskey combo went down.

'Then I gotta tell you that name is correct.'

I looked at him hard. 'For fuck's sake, Finn.'

'No regrets.' He sounded remarkably upbeat. 'It was a gas.'

In some ways the idea of Finn Sheldon as a Soviet double agent shocked me; in other ways, I should have figured it out sooner. Some of it went back years; some of it had only become clear in the last hour.

Like Bobby Peeples regaining consciousness and talking about a crazy-looking fat guy coming at him from the shadows with a baseball bat.

And like the match between the floral pattern dress Stacey had been wearing that morning and the one worn by the woman in the photo I found in Marsha's apartment. The woman – confirmed as Stacey by Stacey – was pictured leaning into the driver's window of a light coloured Ford Pinto with a peace symbol bumper sticker. And although the Pinto was among the most common cars in the country, a light coloured model with a peace symbol bumper sticker just happened to be parked in a lot next to Sheldon's hotel. That had to be more than happenstance. Clearly, Marsha had managed to photograph Stacey rendezvousing with her handler – Finn Sheldon.

'It was a neat op, though, you must admit.' He sounded weirdly reflective. Like I was interviewing him as the originator of a work of art. 'There was a poetic symmetry to it – in the meticulous planning, the intrinsic flexibility.'

'For Chrissakes, Finn, you weren't doing an exercise in abstract thinking.' I gave him an exasperated look. I could tell by his expression, though, that this was exactly what he thought he was doing. And it chimed with the exhibitionism I'd seen in the evidence. What had Caraway said? *Too tricksy for a mob hit.* 'You were showing off,' I said. 'Weren't you?'

'I prefer to say demonstrating my skills.'

'In multiple homicide?'

'Problems and solutions is all.' He polished off the cheeseburger, picked up the pack of Oreos.

'They'll throw away the keys.'

'Maybe they will.' He splayed his podgy fingers horizontally and waggled them. 'Maybe they won't.'

I couldn't imagine any outcome that didn't involve him going to prison for the rest of his life. He was looking at treason and five murders. Even the death penalty couldn't be ruled out.

'It was seemingly complex but basically simple,' he said. 'You did well to unpick it. I'm glad you got there ahead of that asshole Schwenk. It'll help your girlfriend Caraway and make one hell of a story for your paper.'

'Fuck the story.' For once, I meant it. 'Five people are dead. You've handed the Soviets a major strategic advantage. And twelve hundred families could lose all they got.'

But Sheldon didn't want to talk about that. He wanted to tell me how smart he was. 'You and Caraway and the Feds, you all thought the hit hinged on Hazeldene. Since he was the only victim whose movements were predictable, it made sense. But you couldn't have been more wrong.'

He made me wait while he ate more cheeseburger. He was playing this like a stripper, the slow reveal tantalising the audience. 'See, my original plan involved a double homicide: Marsha McMeekin the mark, Ray Carmody the decoy.'

Another bite of the burger; another few seconds of wait-and-see. 'I'd been aware of the CIA investigation into High Rock Mine since the end of last year. Then in March, I made Marsha McMeekin as a federal agent and realized she'd have to be eliminated at some point. But it would have to look like an accident so as not to alert her FBI handler. That way I could keep Stacey Honeysett in play and the faulty torsion bars in production. So I volunteered to join the investigation and my chief at Langley was only too happy to get me out from under.'

He stopped the show again, this time for an intake of Oreos and whiskey. 'That was when I formulated phase one of my plan. It could be executed at very short notice – and, best of all, it was highly adaptable, thanks to my discovery of Rex Hambly's troubled past. A call to the INS and he was in the bag. With Hambly as my proxy, I could have him set up a meeting with Carmody at any location I chose, whenever I wanted. Since Marsha worked at the Million Dollar Nugget and lived nearby, the Desert Diner was already on my list of possibilities. Then I learned from Stacey about Gerwitz's intention to bare his soul to Hazeldene – and I knew from your story in the *Herald* that the congressman was scheduled to visit the New Life Episcopal Church at 2.00pm on Thursday September 13.'

He paused, now raconteur-like, and pulled on his cigarette. 'Most people would have seen this as a big problem, but you know what I saw, Wat?'

'I'm sure you're going to tell me, Finn.'

'I saw a big opportunity. In less than 24 hours I evolved

phase one into phase two. A double homicide became a *triple* homicide. It killed two birds – McMeekin and Hazeldene – with one stone. And it meant I could move all three principals to the same spot, at the same time, while giving the appearance of unfortunate coincidence.'

'You played them all from that phone booth, didn't you?'

The big man nodded. He was in his element. Even the conveyor belt of food, booze and tobacco got put on pause. 'That morning I had Hambly tell Carmody he was antsy and needed to talk someplace outside the mine – the Desert Diner at 1.30pm. Carmody obliged. Then, as Hazeldene began leaving the church, I called the diner. I told the manager I was Hambly and asked him to tell Carmody there was a major incident at the mine. I knew that would make Carmody drop everything and go to his car – and it did. Next, I called the Million Dollar Nugget and told the deep cover fed that Hazeldene was about to get hit. Like Carmody, she moved cooperatively into the parking lot. All three marks were assembled in a little over thirty seconds. And bingo.'

It was as if he'd won a prize.

I probed a little deeper. 'How did you make Marsha as a fed?'

Sheldon reached for the whiskey glass and traced his podgy fingertip around the rim. 'Marsha was good, but she rushed into it way too fast. Stranger comes to town, gets tight with my asset and starts dating the asset's mark, that gotta get me asking questions. The answers came back soon enough from my comrades in LA.'

It was childish of me, but I just had to prick Sheldon's bubble. 'You were real pissed off, though, when Marsha tipped off Gerwitz and he skied out.'

'That was one to her, no doubt about it.' Sheldon drank some whiskey. 'I'm not saying she wasn't smart. Just not as smart as me.'

I wanted to say that if Sheldon was as smart as he thought, he wouldn't have gotten caught. But I needed to quit provoking him if I wanted him to carry on feeding me information.

He went back to the story he was longing to tell. 'Gerwitz had to be eliminated, but that could wait. As with Marsha, his removal would have to look like an accident in order to keep the torsion bar deal running.'

I couldn't prevent a hint of weary contempt sneaking into my voice. 'Let me guess. Two or three weeks later, Gerwitz would have gone missing – this time never to return – after Stacey got him to write some cryptic note saying he couldn't take any more pressure?'

'You know me too well, Wat.'

'That's the problem, though, Finn. I really don't know you at all.' That was tough to admit. Not because I valued his friendship, but because it was an admission that he'd played me too. And not just here in Hicks – all the way back to Vietnam.

He went for a fries-Oreo mix, shovelling the cold fries and warm cookies into his mouth as if not having eaten for five minutes made him extra hungry. 'You took longer than I expected to figure out the two shooters.'

'Sorry to disappoint.'

He gave me a taunting glance. 'If the second guy had cleared away his casings you'd never have gotten me.'

I gave him an unsympathetic look. 'That was on you, Finn. Your plan left no time for that.'

I made my next question sound casual, as if I was only vaguely interested in the answer. 'I presume the shooters weren't locals?'

'You presume correctly, my friend. That side of it was arranged by comrades in LA. They sent the shooters. All I did was give the time, the place and the targets.'

This I could believe. Both killers would have been long gone soon after the hit. Chances of catching them had always been small.

'What about Lucinda Hannity, the barmaid?'

'She wouldn't shut the fuck up. I had no way of knowing what else she might tell you.'

'So you made another call to LA?'

'Had to be done.'

'Did it really, Finn? You could have scared her off and left it at that.'

'This is play for keeps, Wat. You know that. You did enough off-the-books work for Leaping Larry, and not all of it in south east Asia.'

'I was a soldier, not an assassin.'

He gave me a who-are-you-trying-to-kid? glance but said nothing.

Something else came to mind. 'When you went into the kitchen at my place and left your briefcase in the living room, you knew I'd take a look, didn't you?'

The big man grinned and popped an Oreo. 'The moment you looked at those documents the High Rock decoy was up and running.'

Another question occurred to me. 'Why did you hit Bobby Peeples yourself?'

'The inbred bastard's come around, then?' This was more

an observation than a question. He sucked a slick of runny Oreo cream off his finger. 'It was a spur of the moment thing. I needed to thicken the smokescreen for you and Caraway. Peeples stepped right into my sights. Like we used to say in the Nasty, if you don't take your opportunities, they'll take you.'

His mention of Vietnam made me realize something else – something that went back way farther than my time in Hicks.

'All that shit in-country, that was a smokescreen too, wasn't it?'

He gave a look someplace between condescension and pity. 'Gotta say you're right, old buddy.'

I thought back to Gia Lai province five years ago. The liftbird, rotors flattening the tall grass. Sheldon breaking cover, trundling toward and past me. Charlie coming out of the bush in big numbers as I withdrew. One Viet Cong appearing from the tree line, thirty yards to my left. Sheldon's single pistol shot taking him down, saving my life.

Except he didn't.

The Viet Cong never intended to shoot me and he never got hit. I recalled thinking at the time how weird it was that he didn't bleed when Sheldon's bullet hit. I put it down to obscured line of sight, the frantic speed of the action. I didn't imagine for a beat that it was anything other than what it seemed. Why would I? That was the moment Sheldon and I bonded, when he won my loyalty and respect. And now I knew it had been staged for exactly that purpose.

'Your miraculous shot in Gia Lai wasn't miraculous at all. You fired wide. Charlie took a dive.'

The big man made a what-can-I-say? shrug.

'And when you vanished into the jungle, you weren't fearless. You were expected. You were passing intelligence to Charlie.'

'Sorry you had to find out like this.'

For once he didn't seem to be talking shit.

'What made you do it?'

He made a faint smile. 'A lot of things coming together I guess. Too many times getting passed over for promotion. Too many times getting sidelined as the fat guy. Genuine contempt for the American Way. And growing appreciation of the potential of socialism.'

I made a quizzical frown. 'How did you become a Russian agent?'

'I'd like to say I was noble. That I went over and volunteered my services. But that's not what happened. I got compromised. They offered me a deal. I agreed to be a double agent. Do I regret it? Not really.'

'You will.'

'I don't think so.' He sounded confident. 'I'll get turned again, I'll become a triple agent. Either that or traded for somebody Langley wants back from Russia.'

I was less certain: Sheldon was soiled goods. I couldn't see him as a viable asset for either side.

For a while we said nothing. He carried on with the fries, the Oreos and the whiskey. When he looked in his cigarette pack there was just one left. He lit it anyways.

I asked, 'How do you handle all that shit?'

He poured the last few drops of whiskey into his tumbler. 'This is my last supper. Leastways for a while.'

In the distance I heard howlers. They got louder.

'That'll be Caraway and Schwenk,' I said.

He finished the fries, the Oreos and the whiskey. Then he sucked in a lungful of smoke and stabbed out the cigarette. 'Then I guess the show's over.'

FIFTY

Schwenk came into my office and said, 'You did good, Tyler. All reporters aren't A-holes.'

I had to look twice to gauge whether he was being sarcastic. Seemed not.

'Just like all feds?'

The faintest tug of a smile threatened his dead-pan mask.

I indicated the visitor chair and he took a seat.

'I still think you're a degenerate hippie.'

'I still think you're a reactionary square.'

His smile widened then vanished. He said he'd called by to thank me for helping to bring Stacey and Sheldon to justice. He was leaving town later that day and didn't expect to return.

I gave him a knowing look. 'Marsha was your protégé, wasn't she?'

He nodded.

'That why you rode me so hard?'

'I got her into this but I couldn't get her out.' There was anger in his voice, regret too. 'I got frustrated. You were a natural target.'

'She was a credit to the Bureau,' I said. 'I wish I could have known her.'

Another hint of humour. 'You'd have gotten along with her a damn sight better than me.'

I went to the percolator, poured two cups of stewed coffee, handed one to Schwenk.

'What's going to happen with Gerwitz and Amalgamated Metals?'

He gave the coffee a suspicious glance. 'We did a deal with Gerwitz. He'll testify against Stacey Honeysett and we won't go after him for felony fraud. What happens to the factory is down to him. After what happened, though, there's no chance of it winning another torsion bar contract.'

'Without the contract the company will fold.'

He sipped his coffee and winced. 'That's what happens when you cheat on the Man.'

'But Uncle Sam will suffer too. The moment Amalgamated shuts down the Soviets will know the equivalent of three armoured divisions have defective suspension systems. And M60 export orders will go through the floor.'

'Big setback, sure.'

'What if the factory stayed open?'

'That's not gonna happen. Not in the real world.'

'But we're not in the real world, are we? We're in the crazy world, the mutual assured destruction world.'

'What are you getting at?'

I drank some coffee. It was bitter and tepid. 'If Amalgamated Metals stayed afloat the KGB would be kept guessing. And the export market would be none the wiser. No doubt there'd be rumours in the Kremlin, but the question at the back of everyone's mind would be: *If Amalgamated supplied flawed torsion bars, how come the firm is still trading? How come it's still supplying torsion bars?*'

'You serious?'

'And twelve hundred Americans would be kept in work.'

He drank more coffee. 'You got one hell of an imagination, Tyler.'

I smiled. 'So let me develop my imaginary situation one stage further. What if Stacey Honeysett got turned and put into the factory as Gerwitz's number two? How confused would the Soviets be then? They'd have no clue whether defective torsion bars were still being supplied, or whether we were rectifying the problem.'

Schwenk raised one eyebrow just a fraction. 'The idea of keeping the factory open and the Russians in the dark is vaguely plausible. Working with Stacey Honeysett, not so much.'

I kept smiling. 'Just ideas.'

'Yeah – the kind you hippies get when you drop acid.' He placed his undrunk coffee on my desk and headed for the door.

*

I picked up Caraway at the police station and we drove out to her family home. With Stacey out of the picture, Lee had even more stuff to take care of and we agreed to spend the night in her old room.

The empty mansion felt like a mausoleum. Caraway refused to let this get her down, though. She cooked chilli con carne and the Rest & Relaxation deal was topped off by wine and Roberta Flack's *Killing Me Softly* album. Her dad had an expensive hi-fi system but the little mono record player in Caraway's room somehow caught the mood better.

We went to bed early. Sex was tender yet urgent; easy then wild. We got down. We juiced up. We went to it with hunger and thirst. We went to a place of real gone righteousness.

But we knew we couldn't stay there.

Next morning she laid her head in the crook of my arm. 'We can't be together can we?'

'We can try.'

She kissed me smooth and slow. 'You're saying that to be kind.'

I kissed her back. 'What do you want?'

'Same as you. Outta Hicks. We can't stay here. We don't belong. And any future outside Hicks would take us in separate directions, sooner or later.'

I lit two cigarettes and handed one to her. 'Where will you go?'

'An old LAPD buddy just moved to San Francisco detectives as a lieutenant. Says he could use a sergeant. You?'

'Anyplace I can get a job.'

She touched my face with the back of her fingers. 'We'll be okay, won't we?'

I grinned. 'Sure we will.'

*

We ate scrambled eggs for breakfast then I drove us into town.

We were two miles south of I-15 when the left front tyre popped. Then the left rear. The Bug heeled over like it was going to roll. It slewed off the dirt road and ploughed through the rough ground toward a big rock. I felt the bite of the seatbelt across my stomach. I gripped the wheel real tight and braced for the impact. But it never came. The bug ground to a halt with maybe two feet to spare. I looked sideways and saw that Caraway was okay. But the Bug wasn't. The Bug was kaput.

We got out, nursing our necks and went back to the road.

Flat-butt tacks scattered on the surface told me the double blow-out was no accident.

Over to my left I heard the sound of a round being chambered.

What were the odds on a .45 hollow point?

FIFTY-ONE

I smelled Norm Dibbitts before I saw him: Hai Karate and old sweat rode the downwind breeze as he came from the cover of a cottonwood tree. It was the only one for miles around. He'd picked his spot with some care.

He carried a Browning automatic in one hand and an almost empty bottle of Scotch in the other. His eyes were agitated. Maybe he'd be on the Maryjane as well. I didn't let that fool me, though. If anything it made him more dangerous. I'd seen his marksmanship on Harvard Road. If he could hit a knife at one hundred yards, he couldn't miss Caraway and me at three. Did he have the salt to put bullets into us? After the shit he'd pulled these last three weeks, you better believe it.

I put my hands on my hips and made a rueful smile. 'Gotta say, Norm, you suckered me good.'

He smiled back, but it was wistful. No hint of gloating. 'Ain't I the motherfucker, Wat?'

'You sure are, buddy.'

'Even you didn't suspect me, Miss Caraway, did you?' He addressed her with curious old fashioned respectfulness.

'None of us did, Norm,' she said. 'Not me, not the feds.'

Norm made a philosophical shrug. 'Running the Million Dollar Nugget put me in the perfect place. Nobody saw me sneak out before Marsha got the call. Nobody even questioned me, never mind asking for an alibi.'

I said, 'Your fruitcake act was great cover too, Norm. Real convincing.'

He frowned. 'That was no fucking act, man. I got mental problems. And them words is mighty unkind.'

'Sorry about that, Norm.' I noted his dejected expression. 'Really I am.'

'Don't matter, Wat. You're right. You're always right. But a big part of the time I *am* crazy as a loon. I was on point when it mattered, though. Second shooter was the toughest job of all. Lynchpin of the whole op.'

'I never had you figured for a murderer, though.' I kept my tone disappointed rather than accusing.

Norm looked at me sharp. 'Ain't murder when you're serving. You know that, Wat.'

Caraway asked, 'Serving how?'

I found myself replying with another question, 'You took your orders from the CIA, didn't you, Norm?'

Norm nodded.

'And Finn Sheldon was your case officer, wasn't he?'

Again Norm nodded. 'Mr Sheldon explained how Marsha was a rogue FBI agent working for the Russians. How she blackmailed Gerwitz to make sure Amalgamated carried on supplying them faulty torsion bars.'

Flipping reality was smart play by Sheldon.

Caraway asked, 'What about the others?'

Norm glugged some Scotch. 'Hazeldene was another a red under the bed, helping to keep the whole sabotage operation hushed up. Ray Carmody was the moneyman. He didn't get rich quick, he got paid by the KGB.'

I asked, 'How did Stacey fit in?'

Norm's expression softened. 'Miss Honeysett was on Mr Sheldon's team too – the commie stuff was just a front.'

More sleight-of-mind from Sheldon.

I braced myself for the next question. 'Who do you think we're working for, Norm? Me and Sergeant Caraway?'

'You're on the level, Wat, both of you. No doubt about it. But you got played.' He drained the whiskey bottle. 'You took Mr Sheldon down and you let the bad guys win. You didn't mean to do it, I know that. But the fact remains that you did.'

I sensed what was coming. 'Listen, Norm – '

'Mr Sheldon's last orders was real clear. *Don't let the bad guys win.* That's what he said. *Do whatever it takes to stop that happening.* Sorry, Wat, but orders is orders. You know that.'

Looking the wrong way down the barrel of the Browning, I nailed another facet of Sheldon's cleverness. When he told me both shooters were sent by KGB agents in LA, he wasn't being loyal to Norm. He was keeping him in play so he could take out Caraway and me. Dollars to dimes Norm had a bullet with Schwenk's name on it too.

'You really gonna kill us, Norm?' I kept my tone steady. I wanted to make him think this through logically. 'Me, a fellow vet? And Sergeant Caraway, an officer of the law?'

In the edge of my vision I saw Caraway backing slowly toward the Beetle. It had left the road and come to a halt twenty feet away. Both doors were open and I recalled that she'd placed her Smith & Wesson in the glove compartment when we set off from the mansion.

'I don't wanna.' Norm kept his eyes on me, but his voice

scaled up half an octave as he spoke to Caraway. 'But I'll shoot you down right now, Miss Caraway, if you take one more step toward that car.'

'Okay, Norm.' I glanced at Caraway. She'd frozen and was holding her hands where Norm could see them. 'Neither of us is going anyplace. Isn't that right, Lee?'

'Sure is, Wat.' Caraway had the presence of mind to keep the mood amicable.

'No more messing, then.' Norm's voice evened out. 'You hear?'

'We hear you, Norm,' I said. 'Loud and clear.'

That said, I needed to get through to him. I said, 'We all make mistakes, Norm, wouldn't you agree?'

'I guess.'

'Finn Sheldon is an old buddy of mine. We served in Vietnam together.'

'He told me that.'

'He told you a lot of stuff, didn't he?'

Norm stayed quiet.

I filled the silence. 'He told me a lot of stuff too. And I believed him, just like you did. See, what he told you about the Soviet plot to supply faulty torsion bars to Uncle Sam is true.'

'Course it's true. Mr Sheldon said it, didn't he?'

'But what he didn't tell you is that *he* was the rogue intelligence officer. *He* was working for the KGB and Marsha was an undercover Fed trying to stop him. Sheldon told the truth about the plot but flipped his role and Marsha's.'

'That can't be right.'

'Sheldon played me too, buddy. He played me in the Nasty, and he played me back here in Hicks. Think about it.'

'I *am* thinking.' Norm screwed his face up as if it would make his brain work better. 'But I was there, man. I saw how Marsha cozied up to Gary Gerwitz, how she got into his head.'

Caraway said, 'That's true, Norm. But Marsha was trying to protect Gary. She persuaded him to go to the authorities about the torsion bar scam.' There was a soothing authority in her voice that played right. 'That was why Gary wanted to meet with Congressman Hazeldene.'

The mention of Hazeldene's name redirected Norm's train of thought. 'Shooting the congressman and Ray Carmody was the easy part. Larry couldn't fucking miss. I took the toughest shot. Mr Sheldon said so. I was on point. I had to hit Marsha so it looked like an accident. Larry could never have taken the shot I took.'

Another part of the puzzle slotted into place. 'Larry's your cousin, isn't he? The one in Hesperia? You told Lucinda you went to visit him because he was sick. What were you really doing down there, Norm? Paying Larry off?'

'Shutting the bastard up.' Norm was about to swig more Scotch, saw the bottle was empty and tossed it into the desert. 'Larry wasn't a good guy. He tried to squeeze Mr Sheldon for more money. Larry was a piece of shit.'

Something else became clear. 'Those guys who attacked me on Harvard Road, they were acting on Sheldon's orders, weren't they? Sheldon told you what was going down and then what? Asked you to keep an eye on things?'

Norm nodded yes. 'Them dudes was sent over from LA but Mr Sheldon didn't trust 'em.'

My next question was rhetorical. 'The shot you made on Harvard Road, that wasn't the work of a rear echelon clerk, was it? You served in the Fighting First.'

Norm looked puzzled. 'How'd you know that?'

I indicated his arm. 'That Bro tattoo. It has nothing to do with your brother. It's for the Big Red One, the BRO.'

Caraway sounded confused. 'Big Red One?'

'First Infantry Division,' I said. 'The nickname comes from the large red number 1 on the shoulder patch.'

'I should've got that fucking tat taken off.' Norm's voice was loaded with strange vehemence.

'It was hardly a big mistake, Norm.' I tried to sound reassuring. I didn't want him getting angry again.

'I stopped being fit to wear the uniform in '67.'

I let the silence run. Caraway cottoned on and kept quiet too. Norm needed to do this in his own time.

He wiped bulbs of sweat from his brow with the back of his arm. 'I got taken prisoner at Ong Thanh. The gooks put me in a camp, fried my brains. I was like them Peace Committee guys. Spoke on gook radio about how we was wrong to be in Vietnam. How our bomber pilots was committing war crimes. If they asked me to say my mom was a whore I would have said it.'

'They tortured you didn't they, Norm?'

'They did all sorts. They got in my head. They fucked me over real bad.'

I said, 'You got nothing to be ashamed of, buddy.'

'Yes I do. Other guys got the same and they didn't crack. I was a disgrace, man, a fucking embarrassment. Mr Sheldon, he offered me a way back. A way to put things right.'

'By killing Marsha? And Larry?' Caraway was angry and I could see why. Norm was vulnerable. Sheldon was an asshole to exploit him. But that's what spies do.

Caraway wouldn't let up. 'You shot Rex Hambly too, didn't you? And then you opened Lucinda's throat.'

Norm went quiet again. I guessed all sorts of shit was pinballing around his head. The muzzle of the Browning wavered between Caraway and me. He might pull that trigger any moment. Ten feet, he couldn't miss.

None of this stopped Caraway. She pushed even harder. 'Why did you use a knife on Lucinda?'

'I didn't. I couldn't. But I got her blood on my hands all right.' I pinned tears rolling down his scooped-out cheeks. 'What happened to Lucinda, that was the baddest thing of all. She could have been my gal.'

I spoke softly. 'What happened to Lucinda, Norm?'

His nose started running. He sniffed it back with a barking noise. 'Mr Sheldon said she was telling you too much, Wat. She had to be "removed from the picture". Them was the words he used. So he called in more goons from LA. He said they was gonna keep her in some safe-house until this was all done. But he needed my help to get her. When she finished work I asked her to step into the parking lot. The goons was waiting with a van. They bundled her inside and drove away. But they never went to no safe house. They just took her to the edge of town and cut her throat.'

I said, 'If that's how it went down, Norm, it's not on you. It's on Sheldon.'

He shook his head violently, like he was trying to eject the thoughts worming around inside. 'Mr Sheldon said Lucinda died because them goons disobeyed his orders.'

'And you believed him?' Caraway struggled to keep her voice level. I got why she was stoked, but this wasn't helping.

'Don't matter none what I believed.' Norm's voice acquired a frayed quality. I sensed self-hate, stifled hysteria. 'Like I said, what happened to Lucinda is on me.

I should have protected her. But I messed up bad. *Again*.'

'You weren't to know what was gonna happen.' I tried to sound sympathetic without encouraging more self-pity.

'I still betrayed her.' He made a bitter laugh. He was right on the edge. 'But "No sacrifice too great", huh? That's what they taught me in the BRO.'

I took a step closer. 'That's what Sheldon told you. But you can make your own decisions, Norm. Remember the other part of the BRO motto, "No Mission Too Difficult".'

Sweat and tears mingled on Norm's face. 'I dunno, man. Sometimes I see things real clear. Other times, everything just gets totally messed up.'

I took another step. Norm was six feet away. 'You saw real clear back on Harvard Road. You used your initiative to keep onside with me. You can do that now.'

Again Norm used his arm to wipe the dampness from his face. Just for a moment his forearm covered his eyes. 'I can't believe Mr Sheldon lied to me.'

I said, 'That's exactly what I thought. But the truth is he lied to you and he lied to me.'

'You're a good guy, Wat. You always get stuff right. But Mr Sheldon, he's the Man. And he's always right too. But you can't both be right...I dunno...'

He mopped his face one more time. He was distracted, though. This time he used his gun arm.

I moved fast. He saw me coming. The gun came back down. I blocked his arm with mine. The round in the chamber went off. I grabbed his wrist, wrenched it down, snapping his elbow and trigger finger at the same time.

Norm yowled and reeled backward. The gun fell to the dirt. I snatched it up.

My buddy regained his balanced. He stood looking at me, eyes awash with anguish and frustration.

I said, 'It's over, buddy. Let's get you to the hospital.'

I saw Caraway moving toward the Bug.

'Too late for that, Wat. It was too late a long time ago.' He made a faint smile. 'No surrender. Not again.'

With his undamaged arm he reached down to his calf a pulled a throwing knife from an ankle sheath. He'd stumbled backward about ten feet. If he threw the knife with any sort of accuracy I'd be in trouble.

'Don't be a knucklehead, Norm. Put the knife down.'

'But I *am* a knucklehead, Wat. I wish I was smart and brave like you, but I ain't. You're a solid hero and I'm a sorry-ass loser.'

'Nobody's a hero and nobody's a loser. We deal with stuff in different ways is all. But we're still buddies. Now toss down that knife.'

'You gotta shoot me.' He shuffled a step closer.

'Stay right where you are, Norm.' My finger tightened on the trigger.

But I didn't pull it.

Norm came closer still. 'No one else I'd rather do it, buddy.'

His knife arm went up.

I tensed.

One bullet went into Norm's shoulder, the other through his forehead. The impact spun him around. In that tripped-out instant, he seemed crazily elegant. Then he hit the ground, sending up a wall of dust. It settled on him like ochre skin.

Caraway was standing by the Beetle. She lowered her Smith & Wesson.

I knelt by Norm. His expression was one of relief, of a soul unburdened.

Caraway placed her hand on my shoulder.

'You okay, Wat?'

'Yeah. You?'

'Fine.'

'You did good, Lee.' I shut Norm's eyes and came to my feet. 'I'm glad it didn't have to be me. And I'm glad he never knew it wasn't.'

FIFTY-TWO

We walked back to the Honeysett place and Caraway called in the incident. Then she drove us back into Hicks in a Range Rover her dad had used when he didn't want to get the Rolls dirty. She went to the police station to file her report and I went to the newsroom to file my last story for the *Herald*.

I called my buddy Dave Tomaszewski in the Arizona rehab clinic. He was cool about me quitting. His recovery was coming along well and he was keen to get his ass back in the editor's chair. Anyways, Jacinta Vasquez and Tom Ferris could run the paper with their eyes shut. I moved my stuff out of Dave's house as fast as I'd moved it in. There was nothing that wouldn't fit into the trunk of a car.

I paid $200 cash for a '65 Rambler Rogue and retrieved my tapes and sound system from the Beetle. The auto repair guy was a generous type and fitted the eight track in the Rambler as part of the deal.

Then I left town and headed for LA. I listened to *Strange Days* by the Doors. That was cool because it took me back a few years and gave me a little distance to think.

I thought mostly about Lee Caraway.

But all my thinking brought me back to the truth of what

she said: Neither of us belonged in Hicks but our routes out would take us in different directions. Me hanging around just for a while might have induced her to stay just for a while. And sooner or later we'd have grown resentful. I'd told her this on the drive back into town. She was hip to where I was coming from. She gave me a long, soft kiss that we both knew was our last. Unless our paths crossed again. This was always possible, we agreed on that.

I knew, too, that she had good prospects. With the high profile Hicks case under her belt she'd get the sergeant's job in San Francisco and soon enough make lieutenant in a big city detective division, sexist assholes or not.

A few weeks later I heard on the news that Chester Peeples got a ten year stretch for his role in funding the High Rock fraud.

Two days after that I read in a business magazine that Amalgamated Metals got its new torsion bar contract with Chrysler. It seemed Schwenk decided to play the KGB after all. There was a picture of Gary Gerwitz standing at the factory gates with Stacey at his side. I never knew what arrangement she came to with Schwenk but I was glad she didn't get locked up. She made some real bad choices, but she wasn't a player so much as a victim of Finn Sheldon.

Norm Dibbitts was another of Sheldon's victims. Despite what Norm had done, it was hard to see him as a psychopathic killer. Norm was a Vietnam soldier who never really came home. In the end, death was a good deal: he wanted it strong and was good to go.

And, of course, I was also a victim of Finn Sheldon. My old buddy played me like he played the others, except they were the singles and I was the album. Didn't beat myself up over it though. We all get played whether we know it or not. You just gotta take it and move on. Did I despise Sheldon? Not really. Like I said, he did what spies do.

I never found out what happened to him. No word of criminal charges or a trial. That could have meant he did a deal after all; or the feds disappeared him; or something else entirely. I could have gotten that information but I didn't. As far as I was concerned Finn Sheldon was never coming back.

So I followed the interstate through the jive desert's mean and distorted beauty. I headed toward the Pacific coast, or wherever some other road might take me. I headed into post-Vietnam America, a place with a headload of napalm, of lost sons and absent boys. In those days, though, none of that bothered me. I wasn't looking for a brighter day. I wasn't copping out. I arrived in Hicks with no plans and I left with no plans. Back then, I took my chances. I stayed on the beam. I got my rocks off. This was as much and as little as I needed.

This book is printed on paper from sustainable sources managed under the Forest Stewardship Council (FSC) scheme.

It has been printed in the UK to reduce transportation miles and their impact upon the environment.

For every new title that Troubador publishes, we plant a tree to offset CO_2, partnering with the More Trees scheme.

For more about how Troubador offsets its environmental impact, see www.troubador.co.uk/sustainability-and-community